the
man
who
wouldn't
say
no

the man who wouldn't say

no

ALBERT LEBOWITZ

RANDOM HOUSE
NEW YORK

For

JOEL

and

JUDITH

*O*ur age reminds one vividly of the dissolution of the Greek city-state: everything goes on as usual and yet there is no longer anyone who believes in it. The invisible spiritual bond which gives it validity no longer exists, and so the whole age is at once comic and tragic—tragic because it is perishing, comic because it goes on. For it is always the imperishable which sustains the perishable, the spiritual which sustains the corporal; and if it might be conceived that an exanimate body could for a little while continue to perform its customary functions, it would in the same way be comic and tragic.

—KIERKEGAARD

part · I ·

Your occupation consists in preserving your hiding place, and that you succeed in doing, for your mask is the most enigmatical of all. In fact you are nothing; you are merely a relation to others, and what you are you are by virtue of this relation.

—Kierkegaard

part · I ·

· 1 ·

She talked in a steady stream, and Halter had trouble attending to the words. Her voice, musical but with a metallic edge, like the call of birds, resisted meaning. He felt threatened and titillated at the same time, and beyond that, beyond the self-pitying sacs of tears locked in his eyeballs, was the desperate awareness that he had to remain professionally detached—had to remain a lawyer.

"I don't know if he loves me or not. I suppose he does. That's not really the question. He doesn't *desire* me, and it isn't as if it came up overnight. It's been going on from the beginning. It hasn't gotten any worse but it hasn't gotten any better, and when something like that doesn't get better, it gets much, much worse. At best we've slept together once a month, and even then, I had to ask *him*. On our honeymoon.

"I tried playing hard to get. Once we went without for six months and he didn't raise an eyebrow. When I bring it up he doesn't say anything, he never refuses, he just puts on that easy, patient smile and disposes of me as fast as he can. I can't take any more. He makes me feel stupid and vulgar. He makes me feel cheap. And I'm not. I'm none of those things."

She wasn't. She was the most expensive woman he'd ever met, and certainly beyond his own, limited means. He couldn't imagine buying her at any price. She was too beautiful to be stripping before a stranger, and Halter struggled to remember that she was confiding, not in him, but in his disembodied lawyerdom. He longed to have her touch his flesh and, eyes glazing, discover he was human. He would talk about Betty and they would cry and tell each other how miserable they were.

He couldn't meet her eyes. Head bent over his pad, he wrote: *cruel and indifferent.*

"Is there anything else, Mrs. Brungard?"

She stared at him. "What do you mean?"

"For example, has he ever *said* he didn't love you? Did he ever strike you? Quarrel? Stay out till all hours of the night without telling you where he was? Are there other women? Is he difficult about money matters? Anything like that?"

She had been self-possessed through her confessional. It had mantled her with a special kind of impunity from public exposure—a Jackie Kennedy handling her husband's funeral, refusing herself the luxury for the first time in her life of letting her hem show. Disjointed by a grief of his own, Halter was unmanned by a personality that embraced its will despite the prying of emotional fingers.

Tears sprang to her defense and he sat quietly, warmed by common need. Only a lover could say or do what she needed. Halter was a mouthpiece. She was paying him to put her words in his mouth, not his own.

He waited her out. She refused to recognize her tears by even a swipe of the hand. "No. Nothing else. He's been a perfect gentleman."

"You haven't quarreled sometimes? All married couples quarrel."

"Never. I don't know anything about married couples. I wish I did. I should think what I've told you is quite enough for a divorce. Are you saying it isn't?"

"Anything's enough in this state if both parties want it. General indignities. How does your husband feel about a divorce?"

"He doesn't feel anything. He won't fight it if that's what you mean." She had recovered her composure and with it reduced Halter once again to her humble servant.

"I'd better get your vital statistics," he said, and wrote on his pad: 38-22-36. "Your full name?"

"Hilda Brungard."

"Your husband's?"

"Vincent R. Brungard."

"No middle initial for you?"

"No. Don't tell me that's necessary for a divorce."

He put together a small smile (tight? tolerant? patient? terrified?). "No. We can manage without it. Your maiden name?"

"Martinson."

"If you get a divorce, would you want your maiden name restored?"

"Of course I would. No, I wouldn't. I have a little girl."

"What is her name?"

"Sylvia. We call her Sylvie."

"Age?"

"Seven."

"Born of the marriage?"

"Improbable though it may seem, yes."

"Were either of you married before?"

"No."

"I imagine you'd want custody of Sylvie. Would there be any trouble about that?"

"No. He's very considerate."

"Would you grant your husband right of reasonable visitation?"

"Yes, of course."

"Have you considered the questions of child support and alimony? What does your husband do for a living?"

"He doesn't do anything. The world owes him a living. He deposits checks."

"Are you saying he's independently wealthy?"

"That's what I'm saying. My husband had the talent and

foresight to be the only child of a man who killed himself and left his wife and son each over five million dollars."

Halter leaned back, got up and stood at the window. Being winter, it was already dark outside. He felt a sense of shock; it was as though Mrs. Brungard and he had lost their separate ways and both, by the wildest of chances, had found sanctuary in the same lighthouse. Hardly knowing each other, or when or whether they would be rescued, how long could they remain strangers? The intercom buzzed and he picked up the phone. It was Miss Rauscher, the pretty, flirtatious one.

"Mr. Halter," she said. "Everybody else is gone and I'm getting ready to leave, unless you need me for something."

He hesitated. He would have preferred her to stay, merely to keep out the suggestions of obscenity that winked from automobile headlights far below. But he couldn't ask her; she wanted to go home.

"That's all right. Thanks anyway. I'll close up. Good night."

"You sure?" she said. "Honest, I wouldn't mind."

"I'm sure," he said.

"Well, good night then. See you tomorrow."

He faced Mrs. Brungard. She, fabulous creature, had become mythical. The brilliant tones of her knit-wool skirt and jacket were soft and banked. Amber eyes and rounded breasts were approachable only through abject devotion. This could be the biggest fee he'd brought into the firm, and it would please Mr. Forrest very much. He leaned across the desk to light her cigarette and opened his lungs to her smoke. He felt restored. There was work to be done.

"Does your husband have an attorney?"

"Indeed he does. Felix Mackey. He handles all my husband's affairs."

Halter nodded. "I've heard of him. Very reputable. An ex-president of the Bar Association. It should make things easier. With money involved, this sort of thing could get messy."

"I don't want his money. I just want a divorce."

Halter doodled on his yellow pad, letting her words hang in the air, permitting her to make her stand.

"You think that's foolish?" she said. "I don't care."

"It's not for me to tell you what to do," he said. "I can only make suggestions. Have you considered Sylvie?"

"Unfortunately she has a trust fund. He's seen to it that she'll live in the manner to which he's accustomed."

"You say, unfortunately?"

"That's right, that's what I said."

Halter made notes.

"All right," he said. "That takes care of Sylvie. What about you? Do you have independent means?"

"I have me. I work. I make nine thousand dollars a year. How much do you make?"

Halter doodled.

"Not much more," he said. "May I ask what you do?"

But of course he already knew that she had to do nothing, merely to be. She sat on an elevated chair, and emissaries came from distant lands to drop rubies and pearls at her feet. She smiled at cameras to advertise toothpaste, skin cream, shampoo, mink coats, bathing suits, miracle drugs, synthetic fibers, automobiles, cigarettes. She had sold the Brooklyn Bridge a thousand times over, and still the buyers were lined up.

"I'm a schoolteacher. I'm an assistant professor in mathematics at the university."

She conceded Halter nothing and took everything, not only his breath but that last resource, his imagination. To be beautiful with mind was to strip him of even his sense of manhood, which he could only have imagined. He was a eunuch in Mrs. Brungard's court and, an amanuensis with pad and pen, had to earn his keep.

"You've given him a good part of your life. Don't you feel that entitles you to something? After all, he can afford to pay for the damage he's done."

"No."

He addressed the tips of her shoes. "Let's look at it from another point of view. You may have problems of prosperity with Sylvie. Unfortunately, as you said, she'll be independently wealthy. That may seriously affect your relationship."

"It's up to me to see that it doesn't. You've done your duty, you've made your suggestions, now let's drop it. Is there anything else you want to discuss?"

He wrote: *Halter the lawyer. Vulgar. Grasping.* All right. He had a license to prove it. He could nick her husband for ten thousand at least. He could still deliver the merchandise—a divorce.

"Have you and your husband separated?"

"Yes. He's living at the Bluestone Hotel. I'm still in the house—for the time being."

"What's your address and telephone number?" he said as clumsily as a freshman to a football queen. Dial a number, and there she was. Walk past her room at night and moon at the shaded lights.

"Three Fitzgerald Lane in Sturdivant. Collins 6-7543."

"What about the house? Don't you want to keep that?"

"I've told you—I don't want anything. I'll get an apartment."

"What about clothes and personal possessions? Jewelry. Does he get those too?"

She looked at him and he managed to look back. Their glances locked in a hostile place on her territory. "No," she said. "Do you want to represent me or not?"

"Yes I do," he said. "I'm sorry."

"All right," she said. "Let's get it over with."

"Your age?"

"Thirty-three."

"Mr. Brungard's?"

"Thirty-four. What's yours?"

He played with his pen. "Mine?"

"Yours."

"Why do you ask?"

She shrugged. "Why not?"

"I'm thirty-one," he said. "When and where were you married?"

"Here. January third, eight years ago last month."

Halter scribbled on the pad and stared at the data. Betty

and he. In the same month, same day, same city. Only the two years separated him from Mrs. Brungard wherever he turned.

"Sylvie's birthday?"

"She was seven last August fourteenth."

Halter examined his notes, wrote *Halter is a lawyer,* and capped his pen.

"I guess that does it for now. Except for one thing. I've always felt it mandatory for an attorney to make an effort at reconciliation. I'd like, if possible, to arrange a meeting here between you, Mr. Brungard, Mr. Mackey and myself." He hesitated and then ploughed ahead. "It's easy to divorce and even easier to regret it. Freedom isn't all it's cracked up to be."

"Mr. Halter," she said. "Are you married?"

He shook his head under the slap of the question. "I was," he said.

"It takes one to know one, is that your credentials? How old are you?"

"I believe I told you. Thirty-one."

"You've said it twice, so I believe you. Haven't you heard anything I said? Vince doesn't desire me physically and never has. What earthly good would a meeting do? He doesn't need marriage counseling, he needs hormones. I think I've come to the wrong place."

Halter rubbed his eyes. Somebody wrote on his pad: *Get the business and worry about it later. Samuel Wentworth Forrest.*

"I'm sorry," he said. "If you want to try somebody else, that's perfectly all right. There will be no charge."

Mrs. Brungard stood up and sat down again. She shook her head. "Is this what they call integrity? Pardon me, but you're an idiot. Since I'm in an idiotic situation, you're what I deserve. I won't go through this again. You still want me as a client? What does your integrity have to say about that?"

"Of course," he said. "You'll attend the meeting?"

"Vince is a perfect gentleman. I'm willing to see him any time."

"Good. I'll call Mr. Mackey and arrange it." Halter stood

up. "Thank you for being so patient. I'm sorry it took so long."

She remained seated. "Call a cab for me, or would that also make you sorry?"

"Not at all," he said. His lips were dry. "I'm leaving now. May I drive you home?"

"Certainly," she said. "You can put it on the bill."

He helped her on with her coat, a fur that was silver-gray, sleek and expensive enough for a millionaire's wife. They went out the front door, and he followed her down the corridor to the elevator, free to examine the elegant turn of her ankle, the gloss of her auburn hair. They were silent on the way to the parking lot. He was conscious of the sexual stares of men passing by, and grateful to be in momentary possession of her, even though law was nine tenths of his possession.

"May I ask how you happened to come to me?" he said.

"Susan Goddard. She's a friend of mine. You got her divorce. She said you were . . . sweet."

"I remember. She was a nice girl," he said.

"It's sweet of you to remember her. Will you be sweet enough to remember me?"

"Yes."

"Well, don't go to any trouble. Just get me the divorce and clear your track for the next Susie to come along."

"I'm sorry. I seem to have a knack for offending you."

"Forget it. This is my first divorce. Next time I'll be as nice as Susie."

On the ride home, closeted with her in the front seat of the car, surrounded by suggestive waves of warmth from the heater, he searched his memory for fragments of himself. He could think of nothing; his memory bank confessed to a zero balance. Frantically he said, "I majored in English literature and minored in philosophy at college."

"Have you read any good books lately?" she said.

"I still read," he said. "When I can."

"And when you can't? I suppose those who can't, do. I'll bet you do a great deal. Handle those giant corporation mergers,

defend murderers, sue railroads or the people who sue railroads.
I imagine you're terribly busy."

He thrust his face forward at the night, having nowhere else
to point. He had never been good at riposte, and if she weren't
his client he would have excused himself and sought refuge
from her beauty in Betty's calm—only Betty wasn't there.

She directed him to her house. He parked and reached for
the door handle.

"Wait," she said softly. "I'm glad you read when you can
and I'm sure you're a sweet lawyer."

He had his own apologies to make—for deferring to her
beauty, for neglecting Betty and desiring this one. His body
leaned over and kissed her a glancing blow on the lips. Her
mouth, cool under fire, did not retreat. "Well," she said. "The
well-rounded lawyer."

"I'm sorry," he said. "It was inexcusable."

"Chalk it up to experience," she said. "I've never been kissed
by a lawyer before, much less a well-rounded one."

He interlaced his fingers and squeezed until they hurt. "My
wife, Betty, died three weeks ago in an auto accident," he recited. "She was on her way to pick up our three-year-old boy at
a neighbor's house, a few blocks from home. She was making a
left turn from Bruger into Clapper Avenue. She was a few
blocks from home when she was killed."

Mrs. Brungard pressed a finger against his forehead. "Okay,"
she said. "Just one thing. I don't like sorry people. Let me
know about the meeting." She opened the car door and went
up the walk toward her house.

Tears leaked into his eyes. He watched her disappear through
her front door, tried to drive away and found he couldn't. For
days he had been feeling torn apart, lost to both past and
future, with no idea of how to keep body and soul together.
He conceived of bodies and souls joined together by faithful
shock absorbers and of his own, now faithless, vibrating separately.

His nose was ticklish and he sneezed. It was too pat and

placed an impossible weight on Betty. His law partners. Would a man with his heart in his work so submit to their heartlessness? He'd submitted for Betty's sake, for the sake of his family. He had not. No more lies, *please*.

Trembling, he wrapped his arms around his shoulders. His mind, not so easily captured, strayed off. What was there left to lose if he went with the grain? What if, instead of trying to pull the pieces together and going crazy, he simply let go?

He stopped shaking. He felt cool and infinitely calculating. There were truths beyond truths if there was truth at all. Who could prove that a man half slave and half free couldn't endure?

Tears evaporating, taking the heat off his cheeks, Halter drove home.

· 2 ·

Halter stood with the collar of his English overcoat buttoned around his chin and examined the front of his house with a listing agent's eye. Two-story colonial, green shutters freshly painted, Italian tile roof in good condition, tuck pointing okay. Depending on the heating plant, the dryness of the basement, termites, foundation, the number of bedrooms and bathrooms, perhaps twenty-eight thousand. It was a house he'd never seen before. He'd always used Betty's eyes, deferred to her taste. The house struck him as being too large, too square, too middle-class. He disliked having to walk to the front door and claim it with his key. Still, if Betty were waiting inside, he would have embraced every stick of Danish furniture, fingered the beige wall-to-wall carpeting. It wasn't her traverse rods he quarreled with, but his privilege of inheriting them. The middle class was a hell of a place for a widow-man. Having to live with a stranger in his own home, he had become the stranger.

Hat in hand, he opened the door and braced himself for Mrs. Gummersell.

White-haired, cheeks rose-petal and spiderwebbed, cued by soap operas, she waited for him in the living room with an immaculate George on her lap. She had him dressed in a candy-striped shirt, blue jeans and red tennis shoes. His auburn hair was slicked back and his little boy's face was clean as scraped celery. Mrs. Gummersell made no bones about it; she was stronger than dirt.

She set George on his feet and said, "Say hello to your daddy, George."

George came forward at his disorganized gallop and said, "Hi, Mommy."

This was nothing new. He'd done it while Betty was alive, and he'd "daddied" her, but now, of course, Mrs. Gummersell produced a professionally sad shake of the head. Acquiescent before the woman's pinkness, clumsy in his overcoat, Halter lifted his son in the air and kissed him on the cheek.

"Hello, big George," he said, and the boy squirmed in his arms. Released, he went for his toy chest behind the sofa. They watched as he dragged out a toy truck and a wooden hammer. He banged on the truck. Mrs. Gummersell got up on stovepipe legs and took the hammer away from him. He started bawling, ran at his father and stood with his arms around Halter's legs, screaming into his crotch.

"George, dear, we musn't break our toys," said Mrs. Gummersell. She reached behind the sofa and emerged with a pegboard. "This is what we bang on, George."

The volume of the crying increased and Halter stood, stone father-idol immune to a child's suffering. In a few weeks' deployment, this woman had him cowed. She was a specialist in the handling of kids, and he, handling only George, was an expert observer of the destruction of toys.

Mrs. Gummersell pried George loose from Halter, guided him to the pegboard and tapped a peg. "You see, George?" she said. "We bang on this."

George turned on his belly and mourned into the carpeting.

Mrs. Gummersell smiled at Halter, exposing the perfect row of her false teeth. "I do think, Mr. Halter, it would work much better if we kept all his toys in his room and brought a few of them down at a time. That way he would be much more orderly and controllable. The man of the house is entitled to peace and quiet after a busy day at the office."

"If you think it's best, Mrs. Gummersell," said Halter, afraid to look at George. He took off his coat and hung it in the closet.

"Dinner is ready whenever you are," she said. "We've already fed George."

"I'm sorry I'm late," he said. "I was tied up at the office. I'll wash up."

He needed a drink badly. Mrs. Gummersell disapproved of liquor and cigarettes. Halter, drinker-smoker, vice king of the block. Meanwhile he kept telling himself how lucky he was. House and children keepers didn't grow on trees any more. Mrs. Gummersell was too good to be true.

She was, but he hadn't realized how frightening goodness was. Her goodness went all the way. She lived by the Good Book. After her second day, a Bible had appeared on his bureau upstairs. After a week the cards had begun to appear on his pillow.

He looked back as he headed for the kitchen. George was pounding on the pegboard with his hammer.

He washed his hands at the sink, poured some bourbon and lit a cigarette. He sat swaddled in his vices, wondering how much sinning time he had left. If she directed him to remove liquor and cigarette from the premises, he would obey.

The tapping stopped in the living room, and he heard George say, "I want Daddy. Play blocks."

"We'll play blocks. We mustn't bother your daddy. He's very busy in the kitchen. We'll take out the blocks and build a house right here in the living room."

"I want Daddy," said George, mildly and without hope.

Halter sipped his drink, wary as a boy stealing apples. It was impossible to remember how a father should behave. He no longer was permitted a private place where his feelings could catch up with him. He sat holed up in the kitchen, afraid to finish his drink, and afraid that she'd decide to catch him at it.

There was Hilda Brungard. Hilda, a name for upstairs maids, but never again. Let's kiss her and babble about Betty. She sits unmoved and lets him approach her mouth. He follows Hilda upstairs to bed and is awarded her unhusbanded body. But of course that is impossible, because Hilda thinks he is a fool. Despising him for confessing to the death of his wife, she gets up, eyes flashing, and vanishes, leaving in her place all that was left to him of Betty, who had become featureless.

That was wrong. Her features were there but kept taking up new positions on her face, and she frightened him even though her voice was the same. She wanted to know if he loved her and how could he say that what he loved was her harmony?

He couldn't prove her features moved; he just *knew* it. Knowing how ridiculous a desperately honest witness could sound, he surely would have made a ridiculous witness. One eye hung like a pendant on her forehead, the other rolled along her cheek. Her nose swung like a pendulum from ear to ear. Halter, nerve ends short-circuiting, leaned forward and touched her mouth, and she dissolved into the cold lip of his glass. He sipped his whiskey.

He was behind at the office. Files were falling over each other. He'd developed the habit of forgetting to look at his appointment book and had missed a hearing in the Equity Division. When the clerk called him, he dashed to court in a sweat, half an hour late, wanting to bleat at the judge *My wife is dead*, remembering in the nick of time his own impatience at lawyers' excuses. The mindlessness of duty. Nothing excused a professional.

The undone, postponed jobs elbowed each other and gave him a headache. His mind was grim at being compromised. A shareholder's option agreement, an estate plan, wills, a motion to dismiss, a law memo for Crenshaw, a deposition already twice continued and others set, a partition suit, various per-

sonal-injury cases. Halter held his head. The work load was
much the same; he wasn't. He used to plow ahead, one file at
a time, and things got done, they got done. Now he gobbled
all the files up at once and sat feeding on his lower lip. He
knew what he was there for—to produce. Forrest, Crenshaw,
Rucker and Halter, and only he was expendable. They would
be irritated at having to order new stationery and a new junior
partner—in that order. If he had to depend on his own clients
(could he depend on Mrs. Brungard?) he would starve, George
would starve, and good Mrs. Gummersell would smile a sweet
good-bye. That was the least of it. If the law wasn't the life of
his body, what life did his body have left?

He was short on bones. He was a plate of jellied tongue.
Halter wiggled his fingers, surprised they hadn't been nibbled
away. He had no idea why lips smacked over his heart, guts
and brain. He wasn't *that* good. Still, he had a law degree from
Harvard. He'd passed the bar. He had a certificate to prove he
was prime. He had papers to prove he was created and that
he still lived.

Mrs. Gummersell came in, holding George in her arms. She
examined the empty glass nuzzling Halter's hand and he put it
down.

"We have to get ready for bed. We're awfully sleepy."

"No bed," said George without conviction. He'd already
learned where the ultimate authority lay, knew his father was
as helpless as he.

"You must do what Aunt Mary says," said Halter. "I'll come
up and kiss you good night." The "Aunt Mary" was Mrs. Gummersell's idea. Security police depended heavily on titles.

"No bed," said George as he was carried upstairs. Father
Halter finished his drink. The heart was going out of George.
He was old before his time, taking on the responsibility for
his good behavior. Halter's heart went out to him, but as a
leaking bucket, drained of content. He poured another drink
and Mrs. Gummersell called from the head of the stairs, "We're
ready for our good-night kiss now."

"All right," said Halter, a sheriff lying, eyes closed, in one of his cells, while marauders swept through the town, shooting off their guns, and Mrs. Gummersell went out and made them wash behind their ears.

Dim under the blue night light, George lay doll-like on his back. Halter recalled the old wriggling and squirming—George's good fight to hang on for dear life to wakefulness and his father and mother. He kissed his son's cheek.

"Good night, George boy," he said, and George, going by Mrs. Gummersell's book, closed his eyes.

She beamed at Halter. "I'll put dinner on the table, Mr. Halter," she said, and walked out.

Halter lingered. George opened his eyes and looked at him. Halter, surrendering, held out his hand. George jumped up, grinning from ear to ear, and ran against the railing of his bed. "Water," he commanded.

"All right," said Halter, "and then you're going to sleep?"

"Yes."

Halter picked up the plastic cup on the bureau and half filled it under the bathroom tap. George touched the water to his lips. "Rock me," he said.

Halter lifted him from the bed to his lap in the rocking chair. George's head found its place on Halter's chest. Halter rocked and glanced up to find Mrs. Gummersell in the doorway. "Dinner is ready," she said firmly. George burrowed deeper. Halter got up, put George in bed and covered him with the blanket. "Good night, George."

George looked at Mrs. Gummersell and closed his eyes.

At dinner, Mrs. Gummersell served beef stroganoff with a marshmallow salad and settled her bulk opposite Halter. Eying her briefly, he dealt with his food.

She was a benevolent-looking creature. With her white hair, pink skin and buffalo nose, she might have been a Walt Disney property hiding the baby in the tall grass until the wicked uncle passed. No one ever bothered to finish the story; she herself gulped down the baby. No one ever confessed that benevolence could be devouring. He wondered how many other appetites it would take before she popped Halter himself in a pot and had done with him.

"Did you have a hard day at the office?" she asked.

"So-so, Mrs. Gummersell."

"My father, you know, was a lawyer [he knew from many times before], so I can imagine how difficult your day must be. He always used to say, 'The law is a jealous mistress.' I can't think of a finer position in life for a man than to be an attorney. I always expected to marry a lawyer, but you know a woman's heart. She goes where it leads her. And Ronald was such a dear. We had twenty-seven wonderful years together. He was an accountant, you know, and all the lawyers who did business with him always told him he thought like a lawyer."

"The beef stroganoff is very good, Mrs. Gummersell."

"Why, thank you, Mr. Halter. It means so much to cook for a man who appreciates it. Ronald used to say that I could make a fortune if I ever sat down and collected my recipes for a book. But you know how it is. One never seems to find the time."

He assumed she was a good cook. He had no way of knowing because he disliked fancy dishes. He didn't like curry and sauces and casseroles. He loved broiled meat and fish, vinegar on his salad. He liked baked potatoes and got them mashed. He liked raw carrots and got them homogenized in a complex paste. He liked spinach and cauliflower plain and ate them diced and creamed. He opened his mouth and shut it around her food and felt trampled under her runaway nose. There was really nothing to say to her, nothing he wanted to say but the forbidden *Please, it's not that . . . but could you . . .?* and she, meanwhile, looked forward to their cozy dinner chats. All he wanted was a hole in which to hide, down which she could throw food.

"Did you have any interesting cases today?" she said. One of the duties of her job, as she conceived it, was to feed not only his body but his mind and soul. The widow-man needn't despair, Mrs. Gummersell was there, mistress of small talk, doctor of sympathy, dispenser of instant faith. She was a good woman. Over and over he came back to this. She was a Sunday kind of housekeeper. Her latest card:

> I believe in God the Father Almighty, Maker of heaven and earth. And in Jesus Christ His only Son our Lord. Who was conceived by the Holy Ghost, born of the Virgin Mary. Suffered under Pontius Pilate, was crucified, died and buried. Who descended into hell; the third day He rose again from the dead. Who ascended into heaven, and sitteth on the right hand of God the Father Almighty. From thence He shall come to judge the quick and the dead.

He knew it by heart. He memorized her cards because this seemed the safest disposition of them.

He might tell her about Hilda Brungard. Lighting an invisible cigarette and blowing odorless smoke in her nostrils, he could say, "Today I lusted after a client. Not only a client but a married woman. You see, she sat there with gleaming knees and discussed this sexual stalemate she has with her husband. Mrs. Gummersell, the house of the Lord has many mansions, and you should see the superstructure this lady inhabits. Oh, Mrs. Gummersell, the stories I could tell."

"Nothing out of the way," said Halter. "The usual things. A contract here, a pleading there. You know."

"Indeed I do. My father, bless his soul, used to come home with his briefcase bulging with papers. Many was the time he worked till all hours of the night. He used to say, 'Service, that's what the client expects and what he has a right to. Service. Not excuses.' He had a sign over his desk just like President Truman: The buck stops here."

"Your father must have been quite a lawyer," said Halter. He was a disappointment to her. He disliked to bring work home; he liked to read unlawful books at night. "I suppose we present lawyers are letting down the old ones. The mistress doesn't seem to be as jealous as she used to be. It's getting to be a lazy world, Mrs. Gummersell."

"Isn't that the truth?" she said, and sighed. "All this talk about reverse taxes. Do you know they've actually proposed *giving* families up to three thousand dollars a year? Can you imagine the generation of loafers we'd have?"

"It's automation, Mrs. Gummersell. The machines are doing the work for us whether we like it or not. Even the Republicans are worried about the poor people. The machines produce and the poor people consume—that's the theory."

"The Republicans have always worried about the poor people," she said. "I know because I'm a Republican myself."

He absorbed the sting of her indignation and stroked her rattle. "I happen to be a Democrat, but I admire many Republicans. I meant no offense."

"Mr. Hoover was one of our greatest humanitarians," she said.

"Yes, of course," said Halter. "But do you think people can afford to loaf on three thousand a year?"

He was paying her four thousand a year, plus room and board—more, really, than he could afford.

"You wait and see. That would just be the beginning. Before you know it, it would be five or six."

"What are they to do, Mrs. Gummersell? If there are no jobs, how can they work?"

"There's always a job for them that's willing to work. That kind of person just isn't, that's all. Mark my words, the country will go to rack and ruin. I could cry when I think of what George Washington or Alexander Hamilton would say if they could see what we've done with our noble heritage." She brightened. "They were religious men, you know. If you want my honest opinion, the basic trouble with our day and age is godlessness. 'By the sweat of thy brow shalt thou earn thy daily bread.' Once a person turns from God, he becomes no more than one of those machines you're talking about."

He ascended into heaven, and sitteth on the right hand of God. She would, Halter understood, give him no easy life, and yet, as long as he could afford it, he would make no move to get rid of her. Unnerving as Mrs. Gummersell's whole sense of being was, she *had* one—and he didn't, wouldn't, couldn't.

Not any longer. He was a poor little lamb, and she had a staff and a rod. But by God—he tried to straighten his back—he was still one of those old-time lawyers who worked like hell whether he brought work home or not. It was either that or Mrs. Gummersell.

She produced the dessert: jello booby-trapped with pecan fragments and topped with whipped cream. Coffee for him, milk for her. She had, she said, read in *Consumer's Digest* that caffein was injurious to one's health and probably caused cancer, besides keeping one up till all hours of the night. Halter sipped his coffee and complimented her on the flavor.

While Mrs. Gummersell stacked dishes and silverware in the washer, Halter, a boy behind the woodshed, lit a cigarette and considered his immediate future. Another night was with him. The house offered the television set, together with Mrs. Gummersell and her sewing basket in front of it. He would like to drown himself in television, but her presence always popped him to the surface. He found himself alien to both his space and time, tumbling like an unanchored astronaut. He had to get away.

"Mrs. Gummersell," he said. "I have to go out. Some business to attend to." He paused. "I may be late."

She scraped a dish and, a lawyer's daughter, nodded. "Will you leave a number in case someone important calls?"

"There's nothing that can't wait until tomorrow," he said. "Good night."

"Good night, Mr. Halter."

He escaped into the cold dark air and drove off in his car with nowhere on earth to go. Halfway across town, he wound up in a drugstore telephone booth. He didn't have to find the number in the book: Collins 6-7543. Though everything else had faltered, his memory for data had become sensational.

He placed a dime on the shelf. What to say? This is your well-rounded, miserably lonely lawyer? But he didn't want to claim her legally. He'd begin again. He'd read of experiments by physiologists trying to prove a qualitative difference in the human heart from those of other animals. After all the cerebration, what a grand project—to establish the heart as an emotional muscle once again.

You don't know me, but I took one look at you and then my emotional muscle stood still.

You don't know me, but I have a hunger and a thirst. My housekeeper doesn't understand me.

You don't know me, but my eyes are equipped with telescopic sights and trained on you this very moment. Adjoining buildings have rooftops. Know me and know death of the heart.

Halter dialed. The phone rang five times before Mrs. Gummersell answered. He'd caught her in the middle of a card, or perhaps she'd been tailing him and it had taken her that long to rush back to the house.

"Hello. Mr. Halter's residence," said Mrs. Gummersell.

Halter breathed heavily into the mouthpiece.

"Hello, who is this?" said Mrs. Gummersell.

Halter breathed.

"Is anyone there? Who is this?" she said.

Halter hung up, and seeking pleasure, bought two packages of Doublemint gum. He drove around aimlessly, stuffing sticks in his mouth until the sugar ran out, then threw pleasure out the window toward the red sign of a bar. He stopped and went in.

Several men sat silently at the counter over beers. It was one of those places where whiskey bottles gathered dust on the shelves and old men came to grow old. Without asking, the bartender served Halter a bottle of beer and a foggy glass. Halter poured, gagged on the first sip, paid and left.

Mrs. Gummersell, what would your father say? Why, if a thing's worth doing, it's worth doing well. Finish the brew and get it out of your system. Boys will be boys, but isn't it time you settled down? Uncompleted tasks, sir, are for the losers. A man who finishes, even last, is still a man.

Halter drove past a movie marquee, went around the corner and parked. Even John Dillinger was safe in the theater.

Halter stared at shapes imposed on a screen. For the life

of him, despite Technicolor and stereophonic sound, he couldn't make contact with the projected bodies. He followed the ray of light to its aperture in the rear, he floated along the ray and tried, without success, to suspend himself in it. He couldn't make sense of the language, though he was certain that if he could only understand the man in the blue suit and the woman in her gold evening gown they would tell him something significant—something he could plug into and turn on with. He stared at the stars, listened to their voices recorded at the wrong speed, and knew that if he ever met them on the street, he'd walk through them before he recognized them for what they were.

When he got home, the card on his pillow read:

> For there is a man whose labour is in wisdom, and in knowledge, and in equity; yet to a man that hath not laboured therein shall he leave it for his portion. This also is vanity, and a great evil.

As he had before, Halter wondered how Mrs. Gummersell, without leaving the house, could follow every move he made.

· 3 ·

After the deposition that had taken most of the morning, Halter was hungry. Given bulk food, the mouthpiece working overtime, he would have crammed chunks in his mouth. He wanted to go to lunch. After all, it was twelve o'clock, whistle-blowing time, but Crenshaw went at one, not twelve fifty-nine or one-o-one, and Halter couldn't tamper with the other man's habits. He was one of Crenshaw's lunch habits.

He settled back to work. The hour wouldn't wait for him. The clock punched out minutes through sleep, dreams, depositions, sloth. Time lived outside of men and respected only events.

He picked up the Gromm file. It was the most arrogant of all work: estate planning, ingenious, sophisticated synthesizing, the ordering of a universe, the summing up of a man's economic life. The objective was to make a time machine leave its office with the sense of having justified forty years of stock-piling, of having its illusory end rounded with purpose—man suddenly made whole again. Mr. Gromm, a bricklayer's son, a little man with most of his weight in his nose, with awkward limbs that must have tortured him in childhood games, was a general contractor undoubtedly bewildered by the houses he had fabricated out of bids and estimates, safe only with his balance sheet and profit-and-loss statement, wanting finally to leave himself behind, rather than rows of zeros locked in a vault.

Halter probed his notes: Federal Estate Tax Summation under Various Plans (see Exhibit A for breakdown): (1) Total Estate Tax without restriction to wife (a) if husband dies first, $179,870 (b) if wife dies first, $151,950. (2) Same as (1) except that assets to wife pass subject to marital trust in husband's will (a) if husband dies first, $132,550, savings, $47,320 (b) if wife dies first, $151,950, savings, None. (3) Same as (2), with addition of irrevocable, inter-vivos trust of $60,000 for benefit of wife, then children (a) if husband dies first, $111,450, savings, $68,420 (b) if wife dies first, $134,260, savings, $17,690.

They loved to avoid taxes. It made them come alive more than anything. The government was immortal, so thumbing a nose at the government was an immortality of one's own. A bloodletting of the President. The last nephews of Uncle Sam left alive were those who dangled the loot and then whisked it away in a casual sleight of hand. Bearded children picketed the White House, burned their draft cards or themselves, while clean-shaven men, amused at the diversion, itemized the cost of entertainment.

Halter warmed to his subject. *Since October 1, 1964, all wills containing marital deduction pecuniary formula bequests must comply with Internal Revenue Procedure 64–10. Otherwise the marital deduction may not be allowed. This is corrected in your proposed new will by requiring the executor to distribute assets to the widow under the marital bequest at distribution value at least equal to the amount of the bequest as finally determined for Federal Estate Tax purposes.*

The Internal Revenue Service gave and it took away. It played hide-and-seek. An oxymoron, it openly hid its rulings and regulations like purloined letters, and the lawyer, blindfolded, stumbled through the maze with golden eyes in the back of his head. Pilings on pilings—would Mr. Gromm build a house that way? Give the robber baron's widow a break. You had to give a little, take a little, and let rich hearts break the bank a little. All this marvelous twentieth-century elaboration. What did people do before then to qualify for citizenship?

It is suggested that the requested provision diverting thirty percent of the corpus to each child reaching twenty-four years, during the widow's lifetime, will diminish her income considerably at a time when, conceivably, she will have become accustomed to the full income. It has, of course, the advantage of reducing her taxable estate by about $85,000 and reducing her death taxes by about $23,000, but it would also diminish her annual income by roughly $3,000. Her ability to make, in her discretion, annual gifts of $3,000 to each child protects her standard of living and, at the same time, permits a continuing reduction of corpus in favor of the children.

Ah, the humanity of it, the sweet, sane concern over family. The hell with taxes—play with them but get serious about the family. Mr. Gromm, think. All is not vanity. You haven't worked in vain. Your wife will never have to wash a dish. Your dollars will tint her hair, service her teeth, lift her face, wheel her limbs to the limousine, harden her tone to domestics. The beauty of it. Thinking of your family, little man, your nose walks taller in the world.

But. Too much of a good thing kills, Mr. Gromm. The other day, remember? You borrowed five dollars from me to take a cab home, and how can I ask for it back? I'm a struggling young lawyer with expenses—a small boy, a housekeeper. In strict confidence, in the richest country in the world, I don't have a penny to spare. Time is money for those who have the time.

A knock at the door made him look at his watch. It was twenty minutes to one—not Crenshaw, who wouldn't knock.

Miss Rauscher stuck her head in. "Could I please talk to you for a minute? Are you terribly busy?"

"It's all right, Miss Rauscher," he said. He had relatively

little contact with her; he was permitted to use her only when the newest secretary, Miss Gregory, was unavailable, and not even then unless it was urgent. One of the reminders of how junior his partnership was.

She sat down, crossing her slim legs and smoothing down her skirt. Usually she seized every chance to show a sweep of thigh.

"Mr. Halter," she said. "I don't know who to turn to. I have a serious personal problem and you've always been so nice to me."

He looked at her lippy, small-boned face half hidden by a sweep of ash-blond hair, at the little, hard-pointing breasts, and wondered how he'd been nice. He hadn't responded to the caress in her voice, the casual exposure of limbs—was this her definition of kindness?

"What's wrong?" he said.

"I desperately need five hundred dollars," she said, and bowing her head, spreading fingers over her face, burst out crying. She twisted so that her skirt hiked above her nylons. Her sobs were loud enough to be heard outside, and he waited for the stampede of Miss Benton's sensible legs. Miss Rauscher's sobs ceased instantly; lifting her head, she stared, gray eyes wet and gleaming, through her hands. He tried to concentrate on the mosaic of irises but instead found himself inside her pupils. She slid forward on her tail bone, rested her head on the back of the chair and closed her eyes.

Halter wondered if it had become obvious to everyone that he could be had for the asking. She must be aware that of all the men in the office he could least afford to give her money. She must know he was the only one who couldn't afford it.

"I'll write you a check," he said.

She didn't move, not even to open her eyes. He watched his pen trace her name, Terry Rauscher, and the amount and his own name at the bottom. It was a lascivious act—male, female, coupled by money. He ripped out the check. "Here you are," he said.

She opened her eyes, sat up and smiled. "Thank you from the bottom of my heart. I'll forever be grateful. Honest I will. Don't you want to know what it's for?"

"Not unless you want to tell me."

"I do. I owe you that much and more. Much, much more. It's, it's for an abortion."

He sat with the check extended, and when she made no effort to take it he put it on the corner of the desk. His name, hers, five hundred dollars and an abortion. Who would believe he wasn't the man? He sat quietly while the check was being handed from lawyer to court reporter, marked *Exhibit A*, delivered to the judge, scrutinized, lip curled over, returned to the lawyer, presented to the witness—to the world. He could go to the bank and get cash—she owed him that much—but the check, impregnated with sin, lay beyond his power of redemption.

"I don't suppose there's anything to be done with the man."

"Are you kidding? He doesn't even know. He's married. I couldn't ask him for money, could I?"

"I suppose not."

"I mean, it would make everything seem so ugly and dirty, and it isn't that way at all." She reached for the check, folded it twice and stood up. "I'll never, never be able to thank you enough," she said. "I'll pay you back as soon as I can."

He nodded, knowing that he would never get his money back. He had committed the unpardonable—a nondeductible act of charity.

She turned at the door. "I can't tell you who he is," she said, "but you know him very well. I owe you that much." She waited with her hand on the knob, he waited in silence, and she walked out five hundred dollars to the good.

He had failed her. She wanted to tell him who it was; all he had to do was ask. She wanted him to know because then she'd get even every time Halter risked a look. It had to be somebody in the office—otherwise her hints would have no point.

Mr. Forrest? Sam, let's drop the formality, shall we? You see, I have these expenses and ten thousand a year just doesn't do it. You understand. Why, even Terry Rauscher was telling me the other day—by the way, she says you and she . . . She was telling me she thinks I'm worth a lot more money.

When even the secretaries feel that way, it's time to sharpen the pencil, don't you think?

Now see here, Crenshaw. You make fifty grand a year, while I make ten. I'm a decent guy—I go to lunch with you every day whether I want to or not. Miss Rauscher tells me you've knocked her up. So let's you assign me three percent of the firm's take. That gives me another six thou and still leaves you a nifty forty-four. Very truly yours I'd take it as a real kindness.

Come on now, Ben. We're pallies, remember? I'm your buddy-boyed, jollied-up lawyer. Three percent and we'll forget about torrid Terry. It never happened. Why would I squeal on a big brother like you? It's just I've got Mrs. Gummersell to pay, my kid to raise. Me, I could live on the magic of your smile, but I've got these mouths to feed. Okay, sport?

He placed Terry and *the* man in a motel bed. Forrest, sharp-nosed, clocking the waste of time (money), testing the chain at the door with his teeth, clearing his throat for a little billing dictation while he dug clams. Crenshaw, dapper in his bare flesh, placing his order for steak well done (he liked his meat bloodless). Rucker nuzzling her hip socket with his pitted but toujours-gay grin. The truth was, he didn't know which of them it was, because even after six years none of them was more than a sketch.

Meanwhile there was Terry, a self-confessed "other" woman who owed him money. What was she worth on the open market? Let's say, to give her unlimited credit, a hundred dollars a night. She owed him five nights.

Halter pushed at his nose with his fingers. It was a part of his stupid body. It didn't know enough to look down at anybody or to poke into anybody's business. The others would have put up a fuss, extracted details, called her parents or given her a dime to call a lawyer. The guilty one would, at the very least, have demanded a doctor's certificate: *To whom it may concern.* Or he might have made her sweat and scared the baby out of her. Look, Rauscher. I've got a dossier on you. John Craven at the Dropout Motel on January 5, Bill Squeamish on March 19 at the Penetration Hotel, et cetera, et cetera.

You try anything and I'll throw the book at you. I'm not a proctor at admiralty for nothing. Go ahead—pick a time and place. Ten people will swear I was with them, playing Truth or Consequences. Why do you think I wore the false beard and putty nose? Did you think I was that perverted? Beat it, Rauscher, I'm busy, busy, busy.

He knew little about Terry. She was an efficient secretary and made eyes at men. She'd come in, rattled Forrest, Rucker and Crenshaw around under shells, and walked off with five hundred of Halter's dollars. Did she live with her parents? With other girls? Would she paper a love nest with his currency? Was she an innocent soul searching for true love and finding Forrest-Rucker-Crenshaw?

Halter sat, lonely and unprogrammed, in an overpopulated, social-worked world. He knew nothing about anybody, though he had a store of information about Betty. Her way of laughing with her eyes squeezed shut, her good will, her shyness, her charm, her delicacy in eating—a lovely girl with a curious, dispassionate but irresistible form of sex appeal. She was an American-dream girl, wonderful to camp and swim with, reasonable with children and winning with servants and waiters. He'd never made a depth analysis while she was alive. Now, when she was permanently out of his sight, he couldn't afford to settle her in his mind. He had new demands. She was, his mind insisted, the product of his imagination, and he mustn't imagine her as more than a promotion gimmick.

There was a vital, newly discovered fact about his mind: it was starving for sex more than his body. Mentally, sex was different from other appetites; it was the ultimate in Chinese food. He collided head-on with four-letter words and wrote them in a flowing hand. Fingers turned arthritic, he scrawled *fuck*. His mind tasted the word and spit it out, hungrier than ever.

Love is a lie, Halter thought. You can't live on it.

He had the living to consider. He had tendered Terry five hundred dollars because she asked for it. He was payable on demand. He'd have written the check for Miss Benton or Mrs.

Gummersell. For Miss Gregory, the secretary he most used and knew least. If he considered her at all it was as a displaced Brownie leader or Peace Corps worker. Quiet, self-contained, she seemed born to service.

And there was Hilda Brungard. Who would refuse her? He reached for his appointment book; her name there was the only evidence of contact. He would see her in two days.

Crenshaw came in without knocking. "Let's go," he said. Halter looked at his watch; it was one o'clock. He got his coat and followed the round-faced, blue-eyed, immaculate man.

"Back in an hour," Halter said to Miss Benton, "—going to McNary's for lunch," as if she didn't know. Once he tried walking out, like Crenshaw, without a word, and Forrest had called him in and said it was essential to let Miss Benton know where he was going.

She nodded and wrote it down on her time chart. The other girls were typing, heads zeroed in on their hearing aids.

If asked for a single, four-letter-word description of Crenshaw, Halter would unhesitatingly have said *hard*, and yet as they walked to the elevator, waited, rode down and proceeded to the street with no communication between them, he resisted settling for the easy word. There were words behind the words, mattresses beyond the "Do Not Remove" tags. His mind was cut adrift from face values because his body alone could handle them. A waterfall was not a cigarette, a tiger was not gasoline, mermaids were not tunas. Labels on human packages were trickier—adjectives instead of nouns—but pasted on just as much.

Crenshaw's eyes were busy taking impressions of pretty girls as they passed. His lips licked them clean. A hungry man and likely candidate as Terry's seducer. A blonde passed; Crenshaw's man, Halter, turned and looked. Crenshaw's eyes met his; he grinned and Halter grinned back, not without a little alarm. It was a frightening prospect, having the same amusements as Crenshaw.

"Some dish," said Crenshaw in his accountant's voice.

At the restaurant, Crenshaw ordered noodle soup, steak well

done and a salad, Halter a ham sandwich and a glass of milk. Crenshaw usually ordered steak but never soup. Tiny cracks in his routine. He rarely threw Halter a grin either.

When the soup arrived, Crenshaw looked at it and then at the fat waitress with tiny banana fingers that give under weight. "Too thick," he said.

"It's noodle soup, sir. Most people like lots of noodles."

"When I want noodles I'll ask for them. When I order soup I want soup."

"Yes, sir," she said. Halter watched her thick ankles, her white gunboat shoes, her underarms, mottled and puffy, vibrating, carry off the soup.

"How you doing on my option agreement?" said Crenshaw.

"I've started it. There are a couple of things I wanted to get straight. Two of the three shareholders have first options on shares but one doesn't. Is that right?"

"What makes you think it isn't? He's not putting money or contacts in, just work. They don't want him to get any big ideas about who runs the corporation. Once a worker, always a worker. It doesn't pay to give him ideas."

Halter played with his spoon. He didn't put in money or contacts either, just work, and Crenshaw let him know soon enough when his soup was too thin or too thick. He had never tested his relationship with Crenshaw or the others; it was enough that they were in business together. Crenshaw was one of the governors above him in the firm. He existed to be obeyed. A man facing a "No Trespassing" sign, Halter wouldn't dream of walking on the lawn. He was no longer sure if he was a lawyer or what a lawyer was, only that he was *supposed* to be one. Crenshaw was a lawyer. How could Halter be one too? Crenshaw, Forrest and Rucker preached what law Halter practiced.

Yet they, in turn, got only as good as they gave. Clients dictated to *them* in the hierarchy of overlording. Somewhere in the concept of power the lawyer drank a magic potion and was transformed into something else—something that everyone but himself could see and, depending upon the sophistication of the vision, patronized, laughed at or feared. The assumption of professionality was the invisible cloak that the lawyer, naked, believed he wore. Yet the only real professionality was the athlete's; man playing children's games—measurable against the amateurs who worked for nothing at the same play.

And there were no amateur lawyers. There were only children being paid for playing at a man's game, in training for an unrealizable maturity. There were, as in all games, the rules: Thou shalt be hard-hitting but clean, partisan but ethical, ambiguous but honest, dilatory but responsible.

A lawyer was a negotiable instrument: a national anthem that stood up only in public.

A lawyer was one who, if true to himself, was false to his client.

Halter, said Halter, you're a fragment of a fragment. You don't know if you're a lawyer. You don't know what a lawyer is.

The waitress returned with another bowl of soup and Halter's ham sandwich and milk. She stood with the empty tray while Crenshaw sipped and then put down his spoon. "There aren't any noodles in this soup."

The woman stared. "There are too. Look." She picked up the spoon and ran it through the soup. Several noodles climbed to the surface.

"When I want your opinion, I'll ask for it. Take it away and bring me my steak."

The woman looked at the soup, at Crenshaw. Her lips slid along each other like noodles. She picked up the bowl and turned away. "It takes all kinds," she said.

"What did you say?" said Crenshaw.

"I said I'll bring your steak right away."

"I heard what you said. Send the manager over here."

"Ed, she's only the waitress. She doesn't make the food." Halter examined his words; they dangled. The "Ed" (he never gave Crenshaw a name, being suspended in the abyss between first and last) rotated and sped back at him like an aberrant torpedo. He saw in Crenshaw's eyes the unshadowed, translucent resources of an executioner. He marked himself for death but reassured himself with the thought that Crenshaw didn't dispose of his machines until they'd exhausted their reserve for depreciation.

"All right," said Crenshaw. He stood up. "We'll eat someplace else. Let's go." He moved toward the exit.

Halter looked at his sandwich and milk and at the waitress as he reached for his wallet. "How much?"

"Sixty-two cents, sir."

Halter put a dollar on the table. "Keep the change," he said, and followed Crenshaw out. He was light on his feet and in his head. His body, the part that was pushed by buttons and pulled by strings, was a bird, a plane. Fluttering in Crenshaw's wake, he abandoned a number of lingering conceits: that he was guarding his career and it wouldn't do to antagonize Crenshaw, that he was being loyal to someone whose name he knew rather than to a stranger, that he was enjoying the ecstasy of self-effacement. There was little question about it. Crenshaw was not merely hard, he was as locked in place as a precedent case—and that was as uncompromising as a lawyer could get.

· 4 ·

Halter began, in earnest, to divorce his body. After a night in which be bathed in his own sweat, stared at the blackness of his bedroom and formed images of Hilda Brungard's body and eyes—eyes larger than body—ducked his head in poverty of spirit, watched the curl of her lips as he prattled to her husband and his lawyer, caught the amused expression of their eyebrows as they endured him, he rose in the morning with two pillow-tossed hours of sleep, shaved, dressed, listened to the breakfast chatter of George and Mrs. Gummersell, drove downtown, got the eye from Terry Rauscher, worked—except for lunch with Crenshaw—on Gromm's estate plan until four o'clock, and, solid, inscrutable, alert, faced without a tremor Hilda Brungard, Vincent R. Brungard and Felix Mackey. His body, a trained instrument, was entirely at somebody else's disposal.

"Thank you, Mr. Brungard and Mr. Mackey, for consenting to have this meeting. I'm aware it's a difficult one, but I'm sure Mr. Mackey will agree we should make every effort at reconciliation."

"I do, indeed, agree," said Mr. Mackey, a tall, smooth-faced man with a shock of silver-gray hair falling over his forehead. His legs were crossed and the exposed silk sock traveled out of sight up his leg. His voice sounded as if he had a marble in his mouth; Halter knew he could associate with him only on the other side of a case. "I wish to say for the record that Mr. Brungard is perfectly willing to have a reconciliation. He wishes to make every effort in that direction."

Mr. Mackey was not a trial man. Only someone with little jury experience would refer words to a nonexistent reporter. Yet everyone knew Mr. Mackey was a lawyer; he looked like one. And he was building his case. His client was a very rich man and must be defended against the push of an avaricious woman. Halter looked at the woman. She was dressed in a well-cut black dress and wore no jewelry or make-up. Unprompted, she was prepared to take the witness stand after careful back-room rehearsals.

"I like that. Every effort, Vince?" said Mrs. Brungard.

"I've always tried, Hilda," said Brungard pleasantly.

He was an extremely handsome man: tall, slim, with deep-socketed eyes. Conceived as a couple, the two of them restored one's belief, not only in happy endings, but in serene middles. They could break promises to witches and dwarfs with impunity. There was only one way they could be mortalized: separation.

"Mr. McKay," said Mrs. Brungard, exercising the aristocratic privilege of misstating names.

"Mackey," said Mackey.

"Mr. McKay," said Mrs. Brungard. "Has Vincent told you our problem?"

"He has indicated that he loves you but that you desire a divorce."

"I see. Vince, tell Mr. Markey what the difficulty is."

"Mackey," said Mackey patiently.

"Of course, Hilda," said Brungard. When he smiled Halter

realized that he was deeply tanned. Bermuda? Hawaii? Where did royalty go in wintertime?

"My wife doesn't believe I'm adequate sexually."

The statement visibly crawled over Mackey's face as he removed a folded handkerchief from his pocket, and flapped it to clear the air. He wiped his nose and said finally, "I believe that Mr. Brungard mentioned something of the sort. However, he insists that you do have relations periodically."

"Relations," echoed Mrs. Brungard. "Hardly. Didn't Vince tell you? Each of us is an only child."

"Mrs. Brungard," said Mackey. "Permit me to say that marriage is a complex mechanism. To be successful, it involves a great many things: mutual respect, consideration, restraint, protectiveness, responsibility, fidelity, loyalty. And, naturally, sexuality. The unfortunate factor in many marriages is that sexuality is weighted so heavily in the beginning that people regard it as the most significant element and keep loading the scales in its favor the lighter it gets. And it does, inevitably, get lighter until one can recall only with difficulty what a heavy load it once was. Mr. Brungard loves you not only dearly but maturely. Only the genuinely mature man can integrate sex with other equally important qualities and offer his wife love in its most genuine form."

Waiting out the speech, Halter gazed benignly at Mackey, prepared to kiss him on both cheeks. The man had saved him from the impossible attempt to conjugate marriage. Even more, Mackey alerted him to another definition of what a lawyer was: a stunt man performing acts for the star, not merely because they were risky but because they were dirty. A star couldn't risk injury to his make-up, and neither could a client. Only a lawyer or stand-in could afford, was hired, to play the fool.

"Shit," said Mrs. Brungard. Beyond truth to her beauty or beauty to her truth, there was detonation, a four-letter word that went, like Mackey's rimless-glass analysis of marriage, past sex to another place, a place that demanded and could be satisfied only by an original vocabulary. If he could learn to speak her language, he could dial her number, make a date, go dining and dancing with four-letter words.

Mr. Mackey blushed, and as Halter watched, he realized what a rare human experience it was. The body didn't fool around. It surtaxed blood to flee from disaster. "I beg your pardon?" he said.

"Perhaps you'd prefer another word," said Mrs. Brungard.

"What Mrs. Brungard means to say," Halter said manfully, anxious to spell his lady, "is that while sex isn't the be-and-end-all in marriage, it is, nevertheless, one of its *sine qua nons*. Mr. and Mrs. Brungard, unfortunately, seem to be sexually incompatible."

Mackey trained his blush on Halter. "Mrs. Brungard has made herself abundantly clear," said Mackey. "To say I'm surprised at such language from a member of the fair sex is a gross understatement." He turned to Brungard. "I see no point in continuing this meeting any further."

"I do," said Mrs. Brungard. "I'm not a 'member.' I'm his wife. And Vincent's a rich, rich man. Do you think it's prudent to walk out on me, Mr. Muckey? It might cost your client money."

Mackey examined his fingernails. The cuticles were hedged and sculptured. The moons gleamed in the pale light of common reflection; Halter suspected that they were as hard on waitresses as Crenshaw's. The man was in imminent peril of committing a lawyer's unpardonable sin: champerty. Hilda had been willing to secede from the union without looting her husband's territory.

Talking to the boundaries of his moons, Mackey tried to back off onto neutral ground. "You're right, of course," he said. "Thank you for pointing out my presumptuousness. I am merely Mr. Brungard's lawyer. You have a perfect right to look to your own counsel for guidance. Domestic relations have a habit of obscuring a lawyer's duty. He finds himself fancying from time to time that his real client is the marriage. I'm sorry if I offended you."

He raised his eyes to Halter and blamed him for everything.

Masked, Halter stood ready to operate as soon as Hilda told him what the operation was.

Mrs. Brungard sat still for a moment, then shook her head. "No good," she said. "I won't play."

Halter, cool-minded, watched his hands tremble. He caressed one with the other.

"Hilda, my dear," said Brungard, and Mackey raised a finger. Brungard's lips curved into silence. Halter could make no sense of the man. Hilda and he must put their heads together and talk clinically of her husband.

"Mrs. Brungard," said Mackey. "I'll be perfectly frank. Mr. Brungard and I have discussed the possibility of resolving this matter amicably. I confess I consider your husband to be an exceptionally generous man. He is prepared to make a lump-sum settlement of five hundred thousand dollars. I think you'll agree that's more than fair."

"I agree with nothing," said Mrs. Brungard. "Nothing's fair in love or marriage, don't you agree? You'll hear from Mr. Halter."

"Hilda, my dear," said Brungard, and this time Mackey couldn't stop him. "Your happinness means everything to me. Whatever amount will make you happy, that's what I agree to. I wish there was something more I could come up with than money."

Halter decided he was a nice man. Hilda was a lot to lose, and it wasn't his fault that she was more than money, consideration, restraint, fidelity and loyalty could buy; that instead of mouthing her wounds, he could only cover them with unguent.

Hilda got up, kissed Brungard brusquely on the cheek and returned to her chair. "You're a dear," she said. "Still the best friend I've got. But the money's something for the lawyers to worry about. It's nothing between you and me. Let them fight it out."

"I agree, Hilda."

Their battlefield entente shifted delicate weights in Halter. Miraculously, it seemed, a lawyer and client necessary to each other had found each other. He was, he understood, to regard his humanity as incidental, a poor, humble status into which he had been born. He was to wear her colors. He and Mackey were cocks in a fight to the finish, and one of them was not to walk away.

Halter flapped his wings and crowed; he flexed his fingers and cleared his throat. His open mouth breathed dedication. The chips were down. He'd learn what an ordered body could do. He was no hero, but this was the stuff of heroes. He had to put up or shut up forever.

Mackey was immobile. He had come in peace, offered a cheek of reconciliation and another of largess, and been cut for his pains. Rather than being handed bandages, he was invited to gut-fight in an alley. He was, Halter reflected, miscast —too much of a lawyer who went to equity with clean hands. Hired mercenaries should do his dirty work, take the long walk past the livery stable, the general store, the saloon. He was too much the all-American lawyer, practicing an indigenous sport and crowning himself world champion.

Mr. Mackey stood up. At six feet three or four he was the tallest man in the room. "I'll be in touch with you," he said to Halter, and to Brungard, "Shall we go?"

"Good-bye, Hilda," said Brungard. "I might drop over from time to time if you have no objection."

"Of course I don't, Vince. Mr. *Mackey*. It was certainly a pleasure talking to you. See you in court."

Alone with Hilda, Halter faced the fact that he could no longer take refuge behind professionality. She wanted nothing from a husband who was willing to give everything. What could a lawyer do for her?

He could give her a good show, though only a bit player, he was a member of the performing arts, and he would learn his part or be disbarred trying.

"I hope you get your money's worth," he said.

"Don't worry, I'll get it. Well, you had your meeting, and I despise your Mr. Mackey."

"You shocked him."

"That was my intention. Did I shock you?"

"I guess it was the word to use. I'm glad I'm *your* lawyer."

She caught him with a glance, turned him upside down and set him back on his feet. "You better be. You've got work to do. That man disgusts me. What are you going to do about it?"

"He was just being a lawyer. Just trying to do his job."

"Let him practice on somebody else. I can't stand fools. Especially those who try to make a fool of *me*. I've already told you I don't care about the money. Just make him realize what a fool he is. That's all I care about."

Benighted, Halter nodded, floating on waves of feeling toward eyes that generated their own sunlight. He made their roundnesses his own, gave up the ghost of his lawyerdom and swelled outward into curved hips. He unearthed romance for himself, a suitable substitute for love, and its name was Hilda.

She stood up to go and he helped her on with her coat, taking care not to touch her. "May I drive you home?" he said.

"I have my car."

He pushed toward open, vulnerable ground. Perhaps, like Brungard, he had the right of visitation.

"I wonder if I might drop over tonight. We have things to discuss."

She smiled. "I won't be home tonight. Call me tomorrow."

"All right," he managed. She turned the knob and left him confronting the slowly constricting view of her calves. He reached out to get through to her and scratched at the hardwood. With knuckles of its own, the door knocked and came at him as Terry Rauscher.

He stood, head bowed. There was no end to what closed doors could do.

"Is something wrong, Mr. Halter?"

He looked at his watch; the hands informed him it was something he used to call six o'clock.

"No. You surprised me. I didn't know anyone else was still here."

She said flatly, "I've been waiting for you. I haven't had a chance to tell you how grateful I am."

She put her hands on his shoulders and kissed him on the mouth. Her kiss matched the tone of her voice. For some reason he was pinned down under bombardment, and he would have no part of it. It was up to his body to defend itself. Abruptly he swung her to the floor, where she lay beneath him, flat against the carpet. She heaved under his heart and then lay still. His hands explored her surface, searching for a way through to freedom. She shuddered and swung open. Breathing hard, he took the escape route, and sweating, broke into the clear.

Halter got up. As far as he could tell she wasn't crying. She lay on the floor, her eyes closed. "I guess I had it coming," she said. "I sort of hoped . . . Well, never mind. What difference does it make?" After a moment, she added, "I hope you got five hundred dollars' worth."

She stood up, smoothed her dress and sat in a chair. She appeared completely untampered with, but she was totally changed. He couldn't believe that her years as a frivolous, hip-swinging creature could be wiped out irrevocably in a few minutes. Yet it was so, notably so. His victim had been cardboard mask; only now, after the fact, was he allowed to see her as a person.

Unable to believe himself even as he spoke, he said, "It's no excuse, but since my wife Betty died, I've been fouled up. Until now I didn't know how much."

"It was my fault as much as yours," she said. "You want to hear something funny? I was scared of you before this happened. Now I'm not any more. So in a way you did me a favor. Could I have a cigarette?"

He handed her one and lit it for her. How could he have frightened her? In any event, he was being informed that even rape could be considered an act of kindness. In gratitude, he bent over and kissed her on the cheek, and she began to cry.

"What's wrong?" he said. "Shouldn't I have done that?"

She shook her head and tried to talk. "I'll be all right," she managed. "Just give me a minute."

He was willing to give her anything, and in that interval she was no longer Terry Rauscher fighting tears but Betty Halter fighting to stay alive. Betty, returned to him through an earth's turning, unchained from her marriage license, able to tell him off if she chose, or even, if he wasn't careful, to pick up his separate private parts and put them together again.

I won't waste time in lies, he argued. My body has no memory, just hunger. I've got to clear away dead weight. I've got to stop stuffing my mind in my side.

Recovered, Terry managed a smile. "I'm okay now. Would you mind driving me home? It's kind of late for a bus."

He could pay for a cab. Mrs. Gummersell would be getting worried about him. "Of course," he said, and hesitated. "You said that if I cared to know, you'd tell me who the man was. May I ask you now, or is it a bad moment?"

She met his eyes. Her irises were dark and lubricated. "I said you had a right, and that still goes. But why do you want to know now and not before?"

"You don't have to tell me unless you want to, and I don't have any right."

She wouldn't look away, so he had to.

"That's straight enough," she said. "All right."

The telephone rang and they listened to it. The caller persisted. The rings went on beyond counting, shrill messages that poked fingers into his ears. Finally it stopped.

Terry shook her head. "Some clients."

"It's my housekeeper, I think," said Halter. "Dinner must be getting cold."

"Look, you don't have to take me home."

"Yes, I do," said Halter. He moved to the phone and picked it up, staring at the dial. It remained motionless.

"What's wrong? I told you, it's all right. I'll get a cab."

"It's not that. I don't remember my number."

She smiled and he was happy he'd said a right thing.

"I'll look it up for you. That's what secretaries are for." She leafed through his telephone book and wrote his number on a pad.

"Thank you," he said. He dialed and waited through three rings.

"Yes?" said Mrs. Gummersell.

"Mr. Halter, Mrs. Gummersell. I'm sorry I couldn't call you sooner."

"That's all right, Mr. Halter, but George has been asking for you. It's time to get him ready for bed."

"I'm sorry. You'd better not hold dinner for me."

There was silence at the other end. "I see," said Mrs. Gummersell at last. "I rang your office just now and no one answered."

She had him standing blindfolded against a wall with her squad at attention, waiting for ammunition to arrive.

"Yes," said Halter. "Tell George that his daddy misses him and will see him soon."

"All right, Mr. Halter. Would you like to say good night to him? He's right here."

Halter looked at Terry. "Don't you think that might disturb him, Mrs. Gummersell?"

"I don't see why it should, but if you think so . . ."

"Good-bye, Mrs. Gummersell."

"Good-bye," she said, and hung up. The click reminded him to replace the phone in its cradle.

Terry had her back to him. "The man is Mr. Rucker," she said.

"Ben Rucker?"

"That's right." She turned to face him. "Don't you believe me?"

"Of course I do. I'm just surprised. I imagined it might have been Crenshaw. I didn't think it could be Rucker."

Her eyes filled with tears.

"I'm sorry," he said. "I shouldn't have asked you. It was a stupid thing to do."

"Would you take me home now?"

Terry lived in a large apartment building. Not knowing what

to do after he parked the car, he waited for her to make a move, but she sat motionless. Finally he got out and opened her door, and she passed him without a word.

They went to an elevator in the lobby. "Thanks for taking me home," she said, and pressed a floor button.

He still didn't know what to do. "Would you like me to come up for a minute?" he said.

"Would you want to? Don't you have to get home?" she said.

"I'd like to, if it's all right."

"I don't care. The place is a mess."

The elevator took them to the seventh floor, and he followed her down a long shabby corridor until she stopped before a door. "This is it," she said, pulling out her key. "It's not much, but it's mine."

She moved in ahead of him, turning on a light and picking up a sofa cushion from the floor. Some record albums were on the only chair he could see. She moved them to the top of a phonograph. "Sit down," she said. "I told you it was messy."

"It's very nice," he said.

"It'll do." She sat on the sofa and looked at him. Not knowing what to do with his hands, he looked at his watch.

"You came and you saw," she said. "You want to go now?"

"No," he said. What he wanted was to know what she wanted. What *could* she want? He tried to think, but it was no go. His body had done the work, and it was up to his body to clean up.

He walked over, sat beside her, he took her hand, kissed her and leaned back.

She searched his face. Suddenly she bent toward him and kissed him hard on the mouth. She touched his cheek. "See you tomorrow night?"

"Is that what you want?"

"Don't you?"

"Tomorrow then."

· 5 ·

The card was on his pillow. Offended by his body, undressing in the dark, Halter might have missed it if it hadn't grazed his cheek. He found the lamp switch and read Mrs. Gummersell's revelation:

> Of the nations concerning which the Lord said unto the children of Israel, Ye shall not go in to them, neither shall they come in unto you: for surely they will turn away your heart after their gods. Solomon clave unto these in love.

He tore the card to pieces. It was not the kind of communiqué that should fall into hostile hands, and his enemies, his crawling skin, his shrunken limbs, were everywhere. How could Mrs. Gummersell *know*? He was defenceless against her forces. Lacking imagination, they were invulnerable.

Halter: attorney, devoted widower of Elizabeth Halter and

father of George Timothy Halter, deferential employer of Mrs. Gummersell, servant of Hilda Brungard, invader of Terry Rauscher—a respected member of the community. The sum total of his labels was that he didn't matter. His body could make do without him. Time and space could do without him. A born loser, what more could he lose than time and space?

He could lose his mind.

The notion appealed to him. He fancied the idea of dropping it into the garbage can and clamping the lid on it. The collectors would take it to a rendering plant and run it through with the slunk, tripe, guts and the rest. A machine could do anything if man put his mind to it. And Halter's vital organs could glut themselves on each other.

Halter's body rose, heady with freedom, into sleep, but when he awoke, shaved, dressed and was eating eggs across the table from Mrs. Gummersell, wincing at the cartoon noises from George's television program, his mind was back in the chain of command, thumbing its nose at his body as if it had never been dumped.

"These eggs are excellent, Mrs. Gummersell," he said.

"Yes, aren't they?" she said. "I've found a wonderful man who delivers them fresh from the farm. I think it's terrible what happens to eggs by the time they get to supermarkets."

"I suppose it is," said Halter. Lifting his coffee cup, he found that his hand was shaking. Afraid to meet her eyes and read in them that the wages of sin is death, he said, "I'm sorry about last night. I should have called you earlier."

"Well," she said. "The Lord knows you're a busy man, and my father always said that a woman who stuck her nose in a man's business deserved to have it bitten off."

She smiled, and Halter hopefully considered the possibility that the bargain between them had become a marriage of convenience.

"But George and I do worry about you, don't we, George?" she said.

George, sitting on his legs, was pinned to his chair by television rays.

"George," said Mrs. Gummersell, sharply enough to slice through any spell. "I'm talking to you."

The boy jerked his head.

"Say after me," said Mrs. Gummersell. "We worry about you, Daddy."

"We worry about you, Daddy," said George to Bullwinkle.

"My clients were from out of town. They wanted to have a little fun while they were here," said Halter. He was a bad liar; even if he weren't, it was impossible to fool someone who was so sure of the difference between right and wrong.

"Of course, Mr. Halter. Boys will be boys. It would never do to offend a client. But if you could just tell us when you're not coming home till late so we won't worry—"

"You're perfectly right. I apologize and it won't happen again."

He wiped egg off his chin and went over to George, sitting a foot from the television screen. "I'm going to work now, George boy. How about a kiss good-bye?"

"No," said George out of the side of his mouth.

"Handshake?"

"No."

"Well then, good-bye, George."

George didn't bother to answer, and Mrs. Gummersell followed Halter to the door. "We're terrible when we watch cartoons. Nobody can get our attention. But we do enjoy them so. And we may still be the teeniest bit angry at you for not being home to kiss us good night."

"I'll read him *The Cat in the Hat* after dinner," said Halter. "That might patch things up."

"I'm sure it will. That's a wonderful idea."

Halter escaped to his car. Escape from one situation led to an escape from another. He was constantly skirting danger. Danger from what, of what? Losing his temper? Assuming he took a stand against Mrs. Gummersell, told her to keep the house, not him, told her he'd blow his own nose and all she need do was launder the handkerchief, what was the problem? She could quit and he could get another housekeeper to whom he could lay down the law from the beginning. That was no calamity, certainly not a clear and present danger.

Yet the only puff that held steady above his head was the imperative "Be not assertive." What was so ominous about the invitation to become a "man," which was to say, become a commander?

Mr. Halter, to be a man, one must give up a rib. That statement was in the cards.

Okay, Mrs. Gummersell, he said to the steering wheel, Halter remains your obedient employer.

Downtown, past the carefully impersonal glance of Terry, the cool, freckled nod of Miss Gregory, the watch-checking chirp of Miss Benton, he found Mr. Gromm waiting in his office with a copy of the estate plan in his hand.

"Hello, Mr. Gromm. Thank you for coming in. Have you read it over?"

"Sure, I read it. Last night. That don't mean I understand it. Give me bricks and mortar every time. You boys can have the paper work."

"It's not really too difficult, Mr. Gromm," said Halter, sitting down behind his desk and picking up a copy. "If you left things as is, you'd leave everything outright to your wife. You understand that."

"Sure. Gladys knows that. Everything I got I want to be hers."

"The trouble is that after you've both died, it would cost your children about seventy thousand dollars. You'd be giving the federal government seventy thousand that you could save for Jimmy and Dorothy."

"Listen," said Mr. Gromm. "I got nothing against the federal government. This country's been mighty good to me. But it ain't the same any more. They're taking away our initiative, and don't let anybody fool you. That's how we built up this country. Now it's soak the hard-working citizens and taxpayers and give it to the bums. I'll tell you what they ought to do with the bums. Put 'em on a boat and ship 'em to Siberia. That's where they belong."

"Yes . . . Well, you can save seventy thousand in estate taxes, and it's what they call avoidance, not evasion. The government *wants* you to take advantage of the tax laws. That's why Congress passed them."

"I'm with you there. We got nothing in this country if we got no respect for the law. So what do I have to do? I tell you, I got nothing against the government, but we've come to a hell of a situation when you got to go to a lawyer to find out what's legal and what ain't."

"It's simple, Mr. Gromm. First we set up a sixty-thousand-dollar inter-vivos trust, income to Gladys for life, then to the children, to provide for their education and support, which you'd have to pay for anyway. Then, after Gladys dies, to the kids outright if they've reached thirty, I believe you said, or if they haven't, left in trust with income to them until they do. The rest of the estate you dispose of by a testamentary trust. Gladys gets the income and whatever principal the trustee thinks she needs for her support. Half of it is tied up for the children, and the other half she can leave to them by her will. That's all there is to it, and you save seventy thousand."

"I got you. I save seventy thousand. Let me tell you about my family, Mr. Halter," said Gromm. "Don't get me wrong, I love my family. I'd do anything in the world for them. Why do you think I work sixteen, eighteen hours a day if not for them? A man would have to be crazy if he wasn't doing it for the wife and kids. But you know? Kids ain't the way they used to be. It's like the world owed them a living. Take my boy, Jimmy. He's eighteen years old, still wet behind the ears, and already he tells me he'd starve before he went into his old man's business. Like it was a crummy two-bit outfit like the way it was when I got into it. And I'm telling you, he's a good boy. I don't know what it is. The ideas, maybe, they put in his head at that fancy college of his. I tell him college ain't up in the clouds when it comes to sending bills. Four thousand dollars a year they nick me for and act like they're doing me a favor. My worst customer I don't treat like that. Okay, I tell him, so even if you think my business stinks, what do you suppose pays for you to stay a pupil? 'Pop,' he says, 'I'm doing you a favor.' Got that? He's doing *me* a favor. Everybody does me a favor by taking my money. 'You like to spend your money on us,' he says. 'You keep telling us you're slaving away just for us. Besides,' he says with a big laugh, 'if you didn't make so much money I could get a scholarship and go free.' He could too, you know. He's quick as a whip, an honor pupil.

"And Dorothy. She's only in high school, but you think she's any better? Sixteen years old and she's got to have her own car. You ever see the clothes those youngsters are wearing? The dances they do? Everybody talks about what the modern generation is coming to, but I swear to God, so help me, these kids are something else. You think she listens to a word I say? I can't even come in and meet her friends. It's a rule, she says. Any house they got to meet the parents is off-limits."

"I guess you're right, Mr. Gromm," said Halter. "The modern generation is difficult to handle. They're just against, not for."

"Now you said it. You hit it right on the nose. Rebels without a cause. You're their father, you're dirt. You stand on your head and it don't do any good. I told her if she came home one more time at three in the morning I'd take away her car, and you know what she told me?"

Halter shook his head.

"Try and guess. Go on," said Mr. Gromm.

"Well," said Halter. "She said she'd never forgive you."

"Are you kidding? She said she'd walk into a police station and accuse me of doing something bad with my own daughter. Can you beat that? The little devil."

"I guess," said Halter, "the problem is, they're your own flesh and blood and you have to admire their guttiness."

Gromm nodded eagerly. "That's it in a nutshell. I love those crazy, stubborn kids. They ain't got the sense they were born with, but I love 'em."

"Getting back to the estate plan for a moment," said Halter. "I gather you'd rather let them have the seventy thousand than the federal government."

"Yeah, let 'em have it. Let 'em tear up the town. What you gonna do?"

"Fine," said Halter. "I'll draw up the papers. Everything should be ready in about a week."

He stood up and then sat down again. Mr. Gromm wasn't going any place.

"Let me tell you something," said Mr. Gromm. "I went to work as a carpenter's apprentice when I was fifteen years old. High-school dropouts—big deal. I been on the job thirty-five years without a vacation. I ain't griping. That's the only honest way to make it, and nobody can tell you different if they're honest."

"Times have certainly changed. But you've earned a little time off, Mr. Gromm. It would do you good to get away for a while and relax."

"You're right there. Not to have to look at the mugs of those union bosses for a while. You don't own your business. They do. Look at them sideways, and they tell you to go jump in the lake. A rat race is all it is. I should quit and clip coupons. That's what I ought to do—let some other sucker get the ulcers."

"It makes sense, Mr. Gromm."

"Sure, that's the ticket. Pete Gromm lying around the old beach. You know what I'd do? I'd go down to a construction job and stand there, watching those goons pounding nails. Just stand there. I tell you I've earned my rest."

"No denying that, Mr. Gromm."

Mr. Gromm silently shook his head. He stood up to go. "Who's kidding who? I'm good for one thing, to put up buildings. You have to be a college boy to know how to sit around doing nothing. I tell you, Halter, it's one hell of a world."

"That's for sure, Mr. Gromm. But you mustn't let it get you down. It's the only world we've got."

"Sure," said Mr. Gromm, shaking Halter's hand. "Tell it to the kids."

Alone, Halter positioned Mr. Gromm, the poor little rich man, on a chessboard. He was a pawn. None of the agility of the knight, no majesty, no oblique clericism of the bishop. His home was not his castle. The perplexities were to decide which of the eight pawns he was and whether he had the first move. Gromm had to stay close to home. He would move one step at a time, straight forward, and only when his family was attacked would he strike catty-cornered at the heart. Mr. Gromm, leader of a company, was still a bodyguard, his life expendable.

And Halter, moving slowly with his head down, he too existed to gain his life by losing it; only he violated the basic rules by being ready to succumb to a passing fancy. Superpawn, he sailed over the heads of braced pieces and wound up breathless, sitting behind his desk. As he started to work on Crenshaw's option agreement there was a knock, and Terry Rauscher came in carrying a file. She waited until the door swung shut before she spoke. "Hello, Mr. Halter," she said.

"Hello, Miss Rauscher."

She sat down with the file opened on her knees. "I had to talk to you," said said. "About last night. You don't owe me anything. You can forget about tonight. I mean it."

He looked at the file in her lap.

"It's nothing. Just in case anybody walks in." She was dressed to go out to dinner, and looked very nice.

"I thought we might go to the Palisades."

"You're sure? It's what you want to do, not feel you have to?"

"I'm sure."

"All right. I'd love to go."

She stood up and walked out. He couldn't get over her transformation. She even walked differently, without the exaggerated swing of hips, and he couldn't swear it had ever existed.

He worked steadily until one, finished the option agreement and turned it in to Crenshaw just before they went to lunch. He decided to volunteer nothing to the man, not even the business references that were their usual line of communication, and see what would be said.

Nothing was said until—Halter checked his watch—one-thirty. Crenshaw's manicured teeth ground at his steak, informing Halter that even if the man spoke, his words would receive the same short shrift as the meat. His speech, like his teeth, was a tool, precision-made, and designed for material use. Since words were immaterial to begin with, Crenshaw dispensed with most of them. The result was that wherever possible they became acts which altered the physical world.

The silence, Halter discovered, was impossible to live with. He even found it difficult to swallow without the oil of nouns and verbs. "How's Constance?" he asked, exploring the first-name ground he'd so recently won from Crenshaw, of a wife he had never seen.

Crenshaw grunted. A word, covered with gastric juices, stood poised in the tunnel of his throat, then turned back.

"And the kids?"

"Randolph's ranking his class. So is Bill. Randolph is captain of the baseball team and Bill's number one on the debating squad."

"That's fine. George is a great little kid too."

Crenshaw stared at him. In Crenshaw's pupils Halter could read only an image of himself standing on one toe, wriggling his ears.

"My son George," he explained.

"Oh."

"I think," said Halter, lapsing into familiar sign language, "that the option agreement's in shape now."

"We'll see. I'll look it over this afternoon."

Jokes. Crenshaw liked dirty jokes. But when Halter tried to think of one, he couldn't recall anything dirty enough, except that it wasn't Crenshaw with Terry at all, but Rucker. Rucker, with pictures of the wife and kids gold-framed on his desk; Rucker, of the "little woman." Crenshaw, eater of meat, hadn't chewed Terry up and spit her out. He was of sterner stuff. Giving other men the business was *his* pleasure.

At the office, two telephone messages were waiting. One was from Mr. Mackey, the other from Mrs. Brungard. Halter sat for some time over Miss Benton's smoothly rounded, little-finger-off-the-paper handwriting, and then ventured to call Mackey first.

"Yes," said Mackey. "About the Brungard matter. Before it

gets out of hand, we should reach an understanding, don't you think? I'm sure our clients will listen to reason if we don't allow them to take over the reins here. You and I should be able to perform a genuine service to both of them."

"I should think so," said Halter. "What do you have in mind?"

"Very good. Now I'm willing to recommend to Mr. Brungard any settlement within reason. What is your client *really* prepared to accept? There's no sense sparring with each other."

Halter meditated. He had to make sure he went beyond reason. "She really wants sixty percent of his estate. I'd say that's more than fair, wouldn't you?"

"It's absolutely preposterous. You know that as well as I do. I thought we wouldn't spar around. Let me put it another way —lawyer to lawyer. What figure would you recommend to her?"

"Sixty percent, Mr. Mackey. I'd be happy to recommend sixty percent."

Halter listened to the older man's breathing. When a lawyer might as well save his breath he wound up squandering it. Words made up differences between reasonable lawyers. Breath without words was the only way to deal with an unreasonable one. Mackey was unaware of the latest mutation of one of his own kind, which required that he behave as an *unreasonable* man would under the same or similar circumstances.

"I see," said Mackey. "You want to make a fight out of this."

"No, I don't. I really don't. My client would be very satisfied with sixty percent. That's the minimum she feels she's entitled to. She's a lot of woman, Mr. Mackey, don't you think? Possession of her comes high."

"All right," said Mackey. "I'll lay my cards on the table. I am prepared to recommend to my client that he settle for one million dollars. I think it's outrageous, but in the interest of making an amicable disposition of the matter, I'm prepared to do it. I can't, of course, guarantee it, but I believe that my client will follow my suggestion."

"Your client has in excess of five million," said Halter. "And sixty percent of five is three. Correct me if I'm wrong. I tell you what—we'll forget about the hundred thousand or two over the five million and just take an even three. We can be generous too, Mr. Mackey."

"Young man, you have a lot to learn about the practice of law."

"Yes, sir. I know that."

"I'm letting the offer stand for two days. Consult with Mrs. Brungard. She strikes me as an intelligent woman. If the offer is not accepted by then, all offers are withdrawn. It strikes me that one hundred and sixty-five thousand dollars for each year of marriage is adequate compensation for any woman. She's not the Queen of Sheba—particularly since she doesn't even have adequate grounds for divorce. I must say, Halter, I'm shocked at your attitude. She'd be lucky to get a fraction of our offer in open court."

"I agree with you on one point, Mr. Mackey. She's not the Queen of Sheba. But I'll certainly present your proposition to her. Is there anything else?"

"No. Good-bye."

"Good-bye, sir."

Halter had problems. He was hired to fight and win a private war with Mackey, and how to do it was his business. There was no blueprint to follow. The prescribed procedures, the common property of any responsible lawyer, were all Mackey's; there would be no Halter victory in the courtroom, whatever the verdict. Whether a lawyer won or lost a trial, it was all in the game and he lived to fight another day. To defeat Mackey, Halter had to seek extralegal remedies. The man must be stripped of his shield of Latin phrases. He had to be driven into personal involvement and be beaten with his own hitherto veiled sense of self.

Their contest would be one of chicken: one of them must turn his wheel away from his own onrushing humanity. One, perhaps both, would try himself and find himself wanting.

Halter called Hilda's number. He was the only lawyer in the world with a hot line to the above and the beyond.

"I'd like to see you," she said. "Tonight?"

Halter hesitated. There was Terry. "Certainly," he said. "I've just been talking to Mackey."

"Dinner, perhaps?"

"Fine. Where would you like to go?"

"I meant here, at my house." Her voice sounded amused. "But let's make it out. You choose the restaurant. Let's say seven-thirty." She hung up.

A saw ran its teeth along Halter's skull: tell me what a man does and I'll tell you what he is. But he couldn't say what he was. A lawyer didn't consort with his female client in the middle of a divorce proceeding; he advised her not to see other men until she got her decree.

To come to terms with himself, he'd have to invert the saw: tell what he was to tell what he did. He was a trained bear, taught to walk on hind legs and carry a briefcase, a lion jumping through loopholes, a trapeze artist performing without either spangles or net.

Miss Benton filled his doorway. He hadn't heard the door open. "Neil, Mr. Forrest wants to see you right away."

Her left eye squeezed shut in an insinuating wink. Before he'd discovered this was a tic, Halter had responded with a quick, eager wink of his own. Miss Benton had been snappy for a week.

Halter hesitated before Forrest's office. He had to knock loudly enough to be heard, softly enough not to make waves. He rubbed his knuckles along the panels, gathering momentum, and rapped sharply. He turned to watch Miss Benton's eyelid squeeze him into pulp as Forrest said, "Come in."

Sitting at his desk, Forrest let him stand. The man's straight, tiny-nostriled nose drew a bead on him. "Halter," he said. "You worry me."

"Yes, sir," said Halter, accepting the cause behind the accusation, whatever it was, as a statement of fact. He stood, a puff of flesh, distending and contracting on trapped air, trying to imagine the moment he, going nowhere, could have crossed Forrest's mind. There was, of course, Terry Rauscher, and there was Hilda. There was Mackey. There was the network of listening doors.

"Gromm was in to see me," said Forrest. "What have you been saying to him?"

"Nothing, sir. We just talked about his estate plan."

"He wanted you to handle all his business, even his corporate affairs. What are you trying to pull?"

"Sir, I give you my word: all we talked about was his estate plan."

"Don't get any ideas. From now on, I'll be seeing Gromm, on the estate plan or anything else. You might be getting too big for your britches."

"Sir, believe me—"

"I wouldn't believe any young lawyer on a stack of Bibles. Remember, I was one once myself. I give you credit for ambition. Just point it in somebody else's direction, not mine, or I'm liable to make you wish you never had any. Sit down."

"Yes, sir." He found the edge of a chair and leaned forward.

"Relax," said Forrest, and smiled. Halter watched the lips move upward while the eyes dared him to move a muscle.

"You know our Miss Gregory?" said Forrest.

"Yes, sir."

"What do you think of her?"

"She does very good work. She's a fine secretary."

"I'm not talking about that. What do you think of her *personally*?"

"I don't know her personally, but she seems to be a very nice girl."

"You're damn right she is. Know who her father is?"

"No, sir."

"C. F. Gregory Department Stores. That's who her father is."

"I see."

"Get the picture? C. F. Gregory."

"Yes, sir."

"All right. We've got a big break sitting right here in our laps if we know how to use it. Miss Gregory got this job on the sly, you understand. The old man had nothing to do with it. We had no idea she was anything more than just another employee. Matter of fact, we never met him until yesterday. He's represented by Burns, McGregor and Mackey and has been for years, but there's no reason it has to stay that way."

"No, there isn't." Halter recognized a divine right of kings. Like Mrs. Gummersell, by use of the royal "we," Forrest permitted his subjects to vote only by proxy, and only for their sovereign.

"I'd give my eyeteeth to get him for a client," said Forrest.

"I wish you luck, sir."

"It takes more than luck, Halter. Around here we *make* our luck. That's where you come in."

"Me?"

"You. Gregory is worried sick about his daughter. This is the first time she's pulled anything like this. She's lived a sheltered life. He wants somebody absolutely reliable to keep an eye on her without her knowing he has a hand in it. *He'd regard it as a personal favor* is what he said. You with me?"

"I'm not sure."

"Look, Halter. You and I are the only bachelors in the firm. I'd give my eyeteeth to be twenty years younger, but I'm not, so that's that. Which leaves you." Forrest smiled. "I don't imagine you have much trouble with the fairer sex, huh? Miss Benton tells me you've got quite a way with the ladies."

"My wife just died, Mr. Forrest," said Halter.

"That's true. We meant to convey our condolences, but we've been so damned busy around here we haven't had a chance. You have our deepest sympathy."   ,

"Thank you, sir."

"But we've got to go on living, you know? It doesn't pay to sit around feeling sorry for ourselves. Work is the great healer. Let me tell you something. Not only will she inherit a fortune, but she's an attractive girl. Damned attractive, if I say so myself. Remember this could mean a lot to the firm and the firm won't be ungrateful."

"You want me to keep an eye on her?"

"That's the ticket. Keep *both* eyes on her. Cozy up. Get to know her inside and out. Make her feel she's got a strong shoulder to lean on. Spend time with her. Just be careful not to get cute. You know what I mean? No cute stuff. We're relying on you, Halter, so don't let us down."

Forrest got up and put a hand on Halter's shoulder. A first. "Halter, *she's his only child*."

The hand radiated bamboo shoots under the fingers, needles in the eyeballs. Halter had to get away. "I'll do my best," he said.

"I know you will. I expect to see a lot of you from now on. I want you to report back every morning at nine o'clock. This is Red Alert on your calendar."

"Yes, sir," said Halter. The hand spread its fingers and kneaded Halter's dough until he was a dumpling, ready for the oven, then tossed him aside.

"Tomorrow morning you start your reports," said Forrest. "All systems are *go* as of now. We don't want Gregory to get another bright idea."

"Yes, sir," said Halter to Forrest's back. On the way to his own office he collected two winks, one from Terry, the other from Miss Benton's autonomous left eye. All he could see of Miss Gregory was her short brown hair and sturdy back bent over her typewriter.

As he fell into his chair Miss Benton came in. "How did it go?" she said. "I hope he wasn't too rough on you."

"No. He was very nice."

"Good. I think I helped. I told him you certainly didn't seem to be the type of person to go behind his back and steal his clients. What did he say?"

"I'm sure you helped a great deal, Miss Benton. Thank you. He said that he would see Mr. Gromm from now on and that I should be more careful what I say to clients."

"That's all? My, you were pretty lucky to get off so easy, weren't you? That's *all* he said?"

"Yes," said Halter. "Thanks again, Miss Benton."

She lingered, then turned abruptly and left Halter alone with his new legal duties. He was now a paid informer. He pressed his buzzer for either Miss Gregory or Terry; he had business with both of them.

It was Terry.

"I'm sorry," he said when she came in. "Something's come up tonight. I can't go to dinner with you. Perhaps we could go out for a drink later—but only if you want to, of course. I'm terribly sorry."

She was silent. "I told you before," she said at last. "You don't owe me anything."

"I want to go out with you very much. This can't be helped. If not later tonight, let's make it tomorrow."

"How late would it be?"

"About ten or ten-thirty. No later, I'm sure."

After a moment she said, "All right. Ten-thirty's okay."

He waited until she disappeared, and buzzed again.

"Yes?" said Miss Gregory.

"Miss Gregory, could I please see you a minute?"

She came in and sat down with her pad on her knees. Halter stood up, to look at her for the first time as Alice. She had, as a credit, nicely spaced, large brown eyes. There was nothing wrong with any of her features, but assembled—the nose springing out a little too much, the lips slightly too thin—she might be any of the legion of women who listened to too many stories about her girl friends' men, saw too many movies with her roommate, spent too many evenings alone washing her hair. Except that Alice was also Gregory. Halter felt for the girl as she watched him and waited; she must be in trouble, to be sitting there at all.

"I hope you won't be offended if I ask you something," he said.

"What is it?"

Her voice, rather boyish, was not unpleasant. Nor was her muscular and slight-breasted body. She looked as though she played a great deal of tennis and spent time on the archery range. Her movements were graceful.

"I wonder if you'd care to go out with me sometime."

She closed her pad. "Why?" she said, without change of expression.

"It would give me pleasure."

She stood up. "All right," she said.

He was disconcerted at how equable she was. It was difficult to be indifferent to indifference. "Thank you. Would Saturday suit you? Perhaps we might go to dinner."

She reopened her pad, wrote on it, tore out the page, handed it to him and walked out. He looked after her. The address was in an apartment area, not a particularly good one, in the middle of town. He put the paper in his wallet, sat at his desk and worked very hard. There were hours to eliminate, between him and Hilda Brungard, between him and Terry Rauscher, and now, between him and Alice Gregory. The brain he was supposed to keep cool was working overtime and getting over-heated. Three women were a lot to keep in a mind that also had to be careful its body wasn't playing tricks on it.

· 6 ·

Hilda wore a sleek black mini-skirted dress cut in a straight line across the middle of her breasts. Halter floated in a submerged, sound-muffling depth of ocean. They were sitting in leather chairs near the entrance. Others were waiting too; men and women, she was what they were looking at.

He was in a public place with a beauty of the world and suffered the consequences because he didn't have the means. She belonged on a private yacht, behind sunglasses and ocean spray, or in a manor behind electrified fences. He prayed for the anonymity of a table. Finally it was ready, and he followed her through the crowd that made way for her and condescended to let him through.

"This isn't bad," she said, examining their alcove as he ordered martinis. In the dim light her body was a magazine illustration, and he was able to absorb the glossy imprint of her eyes.

"All right," she said. "This time I'll ask the questions."

"I imagined you would."

"You must be used to this sort of thing, but I find our relationship unusual. You're equipped with the intimate details of my life; yet you're a stranger. You must have noticed how uneasy you make me. I've figured out why it's different with my analyst. With him I can explain myself, with you it's the hard, unvarnished facts."

"I wasn't aware I made you uneasy," he said. "I wouldn't give myself that much credit."

She smiled. "Don't. It's the facts you possess, not you, that bothers me. I was naïve, wasn't I? You didn't need them. Perhaps I knew that but confused you with my analyst. He'll get a kick out of it."

"The information is safe with me," he said carefully. "It's a privileged communication."

"I'm not worried," she said sharply. "You're annoying, you know, with your legalisms."

"I'm sorry."

"And with your sorrys. Why are you so guarded? I answered your questions. Why don't you answer mine? You have a file on me and can put your hands on me any time you want to, whereas and wherefore I don't have any idea of who your hands belong to. No wonder lawyers are pompous."

He shook his head. "I don't believe I'm pompous. If there's anything you'd like to know, I'll try to tell you as honestly as I can."

" 'Honesty.' The most abused word in the English language. Do you honestly believe you're honest? Would you like me to test you?"

"I don't mind."

She showed him her profile as she looked away. Reviving his sense of her beauty, he couldn't believe that whether she was a file in his cabinet or not, she cared to bother with his vital statistics. The truth was that her "confession," its sexual base, made him uncomfortable. He'd never gone back to his notes, not even in his mind. He preferred not to think of her in sexual terms at all.

"I don't believe you do," she said. "I don't believe you care if you're honest or not."

"Yes, I do. Very much."

"Let's see. How long were you married?"

"Six years."

"What was your wife's name?"

"Betty."

She nodded. "Your wife should be named Betty. She was a marvelous housekeeper, companion and mother to your children. Do you have any?"

"Yes, she was," said Halter. "I have a little boy, George."

"You loved each other very much. No ugly sexual problems. Nothing but sweetness and light."

"That's true."

Hilda sipped her martini. "I find it invigorating to talk to an honest man. It revives my faith in human nature." Her voice was flat. "Lawyer, you've flunked your lie-detector test. The horror is that you don't even know when you're being dishonest. People like you are incapable of facing themselves squarely. Consider yourself lucky. You can lie on a bed of emasculated roses. It's the truth that's thorny."

He had failed her, but unexpectedly she'd failed him as well. Her beauty had. She should have expected nothing but reverence and offered nothing but still-life poses. Nature had failed her; it refused to let her body speak for itself. Whatever she might say to him, he found he could face *her* squarely.

"What's the matter?" she said. "Why are you looking at me like that? Have you finally discovered the truth hurts? But you couldn't, could you, and stay a lawyer?"

"There are all kinds of lawyers. I'm sure the truth hurts some of them."

"What kind are you? For that matter, what kind of *man* are you? I've labeled you and your marriage a fraud. Don't you care to fight back? This is a man's world. You could break me in two. No, you can't forget I'm a little woman and must be protected. You can't lay a finger on me except to pat me on the head. You're filled with lies, Mr. Halter, and that makes you the complete man. Here's a truth for you to start with. Women have known for a long time they're stronger than men because in lying to men, they don't lie to themselves. Look at me, please."

"I am."

"What do you see?"

"A very beautiful woman."

"Of course. That's what you see. That's *all* you see. You allow me my words because you don't see them. I could say anything to you and you wouldn't hear me. The good woman is the silent woman. Your wife Betty opened her mouth to say 'Yes, dear,' and you loved her with all your heart. Isn't that so, Mr. Halter?"

"Yes."

She rolled the stem of her glass. "I know the word that's in your mind. Men use it to define women who tell men what they are."

"I think you're very hard on yourself."

Her fingers stopped fiddling. "Well," she said. "So you can fight back."

He ordered steaks and a bottle of burgundy.

"I'm the little woman," Hilda said in a tight voice. "And that man at the next table has been undressing me for the last ten minutes. What are you going to do about it?"

Halter turned to a man about forty sitting alone. He was short and beefy, with a paunch. Halter went over. "Excuse me," he said. "My friend says you've been undressing her for the last ten minutes."

The man chose to make a stand. "It can't hurt to look, can it? What does it cost you?"

"Nothing," said Halter. "You have a clear sense of values." He returned to the table.

"He's still looking," said Hilda. "The least you could do is knock him down if he doesn't stop."

"All right," said Halter. He went back to the man. "My friend says I should knock you down if you don't stop."

"You do and it'll cost you plenty. Listen, buddy, forget it. A woman who can cause trouble like that, I don't care what she looks like, I'm not interested." He moved to another chair, with his back to Hilda.

"That's better," said Hilda, as Halter sat down. "Although I'd have been more impressed if you'd hit him. Don't you want me to consider you manly?"

"I don't know how to answer that."

"Perhaps you play the violin."

"No."

"Paint?"

"No."

"What do you do? You must have told me, but I forgot."

"I practice law."

"Yes, but I don't like lawyers. Why should I like you?"

"I don't suppose you should. You don't have to like me, so long as I get the job done."

"Oh yes," she said. "The job. Any boy out of law school could handle it, couldn't he? It's really a waste of your precious time."

His mouth was dry. "I mean the job on Mackey."

"What are you talking about?"

"You want me to get him and I will."

She frowned. "I don't like teases. Make sense or I'm leaving."

"You don't want alimony," said Halter patiently. "You told your husband the money was something for the lawyers to fight over. You hate Mackey for treating you like a child and you want to get even with him."

"Is that what you're prattling about? Come on. I don't dislike Mackey. I pity him. He's a lawyer, isn't he? He nettled me for a moment, but I've forgotten about it. I advise you to do the same. You have queer notions."

"I don't believe so. I think you've despised him for a long time. You'd like to see him humiliated."

She was silent. "What makes you think I've ever met him before?"

"I just do."

"All right," she said. She looked at him in a new way. "How did you know? Because he was Vince's lawyer?"

"I just knew," he said stubbornly.

"You have psychic powers."

"Perhaps."

She laughed humorlessly. "You *are* queer. I know him and I don't like him. Do you assume I want to humiliate everyone I don't like?"

"Yes," said Halter.

A silence lengthened between them.

"I don't like you, Mr. Halter," said Hilda.

"I know."

"For your information, I have good and sufficient reason to hate Mr. Mackey. And to humiliate him. That doesn't mean I intend to carry it any further. For my purposes I disturbed him sufficiently at the meeting and that's the end of it."

Halter shook his head. "It's only the beginning. I have a plan that will do more than merely disturb him."

"You're crazy," she said. "I'm really annoyed. Are you trying to pull my leg? I don't think it's funny and I'm warning you to stop right now."

"I'm not being funny. You want me to do a job for you and I'm going to do it."

"I'm telling you. I want you to get my divorce. The sooner the better. That's all I want, and if you think there's more to it than that you're fired. I hired a lawyer, nothing more."

Halter nodded. His body was perspiring, but his mind was cool. "You can fire me, of course. Otherwise I'll get Mackey for you."

"You keep saying that and I keep telling you I don't want you to. You think you can wear me down with repetition?"

"No."

"All right, then. You're fired. Send me your bill."

Halter's hands were shaking and he put them in his lap. "When you get another lawyer," he said. "You might have him get in touch with me, and I'll turn over the file. I'll delete the unessential notes."

"Thank you. That's very thoughtful," she said coldly. She paused. "Now that it doesn't matter, would you mind telling me your plan?"

"I checked on Mackey. His wife divorced him recently after fifteen years of marriage."

"I know that. I know her very well. He was a louse."

"He has a conventional weak spot. He likes pretty, young women. He's been seen around with quite a few of them."

"I could have told you that too. He's a nasty-minded louse."

"I know someone who's young and pretty. I think she'd be willing to help me. I thought we'd get him in a compromising position and take some pictures."

Hilda's laughter was so loud that the man at the next table turned around. "That's very funny," she said. "What's funny is that it would work. It really would. I know him. I'd give anything to see his face. No, I wouldn't. Don't get any more notions."

"I planned to have them meet through some incriminating letters she's willing to give him. Letters from you to me. She'd do it because she's jealous. I wanted to involve his lawyerdom as well as himself."

"Very ingenious," said Hilda. "And would she have the right to be jealous?"

"I can't answer that," said Halter.

"But she'd be willing to do it for you?"

"I think so. I can't say for sure."

Hilda rested her chin on her hand and watched Halter. "It *would* be amusing," she said. "*If* you went through with it. Frankly, I don't think you have it in you."

"I think I do."

"Why? Don't tell me again because I want you to. You must have something personal against him. You're not clever enough to think this up for my amusement. Why do you hate him?"

He'd anticipated the question. Even if she hadn't asked it, it still required an answer. He didn't hate Mackey. What then? What he stood for? What *did* he stand for?

"I don't hate him," he said.

"What then? What are you trying to prove?"

"That his trousers come off at night. That he wears more

than his old school ties. That he has become what he does rather than what he is."

"My God," she said. "You're in big trouble with all those thats. Why didn't you tell me you were an intellectual? Imagine a lawyer being an intellectual. Cheer up. I don't dislike you any more. I pity you as much as him."

"I'm glad you don't dislike me."

"I am too. It permits me to change my mind. I could never find another lawyer like you. You're rehired."

"I can't accept," he said slowly, "unless I'm to go ahead with Mackey as planned."

"Of course," she said. "I wouldn't miss it for the world."

Halter was tired. He realized he had expected to be fired.

"One thing," she said. "The pictures. Who will take them?"

"I've heard of an expert."

"No. You'll take them. Only you. I insist on that."

He hesitated. "All right. I'll need expense money. Quite a lot. For the girl. We can't expect her to do it for nothing."

Hilda smiled. "I shouldn't think so. How much?"

"Five thousand dollars?"

Hilda didn't bat an eye. "I'll get it for you. From Vincent. Don't worry. I won't spill the beans."

"Thank you," he said. He was committed. He saw himself with a tiny, demonic creature perched high on his frontal lobe, Halter's reins held in its hands, locking all his systems in one irresistible go.

He paid the check. At her house she said, "I'll have the money for you in a few days. I expect a run for my money."

"I'll draft the letters and bring them over to you. They'll have to be in your handwriting."

"You do that," she said. "Frankly, I wouldn't know how to sweet-nothing you." She smiled sweetly. "To think you're listed in the yellow pages. Good night."

"Good night," he said, and drove home. It wasn't until he awoke the next morning that he remembered his ten-thirty appointment with Terry.

· 7 ·

It was a loser, Halter decided, but he didn't tell that to the client, Miss Farraday. He stapled the note pages together and told her he'd discuss it with Mr. Rucker. She was overdressed, puffy, with a heavily made-up face and small round eyes.

"He said any number of times he'd take care of me. When I think of all I did for him."

"I know," said Halter. "I have it all written down. We'll call you very soon."

As he went across the lobby to Rucker's office Terry didn't look at him.

"Well, how did it go?" said Rucker. As usual, his desk was a shining blank expanse. He didn't like work staring him in the face.

"I think we should turn it down, Ben."

"Why? It sounded pretty good to me over the phone."

"Seven years ago she needed a place to live. She answered this ad about a room, and the old guy, Bartholomew, rented

· 72 ·

her space for ten dollars a week, with kitchen privileges thrown in. It's a little bungalow, with two bedrooms, a kitchen, living room and bath. Once a week there was a cleaning woman, who's since died. Our lady worked in a department store six days a week, nine to five, during the entire claim period. She still does. After a few months, the old man and she became chummy. She says he thought of her as a daughter."

Rucker winked. "What else? What do you think?"

"I think he's the first and last man she ever slept in the same house with, outside her father. They started eating breakfast and dinner together. Sometimes she cooked, sometimes he did. He bought all the groceries. She stopped paying rent. She washed the dinner dishes, he the breakfast ones. She straightened out the house from time to time—which means she picked up newspapers. Sometimes she emptied the garbage, sometimes he did. Once in a while, a crony of his, also now dead, came over to play checkers and she served them beer. Most of the time he and she sat and watched television. Sometimes they went to the movies together. Sometimes she visited girl friends and left him at home alone. Her girls friends never came to the house. He gave her some expensive presents—a watch, a fur coat, earrings. On these facts, she regards herself as having been his devoted slave, taking care of the poor septuagenarian as if he were a baby, never free to go on the dates she claims she had to turn down. She can't come up with a single live witness."

"Wasn't he sick?"

"No. He fell over dead while mowing the lawn."

Rucker shrugged. "So she'll make her own case. Companion and housekeeper for seven years. Two hundred a month, let's say we shoot for fifteen grand."

"She can't testify. The dead man's statute. I think it's hopeless. She's sore because he pops up with an eighty-thousand-dollar estate she didn't know about. She feels she's been conned with her watch, coat, earrings and free room and board."

Rucker played deadpan, which was rare. His pitted skin, narrow eyes and thin lips turned ugly. Jarred into remembering him as Terry's seducer, Halter waited for the sanctuary of Rucker's smile.

"It's not all that bad, Neil," said Rucker. "I'm sure when she thinks harder she'll recall that her girl friends were at the house all the time."

"They were never there. She was clear on this."

"Sure they were. She just got confused."

Rucker was smiling, but looking beyond him to the unmanipulated view, Halter was unable to smile back. "I see," he said.

"This isn't my client, you know," said Rucker. "She works for a friend of Forrest's. We don't have to push it to trial Forrest just wants her to get a few bucks to make us look good You wouldn't want to let Forrest down, would you? You know me. If it were up to me I'd say to hell with it. No client means that much to me. But you know Forrest."

"Yes."

"File the suit and see what happens. I'll get you some witnesses. If she can't come up with any, we'll drop it, okay?"

"All right," said Halter, and turned to go.

"Wait a sec, Neil. Do you have another minute?"

Halter stopped.

"Say, could you do me a big favor? We've got this big personal-injury case for the Sunflower Railroad. This guy drove through a crossing and got clobbered. I've got his deposition set for two this afternoon and I'm in one hell of a bind. Can you take it for me? I'd really appreciate it."

"All right."

"Terrific. You're one hell of a buddy, and don't think I don't know it. Here's the file. His address is on the inside of the cover."

"Isn't the depo being taken here?"

"No. They're pulling out all the stops on this phony. Haggerty's his lawyer, so you know what to expect. Says he's bedridden, so what can you do? I said, okay, we'll take it in the apartment. You got your car? If not, use mine."

"I've got my car."

"You're really helping me out of a spot, Neil boy. You know I wouldn't ask you if I didn't have to. You had lunch yet? I'll take you to the club."

"I guess I won't have time," said Halter. "It's one-fifteen."

"Gee, that's right. We'll make it tomorrow then, okay?"

"All right," said Halter, and escaped.

He went to Crenshaw's office. "I'm sorry," he said. "Ben wants me to take a deposition at two o'clock on the south side of town."

Crenshaw checked his watch. "How long will it take you to get there?"

"Twenty or thirty minutes."

"Hell, let's get a sandwich across the street."

It would take at least half an hour to familiarize himself with the case, Halter reflected. In a way it was amusing. What Crenshaw didn't know—that he was nothing special—would certainly hurt him. First come, first served, Mr. Crenshaw, is the order of the day. What if he discovered that his only hold left over Halter, available to anyone, was his timing? That the first to demand was the first to be obeyed? That once Halter had denied the priority of his *own* demands upon himself, nobody's had priority—not Crenshaw's, not anyone's?

"All right," he said. He put the file on his desk and met Crenshaw at the door.

"What's the case about?" said Crenshaw as they went down on the elevator.

"I don't know. I haven't looked at the file yet."

Crenshaw shook his head. "You tickle me. When are you going to learn that preparation is ninety percent of a case? Maybe Rucker can get away with it, but take it from me, you can't."

They ordered corned beef sandwiches and coffee. Halter finished in four minutes and watched his companion chew. After the sandwich, Crenshaw ordered ice cream and another cup of coffee. As they left, Crenshaw said, "If there's anything I can't stand, it's a sandwich at a cafeteria. It sticks in my throat all afternoon."

"Yes."

It was one-thirty. He had just enough time to go back to the office, get the file and drive over.

"Where's your briefcase?" said Crenshaw.

"I left it in my office."

Crenshaw shook his head again. Halter went up, put the file and a yellow pad in his case, took the elevator down and walked to the parking lot. It was one-forty when he started the engine, and he realized he didn't know how to get where he was going. He asked the lot attendant, who didn't know, so they went into the office to look at a city map. He drove south at one forty-five. At two o'clock he realized he was lost, and he had to ask a filling-station attendant for directions. At two-fifteen he asked another man. He found the house, a single flat, at two twenty-five.

He didn't know whether Mr. Crowder lived upstairs or down. He tried the downstairs bell. A woman in a housecoat and cleaning cap stared at him through a glass pane. "Mr. Crowder?" he said.

She pointed upward.

"Thank you," he said, and rang the other bell. He found that he was perspiring.

Footsteps pounded down the stairs, and Haggerty opened the door. "Halter, how are you? Glad to see you again, boy. How have you been?" Halter's hand was given the full treatment.

"I'm sorry I'm late."

"Forget it. Listen, don't I know you? If you couldn't be here on time, it's for a damned good reason. It's just that my client is in such lousy shape that I hate to keep him under a strain too long. You'll see what I mean."

Haggerty was one of the most successful personal-injury lawyers. His name was associated with hundred-thousand-dollar verdicts. He wore baggy suits and never raised his voice before a jury, even when he cried. The mild voice and the tears had a devastating effect. Haggerty believed in his tears.

"How's my buddy, Rucker? Couldn't make it today, huh?"

"He's fine, but he had something else on his docket."

"Wait'll you see my boy. It'll tear your heart out. We stand around, jawing about money, and my poor chap's had it. One minute he's got nothing worse to worry about than whether the beer's cold in the refrig, and the next he's a vegetable. I could take every cent the lousy railroad's got, and what good will it do him? You know what I was thinking about while I was waiting for you? I was thinking of going to the president of your railroad and saying, 'Look, Mr. Big, forget the money. Just make him whole and he'll get down on his knees and kiss your hand. Not one word of reproach. He'll just kiss your hand.'"

"I'm sorry," said Halter. "Shall we go on up?"

"Sure we'll go up, but listen. We've got his doctor and a nurse up there. When you start rolling, if the doc says it's too much for him, we'll have to postpone the depo. This man's bad. We'll just have to see how it goes. I'm not kidding you. Wait till you see him."

Haggerty pushed open the door, and Halter saw. A figure was lying on a regular bed, not a hospital bed (Halter made a mental note), encased in bandages from the top of his head to below his shoulders, where the blanket hid the rest. All of his face was hidden except for holes at his eyes and mouth. He looked like Claude Rains as the Invisible Man. Anything could be under the bandages except death: the eyes were alive. There might be the rest of a man under the blanket, a mermaid's tail, the carved trunk of a tree. Or it could be any man or woman lying there: Haggerty's law partner, the United States President, Mrs. Gummersell. Halter saw Rucker at his cocktails or on the golf course or wherever he was and envied him for his quick solutions to impossible problems.

"This is Dr. Garrett and Miss Carroll," whispered Haggerty.

Halter ducked his head.

"And you know Ralph Brown."

The court reporter smiled; never having seen him before, Halter nodded.

"We ready to begin?" whispered Brown, fingers poised over his box.

"Yes," hissed Haggerty.

"Appearances?" whispered Brown.

"Terence Haggerty for the plaintiff," whispered Haggerty.

"Neil Halter for the defendant," whispered Halter.

"H-a-l-t-e-r?"

"Yes."

Brown leaned over the invisible man. "Mr. Crowder, do you solemnly swear that the testimony you're about to give is the truth?"

"My time is TOO expensive AND I'm not your little boy. TELL it like it IS," issued forth from the mouth hole. The voice was unmistakably that of a man standing at one end of a tunnel and calling toward the patch of light at the other. It had the deep, resonant, burly sound of a playground instructor, whistle around his neck, directing juvenile traffic.

The sound barrier having been broken, Halter whispered to Haggerty, "Do we have to whisper?"

Haggerty shrugged. "You're taking the deposition, not me," he whispered.

"Medically speaking, Doctor," whispered Halter. "Is it better for me to whisper?"

"Not necessarily. Just try not to alarm him," whispered the doctor.

Halter bent over the bed.

"Please state your name."

"Papa was a TRAMP low-down POOR. But he was a lover TOO," yelled the witness.

Halter went from face to face. They were grave and attentive. He saw that he was in for it.

"Is your name Billy Joe Crowder and are you the plaintiff in this case?"

"I woke UP this morning, toes OUT of my shoes."

"Where do you live?"

"I'm not YOUR steppin' stone. NO, NO, not ME."

"Were you involved in an accident on, let's see, September eighteenth of this year?"

"TELL it, baby, YEAH. TELL it, baby, YEAH. TELL it, baby, YEAH."

"Did the accident occur at the railroad crossing on Howard Street?"

"NASHVILLE cats play CLEAN as country WATER. Nashville CATS play wild as mountain DEW."

"Was anybody in the car with you when the accident occurred?"

"CAN't face the WORLD with your head to the GROUND."

Halter examined the virginal yellow pad resting on his knee. He drew a whole note, going around and around until the ink weighted the paper. He added a line to make a half-note. He added fins on fins and wound up with a hemidemisemiquaver. "I have no further questions," he whispered.

"I just have one," whispered Haggerty. "Mr. Crowder, you were a popular singer before your unfortunate accident. You sang around town. You sang *The Star Spangled Banner* at baseball games. I notice that in response to Mr. Halter's inquiries, you spoke, rather than sang, lines from popular songs. Would you please *sing* a line for me?"

"OVER in the CORNER," said the witness, "a little mouse lay OVER on his SIDE."

"I want the record to show," whispered Haggerty, "that the witness *spoke* his answer in response to my request that he try to sing. That's all I have. Ralph, my client will waive signature, and I want a copy."

"I'll take a copy," whispered Halter as the doctor leaned over the bandages and inserted a thermometer in the mouthhole.

"I'll walk down with you, Neil," whispered Haggerty.

They confronted each other on the porch. "Rucker doesn't know what he missed," said Halter.

"Sure he does—I told him. But you have to see it to believe it. Listen, I'm not trying to tell you fellows how to run your business, but I'd settle this one if I were you. I'd hate to have to roll my client into court, for your sake as much as his."

"How much do you want? I'll pass it on to Rucker."

"I can get three hundred thousand from a jury. Easy. You know it and I know it. I'll recommend two. They need the money bad, as you can well imagine."

"Recommend it to whom?"

"His parents. They're gonna have to handle him like a baby the rest of his life. Isn't it a hell of a thing?"

"I'll tell Rucker. He'll get in touch with you."

"Right. Just tell him not to wait too long. See you around."

At the office Halter went through the file and read the railroad investigator's report. The accident had happened at two in the afternoon on a clear, sunny day, at the intersection of the railroad and a deserted highway. There was a crossbuck sign at the intersection and a warning sign six hundred feet up the road. No flashing signals or crossbar. The train was going southwest about thirty miles an hour, and the car northwest at sixty. The train engineer, the only eyewitness besides the plaintiff, stated that he first noticed the car when it came from behind a house. The train was then passing a sycamore tree on the right, its whistle blowing. The investigator had measured the distances. The house was eight hundred feet from the crossing, the tree four hundred. There was a report from an engineering expert: under optimum conditions, the braking distance of a car going sixty miles an hour was two hundred and seventy-two feet and the car would have to start slowing down by some two hundred and six feet. According to the expert, this meant that the train would be around one hundred feet from the crossing before the engineer could know the car wasn't going to stop. And, concluded the investigator, railroad experts said that train brakes had no effect on train speed for at least two hundred and twenty feet.

Halter leaned back. The law was clear: the engineer was bound to exercise only ordinary care, and the driver of the car the highest degree of care. If the investigator's summary stood up, the plaintiff would have trouble holding the railroad liable. He might not even get to the jury. Of course if he did, and they saw the bandages . . . Another damaging fact to the plaintiff: the skid marks. They didn't start until a hundred and thirty-six feet from the crossing.

The engineer was quoted: "He was lying there a bloody mess. I threw up. I couldn't believe he was still alive."

Somewhere inside the holes in those bandages lay a twenty-five-year-old boy-man who had sung his ditties, who had been begotten but never would beget, who would have camped on the Provincetown dunes or sprawled in a king-sized bed at a Hilton Hotel, taken his kids to the zoo, watched late, late movies—and who had driven across a railroad crossing.

Murder had been committed. Machines, Inc., had murdered Crowder's mind but couldn't be convicted because you'd never get a confession. The homicidal intentions at the crossing were those of a hundred-and-fifty-ton locomotive and a one-ton car. The humanitarian doctrine looked sheepish in the eyes of physics.

Halter sat and wondered where Crowder was hiding out. He was least of all in his bandages. Trapped from the neck down, he might still be alive, but petrified in memory of song fragments, he was no longer a man. He'd lost more than his life; he had become one of those machines that had killed him.

Halter went to see if Rucker was back. He was, or perhaps had never left, after seeing Halter off to the deposition. Rucker of the pitted face and charming smile that captured juries. Rucker's world was a succession of magic mirrors into which he looked and saw that all was well.

"Well, buddy, how did it go?"

"Crowder's mind and body are completely gone," said Halter. "There's no question about it."

"That's too bad. Still, he can't kill us with his testimony. So where do we go from here?"

"We?" said Halter. "Do you want me to stay on the case?"

Rucker handled the big injury cases, Halter the small ones. It was Rucker's pride to sweep into the office on a wave of astonishing verdicts, and only large money, gained or saved, had the power to surprise.

"Sure I do. It's time you graduated to the big leagues. You've earned the right. If it goes that far, you'll try the case, okay? We'll show Sam Forrest what you can do if you get the chance. What do you say?"

"All right."

Was it the ugliness? Was Rucker afraid to look into Crowder's holes and find his own skin there? Or did he think it was a loser all the way?

"Have you read the investigator's report?" asked Halter.

"Yeah. He doesn't think the engineer could have stopped in time. Just try to tell a jury that."

"Maybe it won't get to the jury."

"Don't bet on it. Haggerty gets to the jury, hook or crook. Did he make you an offer?"

"Yes. Two hundred thousand."

"Why not? What's your idea of a counter? Or do you want to forget settlement and take a shot at it?"

"I think we should settle. A jury could come in with the five hundred thousand he's prayed for."

"How much?" said Rucker.

"A hundred twenty-five?"

"Too much. Fifty and be prepared to go to seventy-five. I know our railroad boys. That's their limit. They expect miracles from this office." Rucker smiled. "I've been lucky."

"I don't think Haggerty will go that low."

"Sure he won't. So you try the case. Win it and you'll be the golden-haired boy around here. Don't say I never did anything for you."

"I'll call Haggerty."

"Good." Halter turned to go. "Wait a sec, Neil. Forrest was telling me about our Miss Gregory. She's not a bad-looking little chick, you know? How you making out?"

Halter looked beneath the skin, underneath the laugh wrinkles, the volcanic skin, the light gray eyes, and examined Terry Rauscher smoothing her skirt. "I'm taking her to dinner Saturday," he said.

"Terrific. You know what her old man's worth? Over a hundred million, I'd say, and he's stopped counting. Little old Alice gets prettier by the minute."

"She's a nice girl."

"Sure she's nice. My God she's nice. Neil, just remember your buddy Rucker. I knew you when. Tell you what. How about you and Alice dropping over to the house some evening? A nice, congenial atmosphere never hurt anybody. I've been bending Mary's ear about you. She's been dying to have you over. How about it?"

Halter had never met Rucker's wife, just as he'd never met Crenshaw's. It was regrettable he couldn't bring Terry. It was only decent for Mrs. Rucker and Terry to get acquainted and to compare notes on how it was to be Ruckered.

"That would be fine," he said. "I'll ask Alice."

"Do that. How about Saturday, since you're already set with Alice? Help you break the ice. Mary'll be tickled to death."

"All right."

Terry was in his office when he got back. "I'm terribly sorry, Terry," he said, "about last night."

She seemed perfectly calm. "That's all right," she said. "I have something to talk to you about and I don't want to discuss it here. If you could manage to see me tonight I won't bother you any more."

"I want you to bother me. Would you like me to come to your place? Any place else? Any place you say."

"My apartment will be fine. Thank you."

She got up and quickly walked out. He couldn't think of a word to make her pause.

· 8 ·

After dinner Mrs. Gummersell had to go to church "to help in the rummage sale," and Halter was alone with George. He did what George did; he watched the monster. Sitting with the light solid weight of boy on his lap, he watched a vegetable on humanoid legs, with death-ray and shaggy-dog eyes, immobilize loving couples in lovers' lanes (a favorite haunt of monsters), and then absorb them into his leafy parts.

Waiting patiently for the vegetable to meet its inevitable fate, Halter felt that some explanation was in order. "George, do you know what that is?"

"It's a monster," confided the profile inches from his own.

"It's a man dressed up in a costume," said Halter. "He's just making believe."

"It's a monster," said George.

"Not really. That's what I'm telling you. It's a man pretending. When the show's over he takes off the costume and goes home to his family like everybody else."

George preferred to ignore him. He was listening to the monster, who in a British accent was informing his current victim that he came from the planet Grunk, where the food supply had been exhausted, and that he, a scout, was checking for galaxy substitutes. Earthling flesh was of the same chemical compound as their own source of food supply. The victim, a police officer, didn't seem to understand and went on screaming until the Grunk finished him off and gathered him in.

Halter tried again. "Isn't it a funny monster, George? It looks like a cucumber with artichoke leaves."

"It's a monster," George said, and impatient with the interruptions, twisted off Halter's lap, dragged his little wooden chair a foot from the screen and sat down.

It was difficult to compete with a creature from outer space, and Halter was left with the question of men and monsters.

There were men: Crenshaw of the round, clean face, condensed blue eyes, the metronome ticking in his brain capsules, making time-space studies, making *sure*. Rucker of the corroded skin and metamorphosizing drug that rearranged his pegged and socketed face into gaiety. Forrest of the nose that sniffed out the moneyed, and the strongbox of a brain that he unlocked only to maintain his economy.

Halter regarded the Grunk. A leafy thing, risking the unknown for the sake of starving Grunkians.

Messrs. Forrest, Crenshaw and Rucker. I've become aware of a serious situation, involving all mankind, and I don't know who else to turn to if not my partners. I've just learned that the world has run out of Wheaties, Cokes and Popsicles. Unless something is done, and quickly, the world as we know it will cease to exist.

Mr. Forrest: How much will it cost me?

Mr. Crenshaw: Here's what you have to do. Do it.

Mr. Rucker: I hate to ask you, but I've got this speech to give at the Rotary Club. Could you take a stab at the Wheaties-Coke-Popsicle affair? It's a real chance for you, and don't think I'll forget it.

Mr. Forrest: Who owns Wheaties? You're missing the boat, boy, and Miss Wheaties is on it.

Mr. Crenshaw: Things better go better with Coke. Wrap it up by tomorrow, and don't fuck up.

Mr. Rucker: I met this terrific, ruddy Popsicle, I mean a real lollipop with all the right connections. Be a buddy. Get him to come to dinner. Mary would love it. What do you say?

It was likely that none of his partners, operating from different perspectives, were humanity-savers. Of course, no one could save mankind, but each person should have his chance sooner or later. Forrest-Rucker-Crenshaw seemed to prize life, and this was bad bargaining for such canny traders because they had so little respect for it.

Startled, Halter twitched in his chair. The front door slammed. Mrs. Gummersell was back, advancing on him, on George and on the Grunk eating his way through New York, himself about to be destroyed. Mrs. Gummersell, invincible in her cloth coat, turned him off, picked George up and laid him against her shoulder.

"It's past our bedtime. Say 'Good night, Daddy,' and then we'll go upstairs and put on our pajamas."

"Good night, Daddy."

Mrs. Gummersell suffered Halter's little child to come unto him and be kissed on the cheek. As she transported George upstairs, Halter considered the miracle of his son's docility. It was safe to say, wasn't it, that a three-year-old boy *wanted*? That *want* defined him? Yet Mrs. Gummersell contradicted three-year-old maleness with impunity. George didn't whimper; he accepted Mrs. Gummersell as an implacable substitute for babyhood.

To be sure, Halter contributed to the miracle with his acquiescence, but how could he justify countermanding Mrs. Gummersell? To use juvenile-court vocabulary, how would it serve the welfare of the child? Imagine them in a custody suit. Consider the equities.

Mrs. Gummersell is a creditable woman—a credit to her community, her church and her employer. Halter will give her the best of recommendations, and without a trace of hypocrisy. His reservations concern himself: he may say she could do her best work with a better employer. George eats well-balanced meals, sleeps the necessary hours, wears clean clothes, has ten-percent fewer cavities, never spits or pees in his pants.

Halter, to give him his due, is a decent man. He does what he can. Just ask him.

We acknowledge that each of the parties seeking custody is not evil. One discovers that it is rarely a matter of the good and bad guy and finding out which is which. More often it's a balancing of equities and determining, not whether one is a better person than the other, but who will best meet the needs of the child. We have heard the evidence and after weighing the pros and cons have arrived at the following Findings of Fact:

Mr. Halter sleeps on his stomach. One arm is curled under both the pillow and his head. Often his arm falls asleep before he does. He allows his toenails to grow too long. Sometimes he tears one off and bleeds. He has not washed behind his ears for a long time. The cuffs of his trousers and shirt sleeves are frayed. If one pulls a hanging thread, an entire garment may come apart. In the morning he coughs, an engine on too poor a mixture.

Mrs. Gummersell sleeps on her right side, pressure away from her heart. She chews pebbles to perfect her speech. She winds her white hair in metal curlers and captures her head in a fishnet. She flies her flag on Independence Day and lights up on Christmas Eve.

Mr. Halter has been known to begin a trying day with his lips drawn away from his teeth like a frightened dog. He shakes with dry heaves and prays for vomit.

Mrs. Gummersell rises, breathes grandly at the open window, does knee bends and touches her toes.

The ultimate fact is that Mrs. Gummersell knows what is good.

The ultimate fact is that Mr. Halter doesn't know. He has been known to go to the bookshelf, get his philosophy book and hide behind the following:

Mrs. Gummersell: God is good is God is good.

Mr. Crowder: Picture you upon my KNEE. GOOD for you, good for ME.

The telephone rang and Halter answered it.

"Mr. Halter?" It was an unfamiliar male voice, muffled as through a handkerchief.

"Yes."

"Neil Halter?"

"Yes."

"With a client named Hilda Brungard?"

"Who is this?" said Halter. "I don't know who you are and why you're speaking through a handkerchief."

"I'm a friend, Mr. Halter, with a friendly tip. Your client Hilda Brungard is about to drink and dance and who knows what else with her husband's lawyer. Tonight. I thought you'd like to know."

"Who is this?"

"Remember. Tonight at the Palisades. A word to the wise. About the handkerchief. I have a cold and don't want you to catch it, friend."

The receiver gurgled off, and Halter lowered the telephone into its cradle. From every point of view it was a vicious transmitter. It dealt in lewd static, obscene threats, unrecorded graffiti. It was the culmination of human irresponsibility—the unbonded voice.

Halter had no doubt the message was true. The precision of the voice couldn't lie. He stared at the telephone. He wanted his voice back. Yearning for the sound of himself, he dialed Hilda's number.

"Hello," she said, and he hung up. How many times in the history of the world would Halters hang up? How many times would he cave in at the sound of her voice? In the past, the history part, Halters had been cowlicked by seventeen-year-olds who had telephoned pseudo-Hildas and been unable to survive the frat-pin-on-the-breast hello. Available to Halter the man was the genuine, beautiful, tough-minded Hilda, and all he could do with history was repeat it.

He had reason enough to talk to her: the anonymous telephone call. Was she really going out with Mackey? Had she scuttled Halter's scheme for one of her own?

Going upstairs to change clothes, he passed Mrs. Gummersell. She put a finger to her lips. "We're asleep," she whispered.

"I'm going out," he whispered.

"When will you be back?" she whispered.

"There'll be blue birds over the WHITE cliffs of DOVER," he whispered.

"What?"

"I'll try not to be too late," he whispered.

"Of course."

Halter hesitated over what to wear. Reasonably a shirt open at the neck, slacks and a cardigan sweater. Easy-come, easy-go clothes. Instead, he chose his best suit and tie and reported to Terry, feeling like a parolee.

She was dressed in a pink caftan with a band of embroidered crimson tape running from her chin to the floor. She looked pretty, dark-eyed and sweet, a fragile bird with crushable bones.

"Thank you for coming," she said. "Won't you sit down?" As he did so, she reached into a pocket and handed him a folded piece of paper.

He opened it. It was his five-hundred-dollar check. "I don't understand," he said. "Why are you giving it back to me? Don't you need it any more?"

"I don't know what to do with it, so you may as well have it back." She pretended to smile. "I don't know what I expected. I guess I thought all I had to do was look in the telephone book. I'm not very smart. I wouldn't be in this mess if I were, would I?"

He put the check on an end table. "What are you going to do?"

"I don't know. I'll think of something. But it's not your worry, is it? It never was. I didn't have any right to get you involved. I'm sorry I troubled you."

He glanced at the check. He could pick it up and walk out, and Terry Rauscher would be reduced once again to nothing more than a secretary in his office. She had stated a clear and unambiguous fact. She wasn't his worry. "Do you still want the abortion?" he asked.

"Why wouldn't I?"

"I'll find someone," he said. "Don't worry. Everything will be all right."

He had no more idea than she of how to supply a missing link, but people did it every day. It was simply a matter of looking up one's sleeve.

"Why?" she said. "Why are you still helping me? Just because I asked you to?"

"You're in trouble. What are friends for if not to help each other?"

She sat down on the couch next to him and made a study of his face. It was as though each of his features was being treated separately, and he wondered if any one of them offered a truth to satisfy her.

"I'm very grateful, Neil," she said. "Someday I'd like to be able to help you in return."

Wanting only to assure her of his friendliness, he leaned forward to touch her lips as if patting her shoulder. She put her arms around him. He returned the pressure and she gave before it. He followed her downward and ferreted out the zipper on her caftan. As he paused, she breathed quietly beneath him.

Hilda Brungard accused him of being intellectual. All right. Intellectuals needed subterfuges: they turned out the lights, tuned in on music, eyed flaming logs. Intellectuals shunned the businesslike light and played in the dark. Here and now, under naked bulbs, in his businessman's suit, he could lay his intellectuality to rest. Here and now he could prove to Terry he could bear scrutiny.

There was this to be said about his body. It was terribly repetitious, but he didn't mean to interfere with it. He wouldn't psychosomatize it.

There was this to be said about his mind. It had a right to its own territorial integrity.

He sat up. "I'm sorry," he said. "I keep forgetting myself."

She remained passive, hiding under her eyelids. Finally she sat up.

"As a matter of fact," he said. "You *can* help me. You can, but maybe you won't. What I have in mind is a lot to ask."

She turned away. He waited a long time for her answer. "I said I would and I will," she said finally.

Whatever he did, his head wound up in a noose. His mind was as lynchable as his body, and equally solipsistic. Gravely he put it to work. If the tie between body and soul was something that didn't exist, what could it be but convention? To generate faith in things that didn't exist was the original sin, and that made it not merely conventional but criminal. There was Terry to think of. Convention had impregnated and raped her and demanded the death of her unborn child, while law, convention's mercenary, stood idly by. It was fitting that she in turn should screw a lawyer.

"Do you know who Felix Mackey is? He's been in the office."

She nodded. "The lawyer."

"Yes. He's against us in the Brungard divorce case. It's important to me to get something on him—something pretty bad. That's where you come in. But only if you want to. I still don't think you will."

"What do you want me to do?"

"I'd . . . well, I'd like to catch him making love. I'd take some pictures."

She stared at him. "You mean with me?"

"Yes."

She was silent. "I guess I don't know about you," she said. "What are you trying to make of me?"

"I expected you wouldn't want to do it. Remember? I don't know who else to ask. Actually, it's not quite as bad as it sounds. We wouldn't let it go too far. Just enough to make him look bad." He hesitated. "It wouldn't be for nothing, of course. We couldn't let you do it for nothing. There's five thousand dollars in it for you."

She thrust her jaw at him. "That makes it perfectly all right, doesn't it? Look what a person like me would do for a measly five hundred dollars, so imagine what I'd do for ten times that. You sure you want to pay that much? I wouldn't want to take advantage of you."

"I'm sorry if I've upset you," said Halter.

"What's to be upset about? What am I? Just another secretary, right? You know what I make. Two dollars and forty cents an hour. I'd be a fool not to leap at the chance. What is it, an hour's work? That'd be five thousand dollars an hour. I bet even Elizabeth Taylor doesn't make that much."

"I think you are upset. Why don't we forget it?"

"I will *not* forget it. Why should I? You made me an offer. It's a deal, and now you're trying to welch out of it. Five thousand dollars. That's what you said, wasn't it?"

"I wouldn't have brought the matter up if I hadn't thought it was important."

"I don't *care* whether it's important. A deal is a deal. All I care about is the money."

She ran into her bedroom and slammed the door. He walked over and listened. She was crying. When he entered she was lying face down on the bed. Her logic was impeccable; five thousand dollars was a lot of money.

"You really want to?" he said.

"I said so, didn't I? You help me, I help you. That's what friends are for. Isn't that what you said? Besides, what does it matter any more?"

"I guess you don't think much of me."

"Do you care?"

"Yes, I do."

"I bet. Well, I can't afford to think anything. We're in business together. Would you please go?"

He turned away. "If you change your mind, let me know," he said. "There's no hurry."

"I'll do that. I'll let you know."

He opened the door. "About your personal problem. I'll take care of it."

"Thank you very much. I wish you'd go."

He shut the door behind him and leaned against it. His head hurt, but he couldn't face going home to Mrs. Gummersell's card. He had to drive to the Palisades to see if Hilda and Mackey were really there.

· 9 ·

Halter sat alone at his table and surveyed the restaurant. Hilda wasn't there. He pondered his sense of relief. Halter the judge put Halter the witness under oath and had Halter the district attorney question him:

Halter the D.A.: Mr. Halter, you realize that you have a constitutional right to remain mute?

Halter the witness: Yes.

Halter the D.A.: You are willing to waive your privilege?

Halter the witness: Yes.

Halter the D.A.: You are doing this of your own free will?

Halter the witness: Yes.

Halter the D.A.: Mr. Halter, you are on trial for your lawyer's life. Why did you become a lawyer?

Halter the witness: When I was a little boy I once pulled the wings off a butterfly. I thought that if I became a lawyer I might be able to put the wings back on.

Halter the D.A.: Do lawyers put wings on butterflies? Answer yes or no.

Halter the witness: No. But I thought they did.

Halter the D.A.: Do you admit that your conduct is unbecoming to a lawyer?

Halter the witness: I do.

Halter the D.A.: The State rests.

Before the judge could pass sentence, Halter took a pill, drank a potion and returned to his table at the Palisades. He looked around. Hilda and Mackey were sitting at the other side of the room. He had no idea how long they'd been there.

Hilda's eyes picked him up and moved with him as he approached their table.

"Well," she said. "If it isn't Mr. Halter. I believe you two have a nodding acquaintance."

Mackey nodded. "Hello, Halter. Sit down, won't you? We've already ordered drinks. What will you have?"

It was a remarkable performance. No start, no quiver, no covering effusions. Mackey eased into an ominous sphere of reference; his dignity carried him a very long way.

"I'll remain standing if you don't mind. Mr. Mackey, I wouldn't have expected this of you. Do you regard it as ethical to be with my client without consulting with me first and getting my approval?"

Mr. Mackey turned white, then red, and stood up to confront Halter.

"What new nonsense is this? I was informed by Mrs. Brungard that you desired a meeting, that you felt the differences between our clients could be reconciled. She said you were tied up and would join us here, and that is the extent of my contact with your client. Since you've introduced the word 'ethics,' you'd better watch your step, young man." He reached for his wallet and flung a bill on the table. "Good night," he said. "Mrs. Brungard, may I suggest that in your own self-interest you tell your lawyer to stop playing games?" He turned and left.

"He's right, you know," said Hilda. "You *should* stop playing games. Why are you following me around?"

"Hilda, I'd like to know what you're trying to do."

"I don't recall permitting a first-name basis. Why are you following me?"

"Someone called, Mrs. Brungard, and said you'd be here with Mackey. Do you know who it might be?"

She smiled. "Of course I do. I had him call. I thought it was a fun thing to do. Don't you?"

"Am I permitted to ask why?"

"I told you. It was funny. It amuses me to watch you and Mackey together."

"Do you think it's wise to play around until the divorce is granted?"

"You really are an absurd man. What else is there to do? You and your scheme. What do you call that? Or is it abandoned already?"

"It's arranged," said Halter slowly.

"Your friend will do it?"

"Yes. For five thousand dollars."

She shook her head. "You're a silly man, and that's the most dangerous kind."

"I don't know what I am," said Halter.

"I'm sure you don't." She reached out and dug fingernails into his wrist. "You have such a winning face for a loser. One never knows. Things are getting complicated. We'd better start again at the beginning. Who am I?"

"You're Mrs. Hilda Brungard."

"How old am I?"

"Thirty-three."

"And who are you?"

"Neil Halter."

"Age?"

"Thirty-one."

"What's the connection, if any, between us?"

"I'm your lawyer and you're my client."

"There you are. That seems tame enough. Now tell me. What are you after?"

"I'm just doing a job for you."

"Of course," said Hilda. "And you know what that job is,

· 95 ·

don't you? To keep me entertained. I need diversions. Don't you want to keep me happy?"

"I'm not very amusing," said Halter.

"You're wrong. You're very amusing." She got up. "Come on."

He stood still.

She took his hand and pulled. "Come *on*."

He followed her out. "Where are we going?" he said.

"Oh, you know. Somewhere we can be alone. Like my house."

"Don't you think," she said in the car, "you've gone far enough? I was sure there was a reason, a real one, for you to hate Mackey. I'm satisfied there isn't. He said he'd never met you before this case, and I believe him."

"I don't hate him."

"You said that before. Would you like to stop? I'll try very hard not to laugh at you."

He drew a deep breath. "You can stop me."

"Very well, you're stopped. That leaves nothing to prove. We can just be lawyer and client again. Don't you feel better already?"

"If you don't give me the five thousand dollars."

"That." She shook her head. "That doesn't amuse me. I won't make it easy for you. You'll get the money. Stop because I tell you to."

"I can't."

"You can't. All right. Which brings us full circle. Don't worry, I'll find out what's making you tick."

"Thank you for even being interested," he said.

"We'll see if you thank me."

For the first time, he went into her house. When she lit a lamp he found himself in the most beautiful room he'd ever seen. He had no sense of particular objects—the long, low couch, chairs, rugs, paintings, tapestries—but a general impression of space unviolated by intrusions, of a harmony of colors and positions.

She gave him no time to appreciate it.

"Come on," she said, and went upstairs. He followed her

into a dark room and waited at the door for light. Instead, the room remained dark. He heard a bed creak, and it was not a sound he wanted to hear. His body expressed no desire; it merely liked to look at her.

He waited for a sign, but she was silent. "Mrs. Brungard?" he said.

There was no answer.

"What do you want of me?" he said.

"I want you to entertain me. That's what you're being paid for."

He shuffled forward, his hands probing the space in front of him, and collided with her knees. She was sitting at the foot of the bed. "I don't know how to entertain you," he said.

She made no response.

Tentatively he reached out and found her shoulder. His hand slid to her breast. She was a statue. He couldn't detect breathing. He withdrew his hand and stood before her, unable to function. His body had quit cold, and his mind stood apart, viewing the shambles.

After a moment she said, "That's *that*. The same old thing. Would you mind turning on the light? It's by the door."

He turned quickly and found the switch.

"You'll have to do better. Much better," she said. "You weren't funny at all."

"Would you like me to go now?"

"Is there any reason you can think of to stay?"

"No." He paused. "Good-bye, then."

"Good-bye." Her lips curved. "Don't leave town. I want you where I can keep an eye on you."

Their relationship was paper thin. What they seemed to want from each other was a ringside seat.

He drove home to the card on his pillow:

For the lips of a strange woman drop as an honeycomb,
and her mouth is smoother than oil:
But her end is bitter as wormwood, sharp as a two-edged sword.

· 10 ·

Halter, a criminal lawyer defending the railroad from the charge of murder, returned to the scene of the crime. It was a nice day, cold but sunny, and at the last moment he decided to take George along if Mrs. Gummersell had no objection.

"We think it's a wonderful idea. We'd love to go on a trip with our daddy, wouldn't we, George?" she said, and trussed him up in a sweater, mittens and wool-lined coat with a hood until he looked like a miniature Arctic explorer.

"I should have him back by midafternoon," said Halter. "We'll have lunch on the road."

The railroad crossing was about eighty miles outside the city. Once he was on the highway, watching the dips and swells flatten beneath him, listening to the hum of his engine, Halter felt moments of pleasure uncomplicated by interpretation. George, who had begun the trip with his legs shooting out straight in front of him on the seat, hands clasped, uncertain of what his father expected of him, was now sitting on his knees staring out the window, or crawling into the back seat. He had produced a toy gun; from time to time, he would shout from the rear, "Bang, bang. Take that, you dirty rat," and Halter would cough to admit he'd been hit.

At last the boy settled down in the front seat and Halter poked a finger in his belly. George looked at him solemnly, saw the smile and broke into a crooked one of his own. "Stop that," he said, and cocked his Olive Oyl arm. "I'm strong," he said.

"Yes, you are," said Halter. "I better not fool around with you."

"I got a gun. See?"

"Yes, I do."

Having established his authority, George turned wide-eyed to the window. He had never traveled a U. S. highway before.

Halter's flirtation with euphoria passed. A sense of pleasure was uneasy around him; it was made to feel self-conscious, and being the shyest of emotions, wriggled free of his fingers and ran off. Other people seemed to do better, often, with less. Crenshaw with a steak knife or Rucker with membership lists. Mrs. Gummersell must have an unambiguous satisfaction constructing her cards. Halter wondered if he even had a sense of humor, but qualified that by speculating that he had nothing but a sense of humor, if you defined it as an appreciation of one's frailties. The ability to water his stock; he had little else. Perhaps a sense of humor, like any superior force, became destructive when it ran wild. There was, he challenged Mrs. Gummersell, such a thing as being too "good." But there was also such a thing as being too frailty-conscious, at least in terms of being able to hang on to a sense of pleasure.

When he arrived at the railroad crossing on the same road that Crowder had traveled, past the warning sign, toward the crossbuck, he had an overwhelming urge to step on the accelerator and take the tracks at seventy miles an hour, to prove to Crowder that his drop into a song-phrase world had not been in vain, that man, by the exercise of will and nerve, could tear up the terrain by its substratum layers and throw it into litter heaps by the roadside. He refrained because George was with him in the car, and because it was nothing anybody required of him. He refused to take orders from himself. George was asleep, bent like a toy against the door handle. When Halter picked him up and carried him out in his arms, he noticed a red welt on the boy's cheek and chastised himself for what Mrs. Gummersell would have to say.

The three railroad men were waiting in a cluster some distance down the track. He walked toward them, and they looked at the boy.

"Mr. Halter?" said one of them, a spare, neat man, and Halter nodded.

"This is Gridley and Stoddard. I'm Gunther. We're ready to start if you are."

"I wanted my boy to watch the train," said Halter. "He's never seen a train close up before."

"Fine," said Gunther.

Gridley and Stoddard turned and walked along the track in opposite directions. Gunther pulled out a stopwatch and held it up. "When the others get set, we'll begin," he said. "The locomotive is waiting up the track in the same condition as during the accident—diesel engine, flatcar and caboose. It'll arrive at the intersection at various running speeds, twenty and thirty miles an hour, and the engineer will apply his emergency brake. We'll clock how long it takes him to pass this point two hundred twenty feet down track. Then we'll clock him when he doesn't apply the brakes. It ought to tell us what you want to know."

"Yes," said Halter, "It sounds very precise."

Gunther waved and other arms along the track waved back at him.

"See Gridley at the intersection?" said Gunther. "With his arm in the air? That's the signal to the engineer to start the run. When Gridley drops his arm we start our watches because the train will have arrived at the intersection."

Halter's arms were beginning to hurt from the strain of carrying George. He heard the train coming and then saw it moving toward the intersection. George's eyes were closed, his body an inert mass. As Gridley dropped his arm the train bore down on them and hurtled past. Somewhere down the track it puffed to a halt, and in a moment started up again, going backwards.

"Five seconds," said Gunther. "That's with application of the brakes at thirty miles per hour. Now he'll do it without applying the brakes."

The train came on again, went by them, stopped somewhere farther along than the first time, then reversed its direction and came back.

"Five seconds again," said Gunther. "The brakes can't slow it down for at least two hundred and twenty feet. How's that for your case?"

"Fine. Just fine," said Halter, his arms aching badly now. He thought of putting George in the car but didn't want him to miss anything if he woke up.

"Why don't you put the kid in the car?" said Gunther. "He must weigh a ton by now."

"All right," said Halter. As he walked back to the car the train passed him along the way on another run. He laid George on the front seat, locked the car and went back to Gunther.

They finished the runs at one o'clock. Halter thanked Gunther, was promised a report and returned to the car. George had slept for three hours. Checking him periodically and finding nothing ostensibly wrong, Halter became worried. The welt was still on the boy's cheek. Perhaps he'd bumped his head and had a concussion or something. Nobody approached railroad crossings with impunity. All he had to do was shake George awake to know that he was all right. On the other hand, maybe this, sleeping all morning, was what Mrs. Gummersell had trained him to do. Behind the pink cheeks there might lie a red-eyed witch who put kids under spells to keep them quiet. If he woke George prematurely he might be cursed into Crowderism and say, "Bang, bang, take that," the rest of his life.

He shook George. The child's eyes fluttered open; he rubbed them and sat up.

"You've been asleep, George," said Halter as he started the car. "You feel all right?"

"I'm hungry," George said.

"Tell you what, George. We'll eat at a restaurant. Would you like that? What would you like to eat?"

"Umbruger?"

"Sure, umbruger. And French fries and a Coke, okay?"

George, not bought that easily, nodded sternly. Halter decided not to mention the train. It was only a grownup's idea of a child's delight, and he was having enough trouble developing his own delight.

At the restaurant, watching George eat a few bites and then smear catsup and Coke on the table, upset the French fries and scatter them on the floor, Halter came to the conclusion that to his son he was a dud. George didn't know what to do with his father, and so was driven to flay his food. A child, it appeared, got no kick out of a permissive parent. Nothing turned him on like a "no."

Halter became aware of the persistent, blaring honking behind him. He was in the middle of a city, facing a green signal light instead of George's catsup at the restaurant—a transformation as magical as those involving looking-glasses or potions, and one extremely annoying to the driver behind him. Halter's car was blocking the way, and he was ignoring the most imperative mandate of his society: the green light. As he drove across the intersection, the man behind, with a shredding of brake linings, squealed parallel and Halter, greeted with eloquent eyes, knotted fist and indecipherable words, smiled and waved. After all, they were allied; they were doing the same thing at the same time and place. They proved each other. But the other man evidently didn't think so. He kept pace for half a block, glaring and muttering, totally possessed, quite capable, it seemed, of killing for the price of a green light. Finally he pulled away, leaving Halter, if he could, to live with himself.

Halter drove home and dropped George off at Mrs. Gummersell's house. He reflected on the kinship of Betty and Mrs.

Gummersell. Betty had run his life with as steady a hand as his housekeeper's. Nothing was as consistent as virtue, and its one point of vulnerability, irony, was a line of attack alien to him, depending, as it did, on the discrepancy between what might have been and what would never be. Like Mrs. Gummersell, Betty believed devoutly in the value of being a good person and had an equally strong idea of what goodness was. Her special talent was restraint. She had no cards up her sleeve; nevertheless she used her good for power. His life with her had been calm, uncomplicated and decisive. She had protected him from Forrest-, Rucker- and Crenshaw-infested waters. They nibbled at him by day, and Betty restored his soul by night. She was his one clear excuse for living and this was good, because only one at a time seemed to work. Her mortality made a lie of her goodness, exposed it as just another illusion of purpose, and this was bad.

There was the law. A supervised playground when he could excuse himself and go home to his wife at quitting time—a riot-filled slum now that he couldn't. Each case—even each person—now created its own priority. Gromm, Hilda, the railroad, Forrest, Rucker, Crenshaw, Terry, Miss Benton, the green signal light, his office door—they all came first. He accepted as truth their demands because they did, and he had no reason not to.

At the office he picked up the phone and called Haggerty. "Listen," he said. "I've a personal favor to ask of you. It has nothing to do with the Crowder case. Could I come over and talk to you if you're not too busy?"

"Sure thing. Come on over in, say, half an hour? I'm in the middle of something, but half an hour would be fine. Okay?"

"Thank you," said Halter. "I'll be over."

Haggerty's office was a block away. Halter fiddled with two new files on his desk. One was from Forrest, a suit to set aside a deed, and he put it aside. The other was a divorce case from Rucker. The husband drank, beat the client, gave her no money, played around with other women and subjected her to perverted sexual activity. Nevertheless, with no children or money to protect, he claimed he loved his wife and refused to agree to a divorce. It would have to be contested and it would be an ugly, stupid business.

Halter held his head in his hands and contemplated his files, the stack on the desk, the rows in drawers and cabinets. He was in a cave of paper, and if Forrest decided to strike a match he would go up in smoke. The files never stopped reproducing themselves. Before one curled up and died, it gave birth to two more. They had inexhaustible appetites and fed on his marrow. The moment he stopped flailing his arms they would close in, and all that would be left of him would be an indentation in the leather desk chair. A commemorative plaque would be struck off by Rucker, who thrived on testimonials: Here sat Halter, a good egg who cracked in the line of duty and was eaten up.

There was a knock. Alice Gregory came in, stopped just inside the door and looked at him until the door closed. "Is something wrong?" she said. "I can come back later."

"I'm fine," said Halter. "Maybe a little tired. I was out all morning on the Sunflower Railroad-Crowder case."

"I wanted to tell you," said Alice, "that I won't be able to see you Saturday. I'm sorry."

"I understand," said Halter. "Please don't be sorry, not to me." Suddenly he felt dizzy and dropped his head in his hands.

"Are you sure you're all right?" said Alice. "Should I get you a glass of water?"

"No, thank you," said Halter through his fingers. "I'll be okay."

She was silent. He heard her open the door. "Perhaps," she said, "if you care to, you might ask me for some other time."

"Fine," he managed. "I'd like to very much."

He felt sick as a dog, and as soon as she left began to gag, lips curled back on his gums, his world constricting into throat exercises. He yawed erratically, zigzagging in desperation between George, Hilda, Betty, Terry, Mrs. Gummersell, Forrest, Rucker, Crenshaw, Alice Gregory, Mr. Gromm, Haggerty, Crowder, even the vast amorphous faces of city lunchtime crowds. This sampling of faces was the album of his life, but his shaking fingers couldn't glue them in.

He stood up and stilted his way past the secretaries into Rucker's office. "I'm sorry," he said, "but Alice won't be able to make it Saturday after all."

The ridges in Rucker's cheeks made no attempt to smile. "Hell," he said. "Mary's been preparing for two days."

He sat and thought.

"All right. So you come anyway." He grinned. "Bring somebody else." He winked. "Just so she's damned pretty."

"All right," said Halter. "Thank you."

"Sure. We'll save Gregory for another night. Just name it. All we'll need is a few days' notice, okay?"

"I'll ask her and let you know as soon as I can."

"That's the boy. Never say die."

Halter hesitated. "If it's all right with you, I think I'll ask Miss Rauscher for Saturday."

Rucker looked blank. "*Our* Miss Rauscher?"

"Yes."

"Hell, bring her if you want. She's a real dish." He laughed. "Just so Forrest doesn't get wind of it."

Halter turned to go.

"By the way," said Rucker, "while I've got you here, how did the tests go at the railroad crossing?"

"Pretty well," said Halter. "I think we can show it was impossible for the engineer to have braked in time. The brakes don't begin to grab for two hundred and twenty feet after they're applied, and the distance to the intersection from the tree . . ." He stopped. Rucker was looking at a magazine. "The tests went well," said Halter.

"What did I tell you?" said Rucker without looking up. "This case is going to put you on the map."

Halter went out and reported to Miss Benton that he was going to Mr. Haggerty's office.

Miss Benton nodded. "The railroad case."

"I shouldn't be more than an hour," said Halter.

"Happy hunting," said Miss Benton, marking it down.

He had never been to Haggerty's office before, and was struck by its shabbiness. The leather in the waiting-room chairs was cracked; when he sat down a spring worried his read end. Two secretaries were busy behind battered, scarred desks. The flowered rug was worn to the nap in places. The office reminded Halter of long-dead giants of the law sprawled with their feet propped on roll-top desks, dipping quills in ink wells, squirting tobacco juice at spittoons. Haggerty came at him, hand outstretched, shirt-sleeved, suspendered, a crooked black cigar in his mouth. "Halter, good to see you. Sorry to keep you waiting."

The inner office contained an old desk and several wooden chairs, a filing cabinet and a dictaphone, the single concession to the twentieth century.

"Cigar?" said Haggerty.

Halter shook his head.

"Okay, what can I do for you?"

Halter looked at the man, trying to find him, trying to ignore his reputation (one of the best trial lawyers in town but not quite respectable) and his trappings (suspenders and cigar). Haggerty had strong, winning features—he wanted to win both the game and his adversary. His nose, starting out sharp, turned into a soft knob. His eyes, landlocked blue ice, thawed with a steady, internal flame. Halter was surprised to realize that the man was little older than himself, no more than thirty-three or four, and that he was substantially shorter.

"I have a problem," said Halter. "And I have no right to ask you to help me with it."

"What the hell." Haggerty poked around his drawer and pulled out a pocketknife. He pried open the smallest blade. "Who do you want me to kill?"

Halter had another definition of lawyer: the advocate of instant drama. Certainly courtrooms were designed to accommodate audiences, and Haggerty invariably played to standing room only. His clients, win or lose, could not help being proud of him. But he didn't lose. Juries were proud of him too. Perhaps there was such a thing as an acting lawyer, filling in until the official one arrived. But the official ones—the Mackeys and Forrests—never came; they regarded the jury trials as circuses, designed to entertain the general public, while they attended to business as usual.

"I have a friend who's in trouble," said Halter. "She needs to find an abortionist, and I don't know where to find one."

Haggerty toyed with his knife. "What makes you think I could help you?" he said.

"I just thought you would. As I said, I have no right to ask you. For what it's worth, I know I can trust you."

Intuitively, he knew more than that. He knew that Haggerty and he were linked, not by being lawyers, but by being more or less than that. Somehow they were both beggars at the bar, with the resulting recognition of what it was to be a beggar; they were ready to extend themselves because they had little they were not prepared to lose.

Haggerty reached for his phone and dialed a number. "Hello. Miss America? How's the beauty-contest business these days?" He grinned into the phone. "Good. Listen, Aunt Jemima, I've got a pancake for you. You hungry?" He cocked his head at Halter. "Okay. I'll send it to you. When you getting out the frying pan?" He nodded. "Right. Tuesday at one P.M. I'll wrap it up and send it to you."

Haggerty hung up and wrote on his notepad, tore off the sheet and handed it to Halter. "No sweat. Your friend has to take along six hundred in cash. Good luck."

Halter stood up. "Thank you," he said.

"My pleasure," said Haggerty. He smiled and got up. They shook hands, Haggerty opened the door, and Halter started back to his office. He was perspiring and wiped his face. Haggerty hadn't even asked the inevitable questions: Why doesn't she have the baby and farm it out? This isn't 1872. Why doesn't she keep the kid? This is a criminal offense, buddy. Why should I stick my neck out? What am I, the daddy? It's your baby and you're stuck with it.

They were blood brothers. Each of them had the blood of the unborn lamb on their hands, but it was Halter versus

Haggerty over Crowder. Brothers on opposite sides of a civil war. What if Halter won against the best trial lawyer in town; would Haggerty still be the best trial lawyer? And there was Crowder, who would have to live in the same dirty bandages the rest of his life. However Halter looked at it, he was in Haggerty's debt. The least he could do was pay him back in kind, by not asking any questions.

Miss Benton, her eyelid tripling its shutter speed, informed him that he had been missed; Mr. Forrest wanted him right away.

It turned out that he had failed to make his morning progress report on Miss Gregory. "I'm sorry, sir," said Halter. "I had to go to the railroad crossing in the Sunflower Railroad-Crowder case. They were running braking experiments."

"Sit down," said Forrest. He stood up behind his desk, and Halter made an interesting discovery: Samuel Wentworth Forrest could be described.

He was short, not more than five feet four. His chest pouted. He wore his trousers high over his hips. He had short arms and chubby fingers. He was a flabby man and would have done poorly in barroom brawls. Even his stiletto of a nose could be broken between a railroad engineer's fingers. Nevertheless, it was the source of his power; if money grew on trees, Forrest's tiny nostrils, expanding into suction pumps, would suck in the foliage. Helpless as a Grunkian, Halter bent his cabbage head and prayed.

"Where were you at nine o'clock this morning?" said Forrest. His cartilages clicked like a rattler's tail.

"I believe I told you, sir. At the railroad intersection. On the Crowder case."

"I made your position perfectly clear. Did I or did I not make nine o'clock a red alert for you?"

"Yes, you did, sir. Every morning at nine o'clock I'm to report to you on my progress with Miss Gregory."

"All right, then. We'll try again. Where were you at nine o'clock this morning?"

Halter considered the question from Forrest's point of view. "Not with you, sir."

"That's right. You were not with me."

Whip cracked, Halter quiescent on his stool, Forrest could afford to sit down.

"Listen good, Halter. I'll spell it out once more. I don't give a damn what you do with your time except for nine o'clock in the morning. What you do with your assigned cases is your business. Have I ever butted in on your handling of a case? Even once? Your mishandling of a client, like Gromm, sure. But of a case? Answer me that."

"No, sir."

Of course there was Miss Benton and her time sheet, but Halter couldn't swear that Forrest ever looked at it. Crenshaw, yes; Forrest, probably not.

"The trouble with most lawyers is they don't know where the money is. They keep forgetting law is a business. You don't have the clients with dough, you know what you can do with the casebooks and digests. Stick them up your nose, that's what. C. F. Gregory is big business for us. We get him, and you can screw up a dozen Crowder cases along the way. Get the picture?"

"Yes, sir. It won't happen again."

"That's the way to talk. I'm counting on you, boy. This is your brass knocker to Easy Street. Don't muff it. Let's have your report."

"I believe I mentioned, sir, that we had a date for Saturday night to go to dinner."

"That's the ticket. You're cooking on all burners."

"No, sir. She broke the date."

"She *what*? See what I mean? You've got to concentrate. What did you say to her?"

"Nothing, sir. She just came in and said she couldn't make it. She did say I could call her for some other time if I cared to."

"And have you?"

"Not yet, sir."

"Well, get on it. Does somebody have to draw you a diagram? Don't let the bird fly the coop."

"I won't, sir. I'll call her tonight."

"What's wrong with right now? She's sitting a few feet away."

"I thought it would sound less official if I called her at home. Put us on a more informal basis."

Forrest nodded. "Good thinking. You may be right. All right, let me know tomorrow. I'll expect to hear a full report at nine o'clock."

"Yes, sir."

Halter arose with full bowels. He had to get to the bathroom. As he moved through the outer office Miss Benton, poised at the time sheet, said, "Where are you going, Mr. Halter?"

Halter risked a broad wink. "You know," he said. "Down the hall." And made another of his daring escapes without waiting to see if she wrote it down.

On the wall of the toilet he read: *This is where Napoleon beat his Bonaparte.* He wondered what Forrest did with his bone at night. Probably buried it in the backyard along with his other treasure.

And he knew that he would report in at nine o'clock every day only because he didn't care whether he did or did not.

· 11 ·

Terry went with Halter to the Ruckers' for dinner. He hadn't
expected her to accept his invitation, but for no discernible
reason she continued to deny him nothing. Her mood was
changed. She acted bright and gay and said she was looking
forward to the evening.

"It's nice to think that everybody in the office can become
friends," she said. "I've never met Mr. Rucker's wife." Neither,
of course, had Halter.

When he met them at the door, Rucker seemed delighted
too. Halter had never felt more in step with the times. Was
this the way it was? Were people no longer accountable to
past experience? Guilts, betrayals sufficient unto the day
thereof? Perhaps Terry was right about the office and there
would be a new beginning. They would drape garlands around
each other's necks. Miss Benton would rub bellies with Halter;
Terry would tweak Rucker's nose while she handed him his

baby; Crenshaw would kiss Alice Gregory's hands; wine would flow from the dictaphone cords.

"Here they are, Mary. Neil Halter and Miss Rauscher. She feels like she's known you kids a long time, don't you, Mary?"

Mrs. Rucker stood up and smiled. "Ben talks about you all the time."

Rucker came at Halter with a martini. "Do me a favor, buddy. Just taste this. If I say so myself, I mix a mean martini."

Halter took a sip. "It's very good."

"Right. Some people say I'm crazy to waste Beefeater's in a cocktail, but quality always comes through." Rucker captured Terry's arm. "Come on, kid," he said. "Let's you and me get acquainted." He winked at his wife. "You didn't know we had girls who look like this in the office."

Halter stayed with Mrs. Rucker. When she smiled again, he knew he'd seen it before, but couldn't pin it down.

"Mr. Halter," she said. "It's so nice to meet you finally. Ben says you're the smartest one in the firm."

"Thank you. It's a nice thing for him to say."

She was not the wife he expected. He had in mind a tall, beautifully dressed woman, attractive despite what God had given her to start with, sophisticatedly, wickedly clever. Instead, she was a pretty-faced woman with a stocky figure and a worried smile, ill at ease, timid even, before her husband's hired hand.

They examined the couple sitting together on the couch. Rucker was bent toward Terry, talking quickly, an arm flung along the top of the couch behind her. Terry's legs were crossed and her skirt showed skin to the middle of her thigh.

"She's one of your secretaries, I understand," said Mrs. Rucker. "She's very pretty."

"Yes, she is," said Halter.

Mrs. Rucker drew her breath. "Are you working on any interesting cases?"

"There's the Crowder case. I imagine Ben's talked about it. The fellow who got hit at the railroad intersection?"

She shook her head. "Ben never talks about cases. He says it gets him nervous. He likes to come home and forget about the office. Forgive me. Perhaps you feel that way too and I shouldn't have brought it up."

"I don't mind," he said. "Our client is the railroad, and one of its trains struck Crowder's car at an intersection. He was injured very badly. He's paralyzed for life, physically and mentally."

"How awful," said Mrs. Rucker. "How much will the railroad pay him?"

"Not enough, I'm afraid. We made an offer, and it was turned down. He could wind up with nothing."

They listened to a burst of laughter from Rucker.

"I've often thought," said Mrs. Rucker, "how unpleasant a lawyer's job can get when he has to fight his natural sympathies. I suppose he just can't function unless he develops a thick skin."

Halter diagnosed the harsh, corrugated back of Rucker's neck. "It gets sticky at times," he said. "But everybody has a job to do."

"Oh yes," said Mrs. Rucker. "I'm sure you do it very well. Speaking of jobs, will you excuse me a moment while I check on dinner?"

"Of course," he said. One more smile did it. He knew who it was: Betty. Rucker didn't know it, but he was married to Halter's dead wife. As if he cared. His arm had fallen off the edge of the couch and pressed against Terry's shoulder blades. He behaved as if he'd just discovered her. Halter wondered if Rucker might fork over the additional hundred dollars needed for the abortion. He could say, "Look, Rucker. After all. How many bygones can you let be?"

Mrs. Rucker returned to Halter, and together they watched Rucker. "Has she been with you long?" she asked.

"Quite some time."

"Is she a good secretary?"

"Very good."

"I'm sure she must be."

"Very."

Mrs. Rucker regarded her husband in silence. "Ben, dear," she said. "Dinner's ready if you are."

Rucker swung around. "Sure thing," he said. "Let's go. Neil boy, wait'll you get a load of Mary's cooking under your belt. She puts out the best meals in town. Bring your drink with you."

As Rucker had said, the food was excellent, though Halter had no idea what he was eating. A candle winked at him through his wineglass, which Rucker kept refilling, and suggested that he'd better watch his step—keep his wits about him. He was offered advice: Listen. Words. What are words? Clouds of smoke snuffed out by air fresheners. Put your hand in mine. Go ahead. See who's real and who's unreal. Rucker and Rauscher. All this shitty talk about the flame of desire.

Halter toasted his forefinger.

"Jesus," said Rucker. "What the hell you doing?"

Halter put his finger in his mouth.

"I'll get some salve," said Mary. She ran out and returned with a tube of ointment for his finger.

"Is that better?" she said. She pursed her lips and blew out the candles.

"Good thinking, honey," said Rucker. "Say, I guess we'd better go light on the alcoholic beverages from now on. Halter, Neil boy, you're a sleeping tiger, you know that?" He winked at Terry. "It's them quiet guys you can't trust."

Halter tuned in on Rucker's clogged channels. He expected Rucker to tell him something, if only another collapsible conceit of self. Admittedly, the law-office Rucker was a bubble held together by charred, rubbery skin. Office lives were vagrant winds ruffling each other's hair, joined together as whispers of the same idea. But somewhere a Rucker must dig his fists in his eyes and tie his shoelaces. Here and now is where Rucker lived, but where was he? Back in the office, trading his idea of a smile for Halter's probe of his substance?

"Neil, I tell you," said Rucker. "This only proves what I've been thinking. Mary, haven't I been telling you a hundred times he's been working too hard? That he ought to get around more or he'll blow his top? Don't get me wrong. You're doing one helluva job at the office. Ask Mary how many times I've told her that. But hell, there's a lot more to life than pleadings, motions and instructions. There's a lot more to *law* than that. The thing is, you've got to move around. Be seen. Be heard. They don't hang medals on you for digging in the books. Let people know you're there. How they going to know unless you tell them? Like organizations. You know this guy doesn't belong to *any*thing? Who ever heard of a lawyer who never belonged to anything?"

"Not everybody likes to join groups," said Mary. "If he doesn't want to, I don't see why he should."

Rucker looked at his wife. His row of ridges were like streaks of war paint. "I do," he said softly. "It's the name of the game."

Mary looked away, and Halter had a sharp sense of her evenings and Rucker's meetings: Rotary, Mason, Elk, Community Chest, corporate boards of directors, campaigns for mayor, governor, President, Boys' Club, Boy Scouts, Big Brother, Chamber of Commerce, Downtown Improvement, Metropolitan Transit, governor's special committee of slum clearance and antiriot procedures, Police Board, Airport Commission, Y.M.C.A., Red Cross, Salvation Army, American Legion, V.F.W.'s, National Guard, the Symphony Society.

"Hey," said Rucker to Halter. "I've got a terrific idea. Nothing too big at first. Just to get you going. You live over in Crocus Heights, don't you?"

"Yes," said Halter.

"I thought you did. Well, Orville Trotter's the president of that association, and he owes me more than one favor. How'd you like to be on the board?"

"I don't know. I've never thought about it."

"I have. It's a perfect place for you to get your feet wet. Take it from me. Someday you'll look back and marvel at how your life has changed. I've got another idea. This is a peach. The Downtown Businessman's Club. They've got a waiting list a mile long, but you just leave it to your pal Rucker. I'll get you in—I mean, like right now. Those guys aren't just the most important people in the city. They're swell fellows. You'll like them and they'll like you. I could kick myself for not thinking of it sooner."

"Thank you. It's very nice of you."

"Forget it, Neil. You and me are buddies, and don't you forget it." He grinned. "Hell, I see more of you than I do my wife. You can't be around a guy eight hours a day for umpteen years without knowing what makes him tick. And let me tell you, in my book your tick comes through loud and clear."

It wasn't true. How could it be? Nothing ticked—nothing, that is, that was human. A tick implied necessity, that after one there must be another. A single one as both beginning and end was unimaginable. Only when he was no longer human could a man tick toward his tock.

Halter surrendered. He held out his hands to Rucker for the syndicated cuffs. Big Ben's pendulum bonged against the temple walls of his cranium. Like an ant busy with its legs, Halter's brain washed its hands of itself. Rucker, or Crenshaw, or Forrest, or Mrs. Gummersell, or Hilda, or Terry, or even Alice Gregory had but to bother. They, anyone, held stopwatches and merely had to press the button to stop him or make him go.

After dinner, Terry helped Mary clear the table, and the men sat down over brandy.

"She's some dish, isn't she?" said Rucker. "It's funny how you barely notice her around the office. You speak into the dictaphone, get your letters back and never realize she's a neat package."

"Yes, she is," said Halter.

Rucker nudged him. "Hey. You plan on getting a little? You can tell *me*."

Halter met his eyes. "Yes," he said.

Rucker buddy-slapped his shoulder. "You stud horse. Okay. *But*"—he raised a finger—"listen to a few words of advice from an old pro. It's nice to take a dip now and then, like to cool you off, but don't jump in over your head. Know what I mean?

Forrest'd blow his top if he knew you were fooling around with one of the office gals. He's big on the old public-image stuff. You know, lawyers, the pillars of the community, solid and dependable. Anyway, that's the way that old fogy thinks. Hell, as for me, you know I couldn't care less. If a fellow can't get his kicks, what's the point of living?"

"He asked me to take out Alice Gregory."

"That's what I'm getting at, you dope. There are secretaries and there are secretaries. Alice Gregory. Look around and count the Alice Gregorys pounding typewriters. You might just as well save yourself the trouble. She's the one and only, and she dropped right in your lap. You want to know what makes her special? I'll tell you. It isn't what you think, just the old man's dough. She's the kind of girl you don't have to introduce, know what I mean? If people don't know who she is, you can forget about them. That's why she's special."

"We didn't know who she was," said Halter.

"Sure," said Rucker. "That's the whole point. We're peasants, Neil boy, but that doesn't mean we have to stay that way. I'm telling you, we play our cards right and we move from Nothingsville to Top Drawer in one quick jump. You know who C. F. Gregory is?"

"Yes. *The* C. F. Gregory."

"That's right. And why is he *the* C. F. Gregory? I'll tell you why. Because he's president of the Province Club. You know what that means? You've got to have it *all*."

"The Province Club?"

"The Province Club. Just to walk in that place, what do you have to be? One of the kings of the world, that's all. And he's the president of the club. With him going to bat, we could move right in on top."

"Is it better than the Downtown Businessman's Club?"

Rucker looked at him soberly, then manufactured his smile. "Yes, it's better. Don't knock the Businessman's Club. It's a hell of a lot farther than most people get."

"If I get the chance, I'll do what I can to get you into the Province Club," said Halter.

Rucker massaged his shoulder. "I know you will. Listen, between the two of us, that Gregory gal doesn't stand a chance. I've got some pretty good ideas about how to handle her. For one thing, she's going to find out damn quick she could do a lot worse."

"You think so?" said Halter.

"Sure I do. You're a great guy. You'd make her a fine husband. You're not a phony. I'll tell you something. You're the one guy I know I don't have to butter up. That's right. I wouldn't try to kid you. I tell people what they like to hear. It makes them feel good, and what does it cost me? I want people to like me. That's why I do it. I'm not ashamed to admit it. You never really know what they're thinking of you, even when you knock yourself out. But you have to try, the best you know how, right? With you I don't worry about it. I feel you'd give me the shirt off your back. You don't raise a beef, you just go ahead and do things for me. Like the Crowder case." He hesitated. "You knew I was ducking it."

"Yes."

"Why the hell didn't you turn me down? You think I'd hold it against you? You know me better than that. I'm not Crenshaw. I couldn't go over and look at that beat-up slob. It bothers me even to think about it. Now you know. No guts."

Rucker's skin was etched with welts. When he was serious he was ugly. He had told part of the truth. The larger truth was that he felt the case was a loser and he wouldn't risk his reputation.

"I don't mind," said Halter.

Rucker had the bit of truth in his mouth, and for the moment he couldn't work his way loose. "I know you don't mind, but *why* don't you? What's the angle? You got religion or something? I like you, but I have to tell you. You bother me."

Halter thought about Mrs. Gummersell's cards. "I don't know," he said. "I just don't mind."

"Okay," said Rucker, slipping past his moment of truth. "This Gregory business just goes to show that nice guys don't always finish last. One lucky break, and anybody can make it.

All we've got to do is convince her old man we're watching out for her."

"I guess that's so."

"Damned right it is. Don't foul it up by playing footsie with Rauscher. Get smart. Drop her before she hits you for a hunk of the action."

"All right."

"*There* you go. See what I mean. No crapping around with you. A guy can talk to you straight without worrying if you'll take something the wrong way. Be careful. Broads can raise an awful stink. Let it peter out." Rucker laughed. "Get it?"

"Terry's not like that."

"They're *all* like that," said Rucker. "Take it from an old pro." He got up and twisted his legs around each other. "Don't go away. Got to visit the little boys' room."

Halter regretted that he couldn't meet Rucker's overtures of friendship; one should like men who confessed their weaknesses. He must suspect that Halter did not find him entirely charming, that looking deeply into the pits of Rucker's skin, he couldn't locate any more reality than behind Crowder's bandages. What had Rucker confessed to? Not to being a fraud. That was pretending to be something you weren't, and Halter had yet to find the something in Rucker. The man buttered people. But that was no more false, surely, than putting salt on their wounds. Where was the truth that defined the falsity? If it existed, truth was neither beauty nor ugliness. Truth operated outside of aesthetics, as any trial lawyer could plainly see, and two uglinesses could make a truth as easily as none—as easily as two fictions.

On the way home, Terry reached for his hand and kissed his burnt finger.

"Why did you come with me tonight?" he said.

"Because you asked me."

She was turning the tables on him, and it was as if he were forced to react to himself. He felt confused, his behavior patterns blurred, and he longed to surrender himself to the pastoral myth—to the time when men thought all they had to do was what came naturally. Even Don Quixote seemed less ridiculous than he; it was easier to fight reality with myths than vice versa, and much more human.

"I was surprised. You have a great deal of courage, going to Rucker's house, and I admire you for it."

"I'm not so brave," she said. "Why did you stick your finger in the flame?"

"I don't know. I wanted to see if it would hurt. It didn't seem real, you being there with Rucker and me and being so lively. As if nothing had ever happened."

She stared through the windshield, then reached into her purse. "Here's your check," she said. "I don't need it. I never did. There's no point in keeping it any more."

"I don't understand. Why not?"

"I wasn't pregnant. I told you a lie. There was never anything between me and Mr. Rucker."

"I still don't understand. You mean you made it all up?"

"Yes."

"But why? Did you need five hundred dollars that bad? I'd have given it to you anyway, with no question asked."

"It wasn't the money. Let it go at that. It doesn't matter why I did it, does it? It's all over with and it didn't cost you anything."

"I guess it didn't," he said slowly. "I don't see what you might have gained." He thought of Hilda. "Did it amuse you?"

"Sure," she said. "It's been a laugh a minute. Let's drop it."

"And Mackey too, I suppose? You were putting me on about that?"

"Who's putting who on?"

"I meant everything I proposed."

"Well, so did I. Like I said, what do I have to lose? If you want me to do it, I'll do it."

"You shouldn't do it because I want it," said Halter. "You should do it only because you want to."

"Why should I? For the money? For the fun of it? Just tell me why."

"I don't know why," Halter said. "That's why I don't know if you're serious."

"You can believe what you like. I don't care. If you don't back out, I won't."

"I don't understand you, Terry."

"Okay. That makes us even."

· 12 ·

It would be, Halter felt, a supreme test of Mrs. Gummersell's extrasensory perception. He was actually staying downtown on business to attend a tool-and-die corporate meeting, and then a late dinner with Crenshaw afterward. The meeting was set for six o'clock; evidently the majority shareholders wanted to squeeze out the minority interest in their spare time. Though Halter had drawn the option agreement for the company, Crenshaw was not particularly interested in his legal opinion but required his company at dinner.

Before that the day loomed. He began by making his nine o'clock report.

"Well," said Forrest. "Did you call her?"

"Yes, sir. She's agreed to go out with me this coming Saturday."

Forrest beamed. "Fine. Now *that's* something I can tell C. F. Where you taking her?"

"I haven't decided yet. I thought perhaps dinner and then a movie."

"Good. Now listen. Be careful with the movie. None of that 'adults only' stuff, if you know what I mean. You don't want to frighten her off. Be a big brother to her, gain her confidence. That's the way to handle a girl with her background. The easiest way to scare off money is to try to pick pockets. But don't be a panhandler either. Be respectful but not familiar. Show her your respect is a healthy one. Get the idea?"

Halter wondered why a man with such an abundance of theories on the mating game had never gotten married, and then he realized that Forrest had and that he was living happily ever after. He went home and became the beast with two backs, one of them green.

"Yes, sir," said Halter. "I'm to handle her with kid gloves."

"But not too much, not too much. Let her know there's a man there too. A real man, who knows enough to keep his hands where they belong, a man she can tell her troubles to because she knows he respects confidences. Let me tell you, Halter, I have a lot of faith in you, but no man's immune to Demon Sex. Keep your wits about you."

"Yes, sir."

In his office Halter attacked his work pile. He reread the option agreement of the Acme Tool and Die Company. No problem there: the purchase price was book value, and the balance sheet had been prepared to the first of the month. Beeby, the minority shareholder, had two thousand of the ten thousand shares outstanding. At forty-three dollars a share he was entitled to eighty-six thousand dollars.

The divorce case, the messy one, *Fletcher* vs. *Fletcher*. The husband, a red-eyed, bull-necked nasty man. Halter drafted a petition for alimony pendente lite and prayed for Mrs. Fletcher's safety.

An overdue memo for a Crenshaw plaintiff: the law pertaining to joint bank accounts and the basis for setting one aside on death of its creator a day after it was opened. Evidentiary requirements on trial required research, which meant going to the office library past the secretaries. Halter resisted running the gauntlet of glances; he put the file in his cabinet.

He settled down with Rucker's defendant on a promissory note. The suit had been filed by Brother Jack against Brother Phil on a ten-thousand-dollar note executed in the days when Jack was up and Phil down. Now Jack was in financial trouble, and Phil's business was thriving. Yet Phil didn't want to pay the money back, and because Jack was a good brother and Phil a bad one, he didn't have to. The note was over ten years old, and no interest had ever been paid. It was barred by the statute of limitations. An easy victory for Forrest, Rucker and Crenshaw. All Halter had to do was prepare and file a motion to dismiss, argue the motion, and the note would dissolve in the salinity of Jack's anguish.

Halter went through the motion and pleaded Jack's case before Phil.

Halter: He did lend you the money. He held out his hand to you and picked you up off the floor. The way I heard it, you were going under.

Phil: Don't kid yourself. He owed it to me. He was my folks' favorite son, their darling little boy. He swiped my Lone Ranger outfit from the closet and stole my birthright. I don't owe him the sweat off my balls.

Halter: Was that the way it was? The ten thousand was really yours?

Phil: Hell, no. I got the old man's dough and blew it in Las Vegas while Jack worked up from scratch. But you legal buttboys need window dressing to do your job, so I'm giving you some. Listen, big mouthpiece, the law's with *me*.

Halter: I didn't say it wasn't.

Phil: Don't you forget it. You're with the law or against it, so get with it. Me, I'm a law-abiding citizen, and I'm not about to slip drinking money to a panhandler. There's a law against vagrancy.

Halter: But Jack's your brother. Don't you want to do right by your brother?

Phil: He's a bum. When he became a bum he lost me as a brother. It's the law.

Halter: There are those who say morality and law have a nasty habit of diverging. That moralities change clothes with the fashions, but law keeps wearing the same old suit.

Phil: Listen, punk, and listen good. I want you to take that note and shove it up Jack's ass.

Halter: Rest assured, sir. I respect the lawyer-client relationship.

His hands were sweating, and his face poured moisture onto his collar.

The Farraday case. The stupid, inconsequential, champertous Farraday case.

Moving to the cabinet, he found the file under *F* for Fear. He checked the date. The first notice to creditors in the defendant Bartholomew's Estate was nine months and two days ago. Miss Farraday's claim was barred by the Statute of Nonclaims.

Halter sat down at his desk with the file, opened it again very carefully, uncapped his pen and wrote the date on a pad. He flipped the months of his desk calendar, and for each month inscribed an Arabic numeral on the pad. It amounted to nine months, carry two days. He repeated the process with Roman numerals and paused at IX. His pen hovered in the air and added a dash and the accursed II. There was no mistake: the world had ticked and Halter was out of time.

He experienced with dread the void that was time. He had no idea what year, month, day or minute it was, only that he was forty-eight hours past Miss Farraday.

Why should he fear her? She was an overweight woman with cosmetics to make up for lack of muscle tone, an unpleasant, suspicious person. She didn't believe in his professional capabilities and would flow on a stream of mascara to the Grievance Committee. For all he knew, Mackey sat on the committee.

Halter wiped sweat off his cheek. He valued being a lawyer and a good one, whatever Mackey might think.

Judge Halter: Before I pass sentence, precisely what is it you wish to know?

Halter the witness: Yes, your Honor. I would like to know what it is I'm in peril of losing. I want to know what a lawyer is.

Judge Halter: A lawyer is a midwife. He helps the court bring decision into the world.

Halter the witness: He makes none of his own?

Judge Halter: He does not.

He examined his notes. No doubt about it. He'd been right from the beginning; Miss Farraday had no legitimate case. Her chances of recovery were negligible—at most, before a jury impatient to get home to dinner, two or three hundred dollars.

His bank balance was twelve hundred dollars. He also had an emergency fund of four thousand in a savings account. Beyond that nothing but a mortgaged house. Perhaps he could tell Miss Farraday there was a thousand-dollar offer and they should take it. Surely even she must realize that a thousand dollars would be a gift, from Halter or anybody else.

His head rolled loosely on its stem and wound up shaking from side to side. It was not the thousand dollars that bothered him, little as he could afford it. He found that he couldn't defraud himself. It was one thing to murder, another to hide the body and try to get away with it. At least he should be able to say that nothing became his law practice like his leaving it.

He went into Rucker's office and watched the plowed and furrowed face flower into its broadest smile. "Neil, old man, come in and sit awhile. I've got great news. You're on the Crocus Heights board as of now. Orville Trotter was tickled to death after I told him what a hell of a guy you are."

Halter sat on the edge of a chair. "Thank you," he said. "But I've blown the Farraday case. I'm sorry."

"Blown it? What do you mean? I didn't know you'd even filed it yet."

"That's the trouble. It was barred by the Statute of Nonclaims two days ago. It's my fault, of course, and I'll tell her so."

Rucker's face shook itself down to bedrock. The eyes probed Halter's woolly head, picking up invisible pieces of lint.

"That lady's no lady. Nobody to fool with. Did you know she brought the only medical malpractice suit we've ever had in this office?"

"I'm sure she's nobody to fool with," said Halter. "I'll make it clear the blame is mine, and not yours or the firm's."

"Come off it," said Rucker. "You're a partner. We're all liable."

"I mean in terms of the Bar Association," said Halter. "If there's a money loss, I'll pay it." He hesitated. "It may take a while."

Rucker smiled. "It's not as bad as all that," he said softly. "We think a great deal of you around here. We're buddies, remember? You think I'd throw you to the wolves? Her claim's not worth a damn, remember?"

"Yes, but I doubt if we could convince her of that."

"Sure we will," said Rucker. "For three grand. She'll be tickled to death, and the firm won't even miss it."

"Three thousand dollars," said Halter. "What will Mr. Forrest say?"

The old Rucker grin was back, filling in his eyes and cheeks. "Don't worry about him. I can handle him. I'll tell him it's a loser but we want to keep his client happy. Like fixing a traffic ticket with our own dough. She's a friend of one of Forrest's biggies. No trouble there. In fact, he'll pat me on the back for thinking it up."

"I don't know what to say."

Rucker winked. "Don't say anything. It's bread on the waters. You'll do me bigger favors. Besides, we've got a forty-percent contingent fee coming. We'll get back twelve hundred."

"Thank you," said Halter. He stood up. Rucker extended his arm and they shook hands, man-to-man, rising above the muck of lost battles.

"I have another date with Alice Gregory this Saturday," said Halter. "Would you like us to come over?"

"Would I ever. Now you're talking. Lose a Farraday and gain a Gregory. I'll settle for that every time. You just rest easy. I'll call Farraday in, and you can watch her laugh all the way to the bank. Say seven o'clock Saturday for dinner?"

"All right."

He returned to his office and sat down, his fingers tingling. Who was Rucker? What was he? Who was Halter? What was he? A comradely act that one should take simply and lay questions to rest. But there were no simple acts of friendship—not for Rucker or anyone else. Acts of friendship arose too easily to be simple. The idea of friendship was complicated enough; *why* it was acted upon became hopelessly complex, tangled up in memory traces of benefits rendered and received.

Rucker's friendship was just too easy. One became his friend by not becoming his enemy. With all the ports of entry through Rucker's skin, one never quite made it inside. Rucker offered yet another definition of lawyer: somebody who never let a client inside. He was friendly to everyone, but nobody's friend. Where did that leave Halter? Without a friend named Rucker who had done him a good turn. Halter owed him whatever Alice Gregory could do. Rucker had no desire to get inside people, only places.

But thanks to him, Halter was free of Miss Farraday by the same route he had rejected for himself: she was being bought off. Someone else was doing his dirty work. His self-deception was no less, his failure no less redeemed, and yet he felt vast relief. It was out of his hands, and he could remain everyone's obedient servant. The return of a favor imposed no burden; it required what he would have done in any event.

Halter wagged his tail in appreciation and faced his work pile with renewed vigor. The basic question, why he wanted so much to remain a lawyer, retired to its dark corner. For the time being, he could say it made him a living, provided him with loyal, stout allies like Rucker, gave him a mechanism by which he could do a job. It was a service profession, existing to implement rather than create, which was all he could reasonably ask for himself if he admitted to two faces. Perhaps it was human to be two- or three- or twenty-faced, and whatever else he lacked, he had a Social Security number to prove that he was human.

He worked behind his door until five minutes to six, when everyone would have deserted the secretarial no-man's land. Passing the hooded typewriters on his way to Crenshaw's office, he stopped. Alice Gregory was still at her desk. "Hello," he said. "I didn't know you were still here."

"Mr. Crenshaw asked me to stay," she said. "He wants me to make a record of the meeting."

"That's too bad. Have the men arrived?"

"Not yet."

"Look," said Halter, dismissing the premonition of trouble with Crenshaw, "we're going to dinner afterward. Why don't you come with us?"

She looked at him. "I am," she said. "Mr. Crenshaw has already invited me."

"Oh. Well, fine."

He knocked on Crenshaw's door.

"Who is it?"

"Halter."

"Come in."

He entered. Crenshaw finished picking his nose before saying, "Well, where's the Acme file?"

"In my office. You asked me to read it over. I'll get it."

"I didn't ask you to take all day."

Halter went back for the file. As he returned he saw two men sitting in the waiting room and another coming in. They were dressed in overalls. He opened Crenshaw's door and went in. "I think they've all arrived," he said.

"This is the last time I'll tell you," said Crenshaw. "I don't want you barging in when my door's shut. Not you, not anybody. Forrest respects a closed door, but not you. What the hell is it with you?"

"Well," said Halter. "I was just in here, and thought—"

"Think about what you're supposed to and you wouldn't fuck up so much. Give me the file."

Halter meditated on the fact that Crenshaw had never knocked on his door before entering.

The buzzer sounded, and Crenshaw picked up the phone. "All right, Miss Gregory. Tell them to come in and bring your book."

He appraised Halter. "I need you like a hole in the head, but you can stay. Maybe you'll learn something for a change. Bring in a couple more chairs."

Halter brought the chairs while the men and Miss Gregory filed in. Crenshaw didn't bother to introduce him. "All right," he said. "Let's get down to business. We all know why we're here. Beeby wants out, and Wicker and Cassidy are willing to buy him out. It's just a matter of the mechanics. Before we go into that, Beeby, did I or did I not advise you to get your own lawyer to represent you at this meeting?"

Mr. Beeby had silver-gray hair and light blue eyes. He was a handsome old man with battered, chipped hands presently interlocked against his chest.

"I don't need no lawyer. You're the lawyer."

"No, I'm not. Not yours. I told you. I'm the corporation's lawyer, and the majority shareholders have first claim on me. I'll ask you again: didn't I advise you to retain your own counsel?"

"What I need a lawyer for? I give you my stock and you give me the money. We don't need to make a fuss."

"Miss Gregory. I want the record to show that Mr. Beeby has been urged to retain his own counsel and has indicated he doesn't wish to do so. *Okay.* Beeby, let's face it. You're a minority shareholder in a closed corporation, so your stock isn't worth a plugged nickel on the open market. But Wicker and Cassidy want to be fair. They feel you've put in some good years with the company. After weighing their desire to help you against their duty to the corporation, they're prepared to offer you twenty-five dollars a share. You have two thousand shares, so that makes a total of fifty thousand dollars. Try to get it somewhere else."

Mr. Beeby blinked. His face heated up, and his head jerked toward Cassidy, who looked away.

"What you mean? We all agreed. Wicker, Cassidy, me, we shook hands. Book value like the agreement says. Eighty-six thousand dollars. You think I'm a country yokel? I know what I'm entitled to."

Crenshaw stood up and shot Beeby with his finger. "I've just told you what you're entitled to. What you can get. You turn our offer down and you know what you wind up with? Two thousand shares of paper you can stick you know where. Cassidy and Wicker told me about your tentative discussion of sales price. That's all it was—*tentative*. It was your amount, not ours. And don't bring up the option agreement, if you please. We don't have to exercise our option unless we want to. *And we don't want to.* An option agreement means what it says: it's optional. You want to read it?"

"We shook hands," said Beeby.

"We'll shake your hand when you say good-bye," said Crenshaw. "That doesn't mean we have a deal."

He tried to soften his voice, but no manipulation could blunt its edge. "I'm telling you, Beeby, you've got a fair shake here. We don't have to give you a dime. You want out? Okay. Nobody's stopping you, nobody's shoving. You're acting like fifty thousand is peanuts. It's not going to be easy for us to raise it, but for you we're determined to do it."

"I worked hard for this company," said Beeby to Wicker, who looked away. "I sweated with you guys for thirty years. I'd trust you with my last nickel. Why you doing this?"

Wicker, a small, wiry man, got lost in his overalls. "We gotta do what our lawyer tells us," he said. "That's what we pay him for. He tells us we're being more than fair."

"I figured with Social Security and the eighty-six thousand I could get by," said Beeby stubbornly.

There was a silence. Crenshaw filled the time by going from

face to face. He settled on Halter. "Tell him, Halter. Halter here has analyzed the corporate picture backwards and forwards. Tell him, Halter, what a good deal it is. Beeby, you listen to him. This is a young fellow who wouldn't lie to save his mother. Halter, be his lawyer. Give him the lowdown."

Halter, hired by Crenshaw to represent Beeby, rose and stood at the old man's side. He was grateful to Crenshaw for giving him the business. "On behalf of my client," he said. "I'd like to point out that the average net earnings of the corporation, after taxes, for the past five years have been roughly a hundred thousand per year. Capitalizing this amount at the conservative figure of eight, we arrive at a value of the corporation of eight hundred thousand, and that of Mr. Beeby's shares at a hundred and sixty thousand. Conceding that the book value of his shares is only eighty-six thousand, I would place the value of his shares at a minimum of one hundred and twenty-five thousand."

"Get out," said Crenshaw. "I'll talk to you later."

"Yes, sir," said Halter, and returned to his office.

It struck him as likely that since Crenshaw had another companion for dinner, his services would no longer be required and that he might as well leave for home. But Crenshaw had some words to say to him, words that must be said, and the pressure of these welded Halter to his place. Besides, he didn't want to go home. He wanted to have dinner with Miss Gregory in order to prepare for their Saturday night date.

Lawyerdom à la Crenshaw was a grim business, but no one ever accused the law of levity except at fortuitous moments. The legal practice had room for executioners. Crenshaw loved to put people to death, or at the very least to whip them until they fell into their places. He hated to risk a case in court and rarely did, for in the courtroom control might move out of his hands. He found Halter useful because Halter was expected to behave and he found *ex cathedra* law valuable for the same reason. Ultimately, it was people Crenshaw was interested in mastering, not the law. Despising Halter, he couldn't do without him because he was the only exclusive servant Crenshaw had. Others, like Mr. Beeby, were whipped when possible, but he felt he could lay it on Halter at will.

He busied himself with composing letters to Hilda on the Mackay matter while waiting for Crenshaw to declare himself.

"Dear Neil," he wrote, and immediately crossed it out. He indulged in the luxury of flowing inside Hilda's skin and being made beautiful. "My darling, dearest Neil, my Sir Halter, my Galahad, Launcelot, Prince Charming, Don Juan rolled into one."

This was more like it. She had to get his name in; otherwise Mackey wouldn't know. "Let me tell you what last night meant to me. I must or I'll split. Forgive me if I abandon my feminine reserve and speak from the core of my being, where you eternally reside. My darling, my darling, I've always been untouched by males. I've suffered their hands upon me and gritted my teeth when my goose of a husband pricked me with his quill. There has been another (I will never hide anything from you), but he was much the same—an unpleasant, repulsive oaf.

"You have had me as a virgin. I swear it. Other penetrations, probes of an enemy patrol, never engaged the main body. Yes, enemy. I killed them before they could enter my mind or soul. So you see, my lovely, firm-fleshed sweetheart, *you* have deflowered me. *You* have captured the flower of my maidenhood and I pray you find it fragrant.

"Your sweat. The pungency of it lingers in my nostrils and drives me mad until I have you, we have each other, again. You see? With you I have no modesty left.

"To think that only a brief time ago I didn't even know you, and that I have my husband to thank for bringing us together. If not for him I would never have come to you and you would never have come to me. Last night my flesh turned to fire under your fingers. When you entered me my whole body shook itself loose from old fears.

"I realize we must be careful until the divorce is settled, but you must be careful for both of us. You must arrange it that no one will discover us. As for me, let the world know. I count the locked moments until you once again set me free. The clock has become my jailer.

"All my love, dearest Neil,

"Hilda"

He read it over. Purple, but it should do. He wasn't happy with only "Hilda" as identification, but he couldn't think of a reasonable way to manage the "Brungard." He must try to insert it internally in another letter; there would have to be at least six or seven. He sighed. It was more painful than he'd imagined. Even the fantasy of Hilda and himself in bed gave him no pleasure. He dove back into her body and tried another: "My dearest Neil, How I love to say your name. I must murmur it a thousand times a day. Neil Halter, Neil Halter, you are my Neil, my Halter. I can no longer bear to think of my own name. Brungard, and the beast that made me wear it. 'Brungard' is a rope around my neck, and 'Halter' strokes my throat like a cool breeze. I love you most of all for making me remember I am a woman and a desirable one. You've driven past my feeble defenses that may have seemed so formidable to other men: my so-called beauty that's supposed to drive men mad but instead frightens them and drives them away because they are fearful they're not man enough—not handsome or rich or famous enough. But you saw through all that, saw that my body is merely a territory of desire like any woman's, and you planted your flag in my earth, staked your claim and took from me all I had to give. Darling, you gave more than you received. You made me feel whole. You made me understand what I had forgotten, that I, every woman, was Mother Earth. Don't be alarmed, sweetheart, I'm not pregnant. I'm being careful, not because I don't want your child, but because it might bear the unspeakable name of 'Brungard.'

"Good-bye, my darling, until tomorrow night.
    "All my love,
                "Your Hilda"

The buzzer sounded. Halter jumped out of Hilda's skin and looked around guiltily, prepared to find Mrs. Gummersell scribbling on a card in the corner. He folded the pages, slipped them in his pocket and picked up the phone.

"Mr. Crenshaw wants you to come to his office right away. The men have gone." Alice's voice was huskier than he remembered it. "Good luck," she said, and hung up.

Did she know something? Had Crenshaw acquired a garrote by special delivery? He wouldn't need it; he could throttle Halter with his bare hands. All he had to do was ask permission.

As a last rite Halter smiled at Alice when he passed her at her typewriter. She nodded, a *donatio mortis causa* which pleased him. She was involved with him in the camaraderie of servitude, a relationship one could never take lightly.

He knocked.

"Halter?"

"Yes."

"Come in, you son of a bitch."

It was loud and mean—no barracks badinage there. Loud enough for Alice to have heard, but she gave no sign.

He went in and stood just inside the door.

"All right," said Crenshaw. His hands were spread, palms down, on his desk. His cuticles gleamed with care. "What the hell got into you? You fucked up the deal."

"I was trying to do what you told me. You said to be Beeby's lawyer. I did my best."

"Don't give me that crap. You knew what I wanted you to do. You cost my clients thirty-six thousand dollars. You got thirty-six thousand? That's what you owe them."

"I don't have thirty-six thousand dollars."

"Damn right you don't, and you never will. You son of a bitch. You're a butt-boy here and you'll never be anything else. You can take your junior partnership and stick it up your stupid ass just like Beeby with his minority shares. So you'll know where you stand, as of this minute I'm for kicking you out on that stupid ass of yours and I'm telling Forrest so. You may be lucky to have thirty-six cents when I get through with you."

"I'm sorry. I did what you told me."

"That's your story, is it? Listen, fuck-up. It won't do you a bit of good. You're lucky I don't beat the shit out of you."

Crenshaw was a head shorter, and at least thirty pounds lighter, but with animus on his side Halter had no doubt he could do it.

"I guess I'd better be going."

"You're not going anywhere. You're still working for me until I tell your otherwise, and don't you forget it. Get Gregory in here."

Halter stuck his head out the door. "Miss Gregory, Mr. Crenshaw wants to see you."

She came in and stood by Halter's side.

"You about through with the agreement?" said Crenshaw. "I'm getting hungry."

"I'd say another half-hour," said Alice.

"Well, let's go eat. You can finish when we get back."

"I don't think so," said Alice. "I'll finish up tomorrow. I don't like to work after dinner."

Crenshaw looked at them both. It was pleasant to Halter to have her standing shoulder to shoulder with him. He noticed that she had pretty hands, narrow, with long, slim fingers.

"I need that agreement tonight, Miss Gregory. I want to get it signed tonight."

"Would you like me to finish it now?"

Crenshaw looked down grimly, consulting his stomach. "Things are beginning to get out of hand around here," he said. He studied Miss Gregory, thought of who she was and nodded stiffly. "All right. I guess it can wait until first thing in the morning." He stood up. "Let's go to the club."

Halter stood mutely as Crenshaw brushed past him.

"You too," said Crenshaw, and Halter followed them out.

On the street in his topcoat, walking toward the Downtown Businessman's Club, Halter was astonished at the coldness. He remembered first meeting Hilda Brungard in a fur coat. Was it such a short time ago? If he were a scientist, he could run a time-space study and determine how long it took to put Terry down on the office floor, or Mrs. Gummersell to write one of her cards, or Hilda to tell him to punch a man in the nose. As it was, he had to rely on the weather and tell time by the thermometer.

During the walk Crenshaw talked to him as if Alice didn't exist. It was, Halter decided, a manifestation of naked power, just as taking him along to dinner or not speaking to him at all was. It was also more: proof that Crenshaw regarded him as something less than human.

"You know what Beeby said to me? 'Thank that young lawyer for me.' I'll thank you all right. You'll get thanked like you never got thanked before." He went into an unlikely spasm of amusement, and Halter waited patiently to find out what the joke was, but Crenshaw wasn't about to tell. He was walking on the inside, with Halter and Alice lagging slightly behind. Halter, the gentleman, was on the outside, protecting Alice from rearing horses.

Crenshaw stepped up his pace, giving Halter the back of his head and the opportunity to examine Alice's profile. He found it more attractive than he remembered. The nose, still prominent, coin-struck, was a clean line to the tip. She had a beautifully rounded chin. He encountered a glance from her notable eyes, gray, wideswept, unclamorous. She was Miss Gregory, *the* Miss Gregory, and he recalled that *he*, not Crenshaw, was in charge of her, that he was her bodyguard, and he was glad. If Crenshaw raised a finger to molest or even annoy her, Halter would break it off and feed it to the pigeons.

At the club Crenshaw went through the revolving door without looking back. Halter ushered Alice through and followed. Crenshaw entered an elevator and they tagged along. Crenshaw moved into the restaurant, nodding at a waitress, who showed them to a table. He sat down and Halter held a chair for Alice.

It had become clear that Alice's Gregoryship applied no brakes to Crenshaw. He was his own man, and there was no other with the possible exception of Forrest. Nevertheless, he was, or his present actions were, an enigma. He respected power, and C. F. Gregory was powerful. Alice's father could make or break men; yet it hadn't occurred to Crenshaw to open a door for Alice. Perhaps if Gregory himself were there, it would have been different. Crenshaw didn't throw his weight around with Forrest; he took orders like any common man. Perhaps the answer lay in the military mystique of chain of command. The man would be inferior only to superior officers.

In the restaurant, Crenshaw proved to be a generous host. He ordered steaks and drinks for them all and proceeded to down three martinis while they were on their first. He ordered their second along with his fourth. Somewhere in the middle of his fifth, with no visible change of his expression, the liquor began to talk. Evidently it was above Crenshaw in the hierarchy of command, because he made no effort to shut it up.

"You ever meet my wife, Halter? You got to meet my wife. She's some gal."

"I don't believe I have."

"You know what she can do? Everything. She can do everything, goddamnit. Anything she sets her mind to. Except one goddamned thing. Be a wife. The goddamned TV dinners she tries to pass off on me. I tell you, the biggest mistake I ever made was to marry an American female. You know that, Gregory?"

"No, but I know it now, don't I?" said Alice.

"It's true, goddamnit. Why you think our boys latch on to those Korean and Vietnam babes when they get the chance? Oriental broads don't crap around. They know their job is to please their man, keep him eating out of their hand. You know the biggest mistake we made in America?"

"Giving women the vote?" asked Alice.

"Crap, no. Educating them, giving them ideas. Barefoot, bird-brained and pregnant was the way the good Lord planned it, and we let ourselves be talked out of it. Give a woman a chance and she'll talk you to death. And don't think they aren't as sorry as we are. They don't know what the hell to do with themselves. Book clubs and card parties where they sit around and spill those half-baked ideas they learned in college. The biggest laugh of all is the 'professional' woman. Treat me like a man, she says—until she's in a tight spot. Then she bats her eyes and wiggles her goddamn girdle.

"My wife's gone back to school. She wants to be a psychological social worker, can you beat that? Meanwhile I'm supposed to eat out of cans. The only time she remembers I'm around is when she needs money. She thinks all I am is a cash register. If she's so independent, why can't she make her own crappy money?"

"When she gets her degree," said Alice, "she'll be able to earn her own money."

"Don't get cute, Gregory," said Crenshaw. "My wife's never going to work. Nobody can say I don't earn enough to support my wife. I let her go to school, and by God that's enough. That's *it*. There's such a thing as being too nice a guy. Half the time I don't have a shirt back from the laundry. There's an American dame for you. Everything she could want—a husband, a big house, two great kids, her own car, all the modern conveniences. All she's got to do is press buttons. She oughta be tickled to death to stay home and take care of her family. But not her."

"Why *do* you let her go to school?" said Alice.

"Because she drove me nuts about it, that's why. All she'd do is sit around and cry. If there's one thing I can't stand it's a woman crying. Like I was beating the hell out of her. Halter, take a tip—love 'em and leave 'em, or else marry a chink. That's my advice."

"I'll try to remember."

"Love 'em and leave 'em. Why buy a cow when milk is so cheap?" His eyes pinned Halter against his chair. "There's plenty of that kind around if you know where to look. You know that better than anybody, don't you, Halter? Like in the office."

Halter looked at Alice and lowered his head.

"You been fooling around with Rauscher," said Crenshaw.

Halter made no response.

"Don't crap around with me. I know it for a fact. Just answer me yes or no."

"Yes."

"Sure. Well, get this straight. From now on you keep your mitts off Rauscher. You don't give her the time of day. Hands off. That plain enough even for you?"

"Yes."

"Read it back to me. What did I tell you to do?"

"Stay away from Miss Rauscher."

"Okay. Remember it. Hands off. We're running a law office, not a pimping service. Now let's eat."

Halter munched dutifully on his steak. How did Crenshaw know? Terry wouldn't have told him. Probably Rucker, and what did Rucker know? Crenshaw seemed to know much more. Perhaps he lurked behind trees in front of buildings to check on his employees. He would fight to keep people in their places one way or another.

The liquor had shot its wad, and there was silence. Halter thought of talking to Alice, but Crenshaw made it impossible.

After dinner Crenshaw signed the check and stood up. "I'm going. If you want something else, my number's seventy-nine. Sign my name. Don't say I never gave you anything."

He paused. "Halter, you're on the edge, and don't you forget it. From here on in, keep your nose clean."

He attended to Alice. "You'll have the agreement for me first thing in the morning?"

"I should think so," said Alice.

Crenshaw nodded and walked out on them.

Halter wiped his nose with his napkin and dared to look at Alice. She broke into a grin. It was a revelation, all the more so when he compared it with Rucker's. Where Rucker hid behind his, Alice emerged. Her features came together in a conquering.

"Thanks for the smile," he said. "I can use it."

"Just comic relief. He ought to charge admission."

"He wouldn't do that. He's generous. He believes in hearty breakfasts. His number is seventy-nine. Would you like another drink?"

"I can't pass up his charge account," said Alice. "I think I'd like Benedictine. I feel holy tonight."

"All right."

"Yes, indeed," she said thoughtfully. "Mr. Crenshaw is a very funny man."

"Do you think so? Along with other things, I seem to have lost a sense of humor."

"If you didn't have one, you'd have told him off a long time ago. How else could you stand him? After all, he doesn't own you."

"He thinks he does, and that amounts to the same thing."

"Does it? Are you that afraid of losing your job?"

"It's where I am. I wouldn't know where else to go."

"You could go anywhere. Everyone knows you do the best law work in the firm."

"Thank you, but even if it were true the law doesn't reward its drones. The ability to get the clients is what counts."

"I'm surprised. I didn't dream you had so little faith in yourself. Someday you'll laugh at yourself for even being worried."

"Excuse me," said Halter. "I wasn't inviting your sympathy. I'm not complaining."

"Perhaps that's your trouble. Maybe you should." She looked around the room. "I'd like to go if you don't mind. I see too many Crenshaws sitting around, and he doesn't seem so funny any more."

Halter signed Crenshaw's name and number to the check, and they left.

"Do you have a ride home?" he asked as they stood outside the building.

"No. Could you drive me?"

"Of course."

As they waited at a traffic light, she said, "Are you in a hurry to get home?"

"No."

"I have a favor to ask. I'd like to walk around for a while. Could we go to the park?"

"All right."

At the park they walked onto the grass. She drew a deep breath. "I needed to clear the air of Crenshaw," she said. "Even his silences are growls. You're right—he isn't funny at all."

"I didn't mean to influence you. Nobody's funny to a person who doesn't feel like laughing."

"You don't like to laugh. I've noticed that. Do you know how frightening that is? Terry and I used to talk about it. We used to have a game about how to make you smile."

He was silent. Finally he said, "They claim that only man laughs. I guess I'm not much of a man."

"Tell me," she said quickly. "You asked me out because of my father, didn't you?"

He laughed. It was what she wanted, and he was easily the most ridiculous man in the world. It was really not a human sound, more like the way a dog would laugh if he could. His legs were aching and he found he could barely stand up. "Would you care to sit down?" he said, and realized how idiotic it sounded.

She settled herself on the frozen turf, and he squatted beside her.

"Your father asked Mr. Forrest to have someone keep an eye on you. I was chosen. I agreed to do it. That's the kind of man I am."

"It's all right," she said. "You're afraid of losing your job."

"I wasn't thinking of my job."

"Then what?"

"Mr. Forrest asked me to cultivate you and I did. It's as simple as that. Would you like to go home now?"

"Mr. Halter," said Alice. "I haven't any illusions. I'm a very ordinary heiress. I'm not pretty, but I'm not a fool either. What could you possibly see in me but money? Why do you think I broke our first date?"

"I can understand your doing that. I can't understand why you agreed to another."

"Because I thought it over and figured I had nothing to lose. I was curious to see how far money would take us."

"It isn't the money," said Halter. "I'm not trying to excuse myself, but it isn't the money. I could wish it were. It would be easier to come to terms with. I admire your honesty."

"You're not doing badly," said Alice. "Someone else could have said I was beautiful. What's so great about honesty, Mr. Halter? Why not pretend a little if the truth hurts?"

"I should ask you that."

"I don't mind pretending," she said. "Where does that leave us?"

"I won't bother you any more."

"Is that what you'd like?"

"No. I assumed it's what you want."

"Would you *like* to see me again? I don't mind your keeping an eye on me."

He hadn't thought of Alice Gregory as a feminine body spread out on the green. A shadow, she became real. Her words in the dark air and her name belonged to the same hard, fast structure of physical dimensions. He touched under her coat and found a shoulder. His hand closed on the roundness and his mouth met hers. The kiss blended with the feel of her shoulder, and he lowered his head to her breast.

She breathed against him. "What is this?" she said. "Honesty or pretence?"

"I wish you'd tell me."

"It doesn't hurt a bit," she said. "If you like, I'm perfectly willing to pretend it does."

He pressed against her, knowing that as soon as he was dislodged, he would once again embrace the whip hands of his various overseers. He bit his lips, and they opened in a surprised "oh"; he strained to hear, above his masters' voices, the sound of his own horn blowing.

· 13 ·

Halter felt discomfort. His body annoyed him, making intrusions and demands, all the more exasperating because he couldn't quite make out what it wanted. He felt the pulse at his wrist and it bucked against his thumb, a wild horse trying to dislodge its rider. He pressed his hand flat against his heart, verifying that it still was there. He retracted his anus. Its chamber was empty, but its parts were oiled and ready. He wished that his body and he had learned to communicate in other than sign language, that they could sit down and have a heart-to-heart talk about where it had been and where it was going.

He was perspiring. He observed that he was wearing Bermuda shorts. He looked up, and the sun took a flash picture of his eyeballs. If one believed in the power of proof, it was summer, but Halter had no idea of how he'd gotten there. Automatically he checked his watch, which informed him that it was twelve-thirty. He was standing in front of his house, so he hadn't been drugged, kidnapped and transported beyond the international time zone.

His legs moved him to the backyard and the sound of hammering. Two men, stripped to the waist and dangerously muscled, were knocking down his porch. It was a moment of truth. He thought of other times: the boys peeling bark off his elm; the balloon of wet mud lofted into his car as he drove past; the itinerant yardman who had broken his mower, shears and wheelbarrow. When did a man knot his fists?

He clenched his hand, and the perspiration oozed from the doughnut formed by his little finger. His knuckles turned white. Taking a deep breath, he remembered that Mrs. Gummersell had decided George needed an all-weather playroom. These men were his employees. There would be insulated walls, window frames, windows, electrical wiring, sockets, heating vents, suspended ceiling, linoleum. Halter's legal concepts would soon be translated into a dwelling place for toys.

He admired the rhythm of the men's bodies. They played a different tune; their minds not only seemed happy at what their bodies were doing, but they were joined in the effort. They exchanged remarks and laughed. Their teeth flashed, ready to pull nails and tear away boards. Halter offered them words to chew: equity, tort, liquidation, merger, *res ipsa loquitur*, due process, double jeopardy.

Jesus was a carpenter, and Hitler a house painter. For better or worse, there must be home improvements. Halter got a shovel and dug a hole in his backyard. He worked steadily for nearly an hour before he had enough room for all his office files. He knew that the men, without pausing in their porch-razing, were watching. He was grateful, almost proud, to be noticed by them. When he had finished he rested a moment, leaning on the shovel, then began filling the hole back up. This was easier, of course, and didn't take long. He got down on his knees and retrieved scattered clumps of earth.

As he walked past the men, one of them smiled and said, "Digging a garden, sir?"

"Files," said Halter.

"Flowers?" said the man. Halter nodded and moved on. They laughed, but he could no longer hear them. Halter hired bodies to do his work for him, but their minds were elsewhere, merely imagining things. The body didn't care whether it grasped hammers or air.

Inside the house, Mrs. Gummersell reminded him that they were going to the zoo. George, tugging at the hair on his leg, agreed. "Come *on*, Daddy." He pulled Halter's leg. He had a piece of his father and was unwilling to let go.

"In a minute. I'll change my shirt and be right down."

"Come *on*," said George.

Mrs. Gummersell swung George away in her arms. "We mustn't ever whine. We must be patient," she said, settling herself on the couch with George in her lap. The boy, off-balance, jerked and speared her dress with a toe, flipping it upward. Halter caught a glimpse of a bruised melon of a knee.

"I hope you don't mind, Mrs. Gummersell," he said. "I've invited a friend to go along with us. A Miss Gregory."

"Of course we don't mind. We like to play with little girls, don't we, George? Another child won't be a bit of trouble, I assure you."

"She's not a child," said Halter. "She's a young woman."

"Good heavens, as if you have to ask my permission."

"The zoo was your idea. I didn't want you to think I'd taken over."

"It's perfectly all right with *me*, Mr. Halter. The more the merrier."

Halter ran upstairs, peeled off the shirt, threw water over his face and chest, scrubbed with a towel and put on a sport shirt. He hesitated, then changed his Bermudas for khaki slacks. If his body was up to no good it might help to keep it under wraps.

Downstairs Mrs. Gummersell was at the door beside George, his hand swallowed by hers. Halter gave his body its head. Fresh from the triumph of digging up the backyard, he picked the boy up and lofted him into the saddle of his neck, George's fingers clutched him wherever they could, and his legs flopped before Halter fastened them with a hand.

At the car he lowered George into the front seat and held the door open for Mrs. Gummersell.

"No sense being crowded," she said. "I'll get in back. Now, George, settle down. We wouldn't want to get sick and spoil the fun, would we?"

George pressed against Halter's side. "I won't get sick, Daddy."

"I know you won't, George," said Halter. "Mrs. Gummersell just wants to make sure."

Halter drove toward Alice's apartment, which was right on their way to the park. He hoped Mrs. Gummersell would be pleased at his thoughtfulness.

"Have you known Miss Gregory long?" asked Mrs. Gummersell.

"She's one of our secretaries at the office."

"I see," said Mrs. Gummersell. "I'm looking forward very much to meeting her. I have a great deal of respect for legal secretaries. My father used to say his secretary was worth her weight in gold."

"Miss Gregory is very efficient," said Halter. "We don't know what we'd do without her. Mr. Forrest, especially, thinks she's worth a great deal to us."

"She must be a godsend. Young girls are usually so unreliable these days. All they think about is coffee breaks and doing their fingernails on company time."

"That's true, Mrs. Gummersell. Miss Gregory's an old-fashioned kind of girl. She's excited about going to the zoo."

"We all are, aren't we, George?" said Mrs. Gummersell.

George nodded rapidly. "Wolfs and tigers," he said.

"Wolves," said Mrs. Gummersell.

"Wolfs," said George.

"And camels and deer and prairie dogs and rabbits," said Halter, to reassure Mrs. Gummersell that he was a proper parent and didn't go around introducing children to only predatory animals. He felt fatherly. Yet on that trip to the railroad crossing George had acted as if he'd been kidnapped. Today the boy burrowed into Halter's side as though he would find his father's marsupial pouch if he dug hard enough. Halter quailed before the boy's need. Mothers, not fathers, had pouches.

Alice was waiting on the front steps of her apartment house and ran toward the car when she saw them. Halter got out to meet her.

"So that's your housekeeper," she said, looking toward the car. "And that's your George."

"Yes," he said. "I confused Mrs. Gummersell. When I mentioned you, she thought that you were a little girl."

"I am. I hope Mrs. Gummersell won't be too hard on me."

"She has a great deal of respect for legal secretaries. Her father was a lawyer."

"And does George like legal secretaries?"

"He'd prefer you to be wolfish or tigerish. Those are his favorites."

"I'll do my best. Shall I show my teeth?"

Halter opened the back door, and Alice, nodding at Mrs. Gummersell, sat down beside her. Leaning in, he said, "Mrs. Gummersell, this is Miss Alice Gregory."

"How do you do?" said Mrs. Gummersell. "I'm *very* pleased to meet you. Mr. Halter has said some very nice things about you."

"How do *you* do?" said Alice. "Mr. Halter says all the time he'd be lost without you."

It might be a classic encounter, Halter reflected as he sat in the driver's seat. Mrs. Gummersell made it perfectly clear that though Halter had not sprung from her belly, she'd picked him from a sea of faces at the orphanage and by scrubbing him clean regarded him as her own. She was not about to surrender him casually to any girl with big ideas.

"This is Alice," Halter said to George. "Say hello."

George burrowed into his side.

"Hello, George," said Alice. "I like wolves and tigers and elephants."

George wriggled deeper against Halter.

"George," said Mrs. Gummersell. "We mustn't be rude. Say hello to Miss Gregory."

"Hello, Miss Gegree," said George, the words muffled by Halter's body.

Mrs. Gummersell beamed at Alice. "My father was a lawyer," she said. "He used to say that God put lawyers on earth to keep people out of mischief and secretaries on earth to keep lawyers out of mischief."

"That's well put," said Alice. "Lawyers have a lot to think about, and it's nice to take some of their worries off their shoulders. You and I have much in common, Mrs. Gummersell. We both try our best to help Mr. Halter as much as we can."

"Yes, indeed. A woman's task is to make it easier for a man to handle the more important things. I get so impatient with women who think they can do man's work, don't you?"

Alice smiled. "I couldn't agree more. A woman's place is really in the home. I like to think, though, that a secretary is the next best thing. Office wives, isn't that what they call us?"

Halter concentrated on driving. It was unfortunate that women might rely on the truth of his seeming. For Alice as much as for Mrs. Gummersell, it seemed that her womanhood depended on the reality of his manhood. The fiction was that Adam was created man. He was born merely human and into the vacuum flowed the conceit of manhood. Halter pressed his rib cage and felt it give way. There were two of them and one of him, but he saw no reason to defend himself. What happened to the claims of good women? Even in fairy tales they weren't allowed a happy ending. Hilda Brungards had rights too. What was good about the good woman? She was willing to serve, but for a price that wouldn't occur to anybody else. She refused to let man forget that he was responsible for her eternality.

When they reached the zoo, social lines re-formed. Mrs. Gummersell moved forward with George while Halter and Alice trailed behind.

"Now I know why you wanted me along," said Alice.

"I didn't think it was any secret," said Halter. "I like being with you."

"Your little boy was going to the zoo with his family. Why complicate the situation with—what would Mrs. Gummersell call me? 'Your nice Miss Gregory.' Did you realize you're her family?"

"It's occurred to me."

"You wanted me to come because Mrs. Gummersell was taking George to the zoo and you wanted to take someone too."

"She's very good with George," said Halter. "I'd be lost without her."

"Well, I've had my own Mrs. Gummersell. Some people appropriate other people in the name of devotion. Watch out or she'll swallow you up, fingernails and all."

"I'm watching," said Halter, and looked ahead at George. Mrs. Gummersell had bought him popcorn and they were standing at a railing, examining the seals. He hadn't once looked back or made an effort to call. The touch of Mrs. Gummersell's hand on George preempted any question of appeal to his father. George was ashamed of his father for bowing to Mrs. Gummersell's superior knowledge of goodness. He couldn't care less about the difference between good and evil. He cared for his father, and though he had little to go on, he knew that his father cared for him. He wanted Halter to hit Mrs. Gummersell in her goodly nose because he loved his father.

And where was his father's love? Definitions of love mourned within Halter in a thousand unintelligible dialects, but he couldn't decipher a single phrase, couldn't move beyond what seemed to him to be only advertising slogans.

They caught up to Mrs. Gummersell and George just as they were moving from the seals. "Mrs. Gummersell," said Alice.

The older woman turned and smiled.

"We've been selfish," said Alice. "Why don't you relax for a while on a bench while we take George up that big hill to the animal nursery? George, did you know they have little baby gorillas and chimpanzees? Wouldn't you like to see them?"

George gripped Mrs. Gummersell's hand and hid his head in her skirt. She nodded. "You're very kind," she said. "I *am* a little tired, now that I come to think about it. George, you go with your daddy and the nice lady."

George threw himself at Halter, who caught him on the fly and lifted him in his arms.

"We'll come back after we've seen the babies," said Alice.

Mrs. Gummersell settled herself on a bench. "Take your time," she said. "I can certainly use a breather. Don't fret about me."

They started up the hill.

"Daddy," said George.

"Yes, George."

"Daddy."

"Yes, George."

"Daddy, can I see the baby grilla?"

"Sure you can. And the baby chimp too."

"Yeah."

"They wear diapers, George," said Alice. "And they're very cute."

George burrowed.

"This is Alice, George," said Halter. "She's a very nice lady, just like Aunt Mary said."

"That's right, George. I can cook, type sixty words a minute and play tennis. Would you like to marry me?"

"No," said George into Halter's armpit.

Alice laughed. "That's definite enough."

They looked at the baby gorilla in his diapers. A female attendant was holding his hand, and the baby was hiding from the spectators in the starch of her hospital dress. George, wide-eyed, gripping his father's hand, watched the gorilla while Halter watched George.

On the way home, George decided he liked Alice and insisted on sitting on her lap. Mrs. Gummersell didn't seem to, mind at all. When they dropped Alice off, George cried. He slept the rest of the way home, and Halter carried him up to bed.

Halter decided to take a nap himself. Mrs. Gummersell's card on the pillow read:

> Surely I have behaved and quieted myself as a child that is weaned of his mother: my soul is even as a weaned child.

Late that night he awoke and called Mr. Forrest, who was very angry at being bothered until Halter reported that Alice was going to introduce him to C. F. Gregory as soon as he returned from Europe.

· 14 ·

Halter was a Senegalese at a meeting of western European foreign ministers. No. He was a small animal, indigenous to one country, crouching in the tall grass of another, disdained by the native animals, saber-toothed and crocodile-jawed. No. He stood fully clothed in a room of exhibitionists and had nothing to show or tell. Backed in a corner, he clutched whiskey in his hand, tasting it on his palm.

He was at Hilda's party and knew no one. She'd opened the door, slammed it shut behind him and left him to the bankruptcy of his own resources. A young man in waiter's livery had brought him a Scotch and soda and moved away, but he'd had no other social contact since arriving. He was disembodied, his brain submerged, aware only that he was not dead. He clung to the whiskey as proof he belonged somewhere.

He watched Hilda being a glittering *grande dame* holding

court, then lowered his weightless head to his drink and re-filled it. When he looked up, it was into her global eyes.

"You. Why don't you mix with my friends?"

"I'd like to, but I don't seem to be able to talk their language."

"Of course you don't. That's the point," she said. "Come on. They want to meet you. They've never met a lawyer this close up before. You're to impress them with your intelligence and charm. This is a *take*. Conquer them, captivate them."

"I'll do what I can," he said.

Hilda led him up to a bushy-haired man wearing a checked sport shirt. Tufts of hair curled at his throat.

"Barney, this is Halter, the mathematical genius I've told you about. Test him."

"Halter," said Barney. "Attend. There are two clocks, one which gives the right time twice a day, the other which is right once a year. Which do you prefer?"

Halter turned to Hilda. She was wearing an abbreviated, multicolored dress, over which concentric strands of amber beads were looped around her throat and breasts.

"The first?" said Halter. "Twice a day should be better than once a year."

"You are wrong, sir," said the man in good humor. "Mathematics is blessed, but time is nature's curse. Time is the envelope in which we are sealed. Hilda, would you please open the envelope?"

"Certainly," said Hilda. "The winner is number two. The first is a clock that doesn't go at all. The second loses two minutes a day but still makes its way to man three hundred and sixty days later. The second is preferable because it saves time and time is of the essence."

"There you have it, Halter," said the man. "Mathematics consists of the infinite capacity for adding up the score. You have much to learn."

He turned his back on Halter, and Hilda produced a beautiful young woman with loose blond hair to her waist and wooden beads that swung from her neck to her knees.

"Gretchen, this is Halter, the French literary genius I was telling you about. Test him."

"Oui. M'sieu, do you agree weeth La Bruyère when he say, 'Un esprit médiocre croit écrire divinement, un bon esprit croit écrire raisonnablement'?"

"I don't speak French," said Halter.

"Very well. I'll write the question for you." She took a pad from her purse, scribbled on it and handed the page to Halter.

"I don't read French," he said.

The girl swung her beads in an arc of admiration. "Sacré bleu," she said to Hilda. "Only an authentic French literary genius could neither speak nor read the French."

She untangled her false eyelashes and stared wide-eyed at Halter. "M'sieu Halter," she said. "Voulez-vous coucher avec moi?" Her beads struck Halter sharply in the crotch.

"Lay off," said Hilda. "Genius has its right to privacy."

She led Halter to a tall, thin old man with white hair parted severely at the center of his scalp and ending in disarray at his ears and neck. He wore a leather jacket and faded blue jeans and spurred cowboy boots. He must have been a favorite, for others thronged to listen.

"Ducky, this is Halter, the philosophic-religious genius I was telling you about. Test him."

"Fly boy, all I want you to unzipper, I mean, are your ailerons on straight, the torch man K., does he beam you? The aesthetic and intellectual principle is that no reality is thought or understood until its esse's been resolved into its posse, and the ethical principle is that no possibility is understood until each posse has really become an esse. What I mean, scout, does your esse chase the posse or does the posse chase your esse? I mean, how's your heat-seeking missal to the Thessalonians deicing these days?"

"I don't know."

The old man fell to his knees and kissed Halter's feet. "You old guru, you. To know it all is to know nothing, right?"

He raised his head toward Hilda. "This baby's infrared time-warped, de-kronosed and de-kairosed."

"Thank you, ducky," said Hilda, and took Halter to a triple-chinned lady in pink tights.

"Ariadne, this is Halter, the brilliant historian I was telling you about. Test him."

"Precisely." She spoke in a breathless, tinkling voice. "Mr. Halter, what did Abiel Foster write to the President of New Hampshire on October twenty-third, 1783?"

"I don't know," said Halter.

She shook a jellied finger at him. "You naughty boy. That might do for Ducky, but not for me. Hilda?"

"Abiel Foster to Meshech Weare, as follows," recited Hilda. " 'Sir, I enclose a copy of a resolution of Congress for a second foederal (*sic*) town on the Potomac, at or near Georgetown, and for adjourning Congress to meet at Annapolis, on the twenty-sixth of November next. The reasons of this resolution were, the uneasiness of the southern delegates at fixing the residence on the Delaware at, or near, the falls above Trenton; and the apprehension of the northern states that no other measures would prove effectual to prevent the return of Congress to Philadelphia, for a temporary residence.' "

"Just so," breathed Ariadne. "Really, Mr. Halter. Why do you hate Mr. Foster so?"

"I don't hate Mr. Foster."

"Good. Let's try again, shall we?"

"No," said Hilda. "History has its privileges but also its responsibilities."

She presented Halter to a small dapper man with a waxed mustache and a velvet cutaway jacket. "Gregory," said Hilda. "This is Halter, the genius of the dance I told you about. Test him."

"Yes, yes. Oh yes. My dear boy, what would you say was the first great technical innovation in ballet?"

"I don't know."

Gregory raised a penciled eyebrow. "Naughty boy." He turned to Hilda. "My dear, if you please."

"The turned-out movement at the hip," said Hilda. "The hip joint is a ball-and-socket. The leg can be rotated on its axis. Thus the legs pass each other without interference as the body moves sideward."

"Exactly," said Gregory. "It's evident, pussycat, you know nothing of hip movements. I'll wager you didn't even *know* you could rotate on your axis."

"Enough," said Hilda. "Mr. Halter won't dance. Don't ask him."

She raised her voice and said sharply, "The party's over. Everybody leaves. At once. Not you, Halter. You stay."

The guests disappeared quickly and silently, and left Halter with the proof, if he needed it, that Hilda ruled by divine right. He sat on the couch surrounded by cigarette butts floating in unfinished drinks, and gave up what was left of himself.

She summoned him to the floor and poured stove matches from a box on the rug between them. "You are permitted," she said, "to pick up from one to five matches each time. The one who picks up the last remaining match forfeits his will."

"All right."

"I'll give you a fateful choice. First or second? If you go second, you can't win. First, you could but you won't."

"Whichever you'd like."

"I'll go first, Halter, because you're a born loser."

She picked up three matches. Halter knew the game. He counted the remaining matches. Twenty-five left. He couldn't win, and he couldn't have lost if he'd gone first. He picked up two and she countered with the inevitable four. All she had to do was total six each round until only one was left. He picked up the last match.

"You lose," she said. "You'll always lose. You're my creature."

"Yes."

"Order. We'll go to your house. There you'll await further instructions."

"All right."

As they drove she said, "Those love letters I wrote to you.

Wouldn't you feel nice if they were true? Confess. Your time's running out."

"No," he said. "I knew I could never mean anything to you."

"Oh, but you're wrong," she said. "Here. Feel." She placed his hand over her heart. His fingers felt nothing. His mind levitated her body to an inaccessible balcony above him. She waved him away.

"You're wrong," she said. "You mean something, and I'll tell you what it is. You're a bug, and bugs should be squashed. Look alive when I talk to you. You humiliated me before my friends. I told them you were a genius, and you're only a bug."

"I'm not as intelligent as your friends."

"You think intelligence would save you? You're a bigger fool than I thought."

Hilda, he realized, had troubles of her own. He'd sniffed out as her ultimate problem the compulsion to make unacceptable offers of faith. Hilda wanted him to rip and tear, and all he could come up with was docility.

"I don't know what you want of me," he said. "I'm sorry."

"Sorry it is. Sorry it is you were ever born. Let's go. We've got work to do," and she led him to his front door. As he scratched at the lock, the door opened and Mrs. Gummersell, in a terry-cloth bathrobe and curlers, looked from Halter to Hilda.

"Thank you, Mrs. Gummersell. This is Mrs. Brungard," said Halter.

Mrs. Gummersell nodded. Her bulk guarded the entrance, and Halter waited patiently.

"Step aside, please. We'd like to come in," said Hilda.

"It's late, Mr. Halter," said Mrs. Gummersell.

"Halter," said Hilda. "Tell this Gorgon you'll knock her down if she doesn't get out of the way."

Halter shrugged. "I'm sorry, Mrs. Gummersell," he said, "but you really should stand aside."

"Mr. Halter. I am paid to keep your house and rear your

child. They are in my safekeeping, and I don't believe it will do your house or child the slightest bit of good to entertain an intoxicated married woman at this hour."

"Listen to that. Have you been discussing me with this *person?*"

"No, I haven't," said Halter. It was useless to explain that Mrs. Gummersell didn't have to be told.

Hilda's laugh vibrated against neighbors' windows. "Go ahead," she said. "Knock her down. What are you waiting for?"

Halter waited, and finally Mrs. Gummersell stepped aside. "I've said what had to be said, Mr. Halter, and there's nothing more I can say."

They went past her into the dark living room. Halter turned on a lamp, and Hilda motioned him to the couch. Mrs. Gummersell sat down facing them.

Hilda stared at her and released another blast of laughter. "I do believe, madam, that a man's best friend is his house-keeper. Darling, get me a drink."

Halter waited. It had worked before; perhaps Mrs. Gummersell would give way again and retire gracefully. She sat pat. He made Hilda a drink. The least he could do for Mrs. Gummersell was not have one himself.

Hilda wouldn't let him off so easily; she took a swallow and held out the glass. "Drink," she said. He reached, but she shook her head and fingered the back of his neck as she put the glass to his lips. "Drink it down. It's good for you. Isn't that what you tell him, Mrs. Gummersell?"

He swallowed and she burped him.

"Fill it up again," she said.

When Halter returned, Hilda was saying to Mrs. Gummersell, "Madam, permit me to ask you a question. Don't you believe in love?"

"With all my soul," said Mrs. Gummersell. "I believe in God. Let me ask you a question. Don't you believe in God?"

"Of course. Which one?"

"There is only one God."

"I beg to disagree. I have faith in good whiskey and wild men, Mrs. Gummersell."

"I pray God may forgive you. Even though you forsake Him, He will not forsake you. I pray you will open your heart to Him. I am afraid you are a vain, wicked woman, but it is never too late to walk humbly."

"You, I'm afraid, are a bore. Your God is a worse one." She put down her glass and leaned back on the couch, eyes closed. "Madam, you may have heard that love is a splendored thing. My darling Neil, baby, kiss me."

He bent down, closed his eyes and kissed her. Her arms came up around him and pulled him down on top of her. Even without the depressant of Mrs. Gummersell's presence, nothing would have been changed between Hilda and him. His sex maintained its respectful distance. Lying on Hilda's body he attempted to shield her from Mrs. Gummersell. But when he looked up she had disappeared. "She's gone," he said.

Hilda pushed him off and sat up. "Some housekeeper. She can't stand the heat. Where does she go when she goes?"

"Upstairs to her room."

"Good. We'll go upstairs to *your* room."

"My boy, George, wakes up sometimes and crawls into my bed."

"So? We'll be a trinity."

His bedroom was dark, and she told him to leave it that way. "Your clothes," she said in a conversational tone. "Take them off. Hurry up. I'm waiting."

Halter listened to her words trot down the hallway to the other rooms. He stripped and awaited further orders, so much typescript waiting to be set. Fairy tales had endings.

"Are you undressed?"

"Yes."

"Good. How does it feel to be a bare, utter ass? Did you think I'd let you lay a finger on me?"

Halter stood naked in the dark. "No," he said. "I don't think you like to be touched."

"The ass has teeth in it," she said. "It has to be me, not you, that's found wanting. Don't you think men desire me?"

"Yes. Very much. I don't think you desire them."

She was silent. Finally she said, "You've finally managed to say something funny. Really funny. In the end, truth is the only thing that's funny. Halter, how would you like to be my new psychiatrist? The old one isn't half as funny as you."

"I'm sorry."

"Of course. We started with that and finish with it. Don't you know how dangerous it is to be sorry?"

"Yes. I can't help it. I'm sorry because you're beautiful."

He had to wait for her answer. "All right," she said. "All right. It's my decision to confide in you. My privilege, I think you said. I lied to you, of course. You invite lies. There's nothing wrong with Vince. I wouldn't let him come near me. And Mackey. Our friend. His wife said he was insatiable, an old goat. I got him excited. At the last minute I told him to stop. I hit him with my fists, but it wasn't any use. He beat me at my own game."

"You have a right to hate him."

"No, I don't. I don't hate him. I raped myself and I hate myself for thinking it might be worth it." She held her breath, then let it out slowly. "That girl. Tell her he doesn't take no for an answer."

"I'll tell her."

"Well now," she said. "I think that wraps us up, doesn't it?"

"I guess it does."

She laughed. "You really are a fool, you know. Do you believe anything anyone tells you? Won't you ever know when you're being put on? Who in the world could quote Abiel Foster? My friends can be awfully silly but never that foolish. Only you could be. You must have known I rigged the whole thing for your benefit."

"No," said Halter. "I didn't think I could be worth that much effort."

"But you are. Don't underrate yourself. We were running out of the games that people play."

As she moved past him toward the door, he started to follow. She laughed. "Don't be absurd. I'll find my way out."

He remembered then that he was naked, and stood quietly while she went down the stairs and let herself out the front door.

Back in his room he turned on a lamp and found Mrs. Gummersell's card:

> Behold, I give unto you power to tread on serpents and scorpions, and over all the power of the enemy: and nothing shall by any means hurt you.

· 15 ·

Halter sat at the long mahogany conference table with ten men and two women and considered his new condition. He was officially a member of the board of directors of the Crocus Heights Association but he had yet to discover what the association did.

The risks were enormous. There was no defense to guilt by association. He looked for a hint of motivation in Orville Trotter's thin, uncompromising lips.

It was one thing to take orders from an individual like Crenshaw, and another from an organization. An organization had nothing else on its mind. It knew it was immortal as long as its orders were carried out. Having only conscious mind, it never faltered before reprisals of the unconscious.

"The first matter on the agenda," said Mr. Trotter, "is the question of the chains across Clapper Avenue. As you all know, we've been presented with a petition asking for removal of the chains. The floor is open."

A man raised his hand.

"Mr. Grasser."

"Okay," said Mr. Grasser. "I don't mind saying my name is on that petition right at the top. It's all right for you people who don't live on Salisbury to have the chains up on Clapper. Your kids play in the street like it's a playground. Meanwhile all the traffic comes down Salisbury. It's like the Indianapolis Speedway. Any day we're gonna have our kids run over. I say, fair is fair."

"Mr. Bottom."

"Mr. Grasser is missing the point. It's not the kids on Clapper we're protecting. That corner leading into Bruger is a deathtrap. Everybody trying to make a left turn is taking his life into his hands. We had three accidents there before the chains went up. Mr. Grasser knows that."

"Sure," said Mr. Grasser. "So what's wrong with putting up a signal light with a left-turn indicator? That's the solution, and you know it."

"Mr. Grasser, you're out of order," said Trotter sharply. "You're aware of the rules. You must be recognized by the chair. Mr. Perditch."

"Mr. Grasser knows very well that we've been after the city for years to put up a signal light. They won't do it because of the light a hundred feet away, where the real traffic flow is. I say the chains got to stay up. Mr. Grasser's lucky and doesn't realize it. The rest of us have to drive all the way to Salisbury to get out of Crocus Heights. I gotta leave five minutes earlier to get to work. Besides, I just happen to know that Mr. Grasser doesn't have any kids."

"I *thought* some wise guy'd bring that up," said Grasser. "I'm thinking about my neighbors, which is something that wouldn't occur to you."

"Mr. Grasser," said Trotter. "The chair won't warn you again. If you speak without being recognized once more I'll have to invoke the rules."

The penalty was at least death, thought Halter. Mr. Grasser must understand that. Lips twitching, he subsided in his chair.

"Mrs. Galley."

"All I can say is I have five children and Mr. Grasser is right. My kids can't even cross the street on Salisbury. It isn't fair."

The chair swiveled a glance around the room. "Anybody else?"

The room was silent.

"We'll take a vote. All in favor of keeping the chains on Clapper will say 'Aye.'"

There was a rumble of ayes.

"Opposed?"

There were a few scattered nays.

"The ayes have it. The chains stay where they are. The next item is the question of bumps on Salisbury. The floor is open. Mr. Grasser."

"It's the least we can do for the kids on Salisbury. We've got to keep those cars from speeding. Those bumps will at least slow them down. Nobody can object to that."

"Mr. Bottom."

"Now there's nobody in the world more concerned about kids than me. Ask anybody in my Boy Scout troop or my Little League team. But I'll tell you. I've heard of more cars being put in the shop from going over those darned bumps than for almost anything you can think of. They rattle your teeth, and I don't care if you're going two miles an hour."

"Mrs. Galley."

"I don't like to agree with Mr. Bottom, but I'm afraid the bumps are out. You see, there's the snowplows. I talked to the street commissioner and he was very sympathetic, but he said that those bumps break the snowplows."

"Mr. Farragut, just a minute. I'd like to hear from our new member. Mr. Halter, don't be bashful just because you're a newcomer. I'm sure you have some good ideas, and we like to hear from new members because they have a fresh point of view."

Halter hung his head. "Well," he said timidly. "What if you graded the bump on one side and the snowplow came from the other side?"

There was a silence.

"Mr. Farragut."

"No disrespect to the new member, but I've never heard of bumps like that. It just can't be feasible. We'd spend a lot of money on something that didn't work."

There was a murmur of assent.

"It was just an idea," said Halter.

"And a good one," said Trotter. "Nothing to apologize for. That's what we need, fresh ideas. Mr. Halter, I'm appointing you a committee of one to check into the feasibility of graded bumps. You'll report back at the next meeting."

"All right," said Halter.

"We'll table the question of the bumps until we have the benefit of Mr. Halter's report," said Trotter. "The next matter is the question of flowerpots on the street standards. Mrs. Gross, I believe this is your pet."

"It certainly is. Man doesn't live by bread alone. We ought to do our little bit for beautification. If Mrs. Johnson can fight the billboard people, we can pretty up our street standards. And it wouldn't cost that much to have a little beauty on our streets."

"Mr. Grasser."

"How much? I don't think we should buy a pig in a poke."

"Mrs. Gross?"

"How should I know? How much can it cost to put up a few flowerpots? If you men would mow your curb grass instead of having the subdivision do it, we could have a hundred flowerpots."

"You're out of order, Mrs. Gross. Curb grass is not on the agenda. Mr. Grasser."

"I move we make Mrs. Gross a committee of one to find out how much the flowerpots would cost. Don't forget, we've got to have a base on each standard to put them on."

"A good idea, Mr. Grasser. The chair doesn't require a motion. It appoints Mrs. Gross a committee of one to check the cost of placing flowerpots on the standards, and the question is tabled until the next meeting. We'll move on to Mr. Pilchuck's camper. Mr. Trevellyan."

"I was thinking about that when Mrs. Gross was talking

about beautification. After all, we've got a nice little subdivision here, with just about everybody pulling together. We've paid good money to have a decent place to live, and this Pilchuck's making it look like a slum. He knows damn well the regulation says no trucks can be parked overnight in Crocus, and he spits right in our eye. I say, sue him. If I had my way that's too good for him. He ought to be kicked out of the subdivision. Once you let trash like that in, there's no way of knowing when it'll stop. He's got no respect for his neighbors or the subdivision."

"Mr. Bottom."

"I agree with Mr. Trevellyan one hundred percent. The camper's making us all look bad. And you can't reason with Pilchuck. I know because I tried. He says a camper is not a truck and we can all go to hell."

"Mr. Trevellyan."

"That Okie needs to be taught a lesson. I say, sue him. Meanwhile I move that we boycott him. Don't even say hello to him. Don't let our kids go near his kids. Don't mow his parking. Don't pick up his garbage."

"It's fortunate," said Trotter, "that we now have an attorney on the board. I don't know if you're all aware of it, but our newest member, Mr. Halter, is an illustrious member of the bar. Mr. Trevellyan has proposed actions by the association that, while they may be commendable, may subject us to legal action by Pilchuck. Therefore, it seems in order to appoint Mr. Halter a committee of one to analyze the legal situation as it pertains to Pilchuck and his camper, and to indicate the legal ramifications. We'll table Pilchuck until the next meeting and Mr. Halter's report. I think that's the agenda, so unless anybody has an objection, I'll entertain a motion we adjourn. Mr. Farragut."

"I move we adjourn."

"I second the motion," said Mrs. Gross.

"In favor?"

The ayes clearly had it.

"The meeting is now adjourned," said Mr. Trotter.

The table broke up into knots of conversation. Halter's getaway was nipped in the bud by Trotter's handshake.

"Halter, I'm tickled to death to have you aboard. We can use a level head like yours."

"Thank you."

Trotter halted Mr. Grasser passing by. "Bob, I want you to meet Halter. Bob's one of our original members. One of the guys that makes the organization tick."

Grasser clapped his hands around Halter's and leaned into his face. "What's your street?"

"Salisbury."

"Terrific. Listen, we've got to fight that Clapper crowd. They think they're the cat's pajamas since they got the chains. Fair is fair."

Halter read Mr. Grasser's fine print. If there was to be a chain, why shouldn't it be on Salisbury?

"My wife was killed in an accident on Clapper," said Halter. "Before they put up the chain."

Grasser squeezed Halter's hands and let go. "Say, I'm sorry to hear that, fellow. You see what I mean about Salisbury?"

"Yes."

"Two wrongs don't make a right, right? Glad to have you aboard," said Grasser. He finished Halter off with a tap on the arm and moved on.

"This is one great bunch of boys and girls," said Trotter. "Take Grasser. He's got fifteen drugstores all over town. Trevellyan is vice-president of the Boomer Bank. There's not a single member who wouldn't make a triple-A client. Remember Mrs. Gross, the flowerpot lady? Her husband's one of the biggest meat packers in the Midwest." He nudged Halter. "Don't say I never did right by you. I like your style. Everything Rucker told me about you is true. You're a good boy. We're gonna work together like hand and glove."

"Thank you," said Halter. How could Trotter be so confident Halter would pull for the association? What had Rucker told him?

Halter trailed after him, then stopped and waited. Grasser and Trotter were blocking the door.

"Bobby, I hope you're not sore. You know if I let anybody break the rules of order it'd be you."

"Hell, why do you think we elected you president? I wanted a guy who wouldn't take shit from anybody, and for my money that's you." They shook hands up to the shoulders, and then moved off. Trotter's arm was around Grasser's neck, and they were whispering.

Once he made it outside, Halter breathed deeply and started to walk home. He had no illusions; he was on probation and not a full-fledged member until his loyalty was proved beyond question. His test, of course, was Pilchuck, someone he knew slightly because he'd walked past the camper once and the man had smiled at him. He was tall, freckle-faced, and seemed harmless enough, except that he did park his camper on the streets of Crocus Heights. But death had been decreed to Pilchuck's camper, and Halter was the appointed instrument. If he succeeded, the hidden purposes of the association might be revealed to him. The window dressing would be removed. Vicepresidents of banks didn't spend their evenings on bumps and flowerpots except to camouflage the vast, complex mechanisms of mass liquidations, international flow of munitions, overthrow of governments, beginning and ending of world wars. His new associates were no fools. He would be watched night and day; if he made the least suspicious move, he would be snuffed out. A car went by and nearly hit him. He could trust no one not to be in their employ. A package delivered parcel post could be a bomb.

Mrs. Gummersell had a message for him. "Your secretary, Miss Rauscher, called. She says it's urgent. How did the meeting go?"

"Fine."

"I imagine you're tired, what with working all day and a meeting at night. Would you like some hot chocolate?"

"That's very thoughtful. Thank you," said Halter, and went to the telephone.

"Something has happened," said Terry. Her tone was noncommittal. "I can't talk over the phone, but it's about Mackey. Could you come over?"

"I'll be right there," said Halter. He hung up and went to the kitchen to find Mrs. Gummersell. "I'm sorry," he said. "I have to leave. Something has come up in one of our cases."

"Of course," said Mrs. Gummersell. "The law is a jealous mistress. Do you have time for your chocolate? It would do you good."

Halter considered. "All right," he said. "I don't think a few minutes will make any difference."

Mrs. Gummersell busied herself while Halter sat at the kitchen table. "I've never seen George take to a young lady the way he took to your Miss Gregory. Quality tells. Even a small boy can tell a lady."

"Yes."

"She's certainly going to make some man a fine wife someday," said Mrs. Gummersell. "Somebody who's smart enough to know it takes more than a pretty face to make a wife." She turned from her stirring and smiled. "My father used to say that a pretty girl was more like a malady than a melody. He said she gets you all fevered up and only when it's too late do you realize what's going on. Miss Gregory may not be as pretty as some, but she's a beautiful person."

"Yes, she is. Your father must have been a very wise man."

"Oh, he was. You can be sure of that." Mrs. Gummersell poured the chocolate into cups and sat down with Halter. He took a tentative sip and considered Mrs. Gummersell's enthusiasm for Alice: a mother's enthusiasm for the "right" girl. He wondered when Mrs. Gummersell had decided to become his mother. There was little doubt that her encounter with Hilda had shaken her up; she never referred to the woman except by implication. A mother knew best. Mrs. Gummersell knew best; did this make her his mother?

But he already had a mother. Mrs. Gummersell must know that he'd drunk milk from another woman's breast. The fact that she'd remarried after his father died, and never bothered to visit him or even write (he had sent a telegram about Betty's death and received no answer), made no difference. As Mrs. Gummersell liked to say, blood was thicker than water. Yet if

Mrs. Gummersell chose to be his mother, he had no defense against her, just as there was no defense against her God.

He stood up. "The chocolate was just right," he said. "I feel much better. I'll try not to be too late."

"I hope it's nothing serious," said Mrs. Gummersell.

"Oh no. All in a day's work."

Terry was waiting for him in a mini-skirt, a broad belt strapped across her hips, and a thin red blouse. She looked young and vulnerable, her own kid sister, dressed in her kid sister's clothes. Her eyes, dark, soft, remained the same. He had begun to dream about them. They kept him blindfolded, tied to a post, awaiting an execution that never seemed to come.

"He's just left," she said. She paused and said, "I like him. He's a nice man."

"You mean Mackey?"

"Who do you think I mean?"

"I can see how you might like him," said Halter slowly.

"I called him this morning at his office and told him that I was your secretary and had some vital information about Mrs. Brungard and could he meet me somewhere to talk it over. At first he didn't want to. He thought it was improper for me to reveal any information about a case, since I was your secretary. I said that it had nothing to do with my job, that it was something personal. Finally he agreed to meet me for lunch, but if he decided that it was unethical to use whatever I had to tell him, he would forget whatever I said. He's a very nice guy."

"Yes. That's what you said."

"I met him for lunch and told him you and I have been going together and have had an understanding. That you were over here one night and forgot your briefcase. That I found these letters in it, which showed what a fool I was ever to believe in you. That I wanted to get even, and show what a cheat and liar you were. He said that if it was true, you were a menace as a lawyer and had to be exposed. That any lawyer who would have an affair with his client pending her divorce shouldn't be allowed to practice law."

Her voice was flat and even.

"He believed you, then."

"Why shouldn't he? I told you, he likes me. Do you find that so hard to believe?"

"No."

"I told him that if he cared to come to my apartment tonight, I'd show him the letters and let him make up his mind whether they were genuine. He said okay. He said that he was sorry I had to get mixed up in it, but that I had done the right thing by coming to him. That there came a time when a person no longer deserved loyalty.

"Anyway, he came and I didn't bring up the letters. Neither did he. We had a few drinks and then he tried to make love to me. I stopped him. I said I liked him but hardly knew him. He said that he'd like me to give him a chance to be known better. I said all right, he could come back Sunday night and we'd wait until then before I showed him the letters. So he's coming again Sunday."

"Do you want me to be here?"

"Isn't that the general idea?"

"Maybe you don't feel the same way about going ahead. He's no longer just a name to you."

"Have you changed your mind?"

"No."

"Then stop talking about it. Let's do it and get it over with. How many times do you have to ask me about it?"

"I'm sorry," said Halter. "I'd like to be sure it's what you want to do."

"Two can play at that game. I have to be absolutely sure it's what *you* want to do."

"That doesn't matter. It's what you want that counts."

She looked at him steadily. "Five thousand dollars for a little flirting around. Why shouldn't I?"

He had no answer. "I guess I'd better check the closet," he said.

"I guess you'd better," she said. He followed her into the bedroom, and she opened the closet door and turned away.

Halter made a space by pushing clothes along the bar and squatted to bring his eyes level with the bed. "I'll drill a hole about here," he said. "A very small hole. I'll patch it up later so you won't even notice it. I'll bring over the drill Sunday morning, if it's all right with you."

"You're the mastermind. I just work here."

"I value your opinion."

"I haven't thought about it one way or the other. You seem to know what you're doing. You're not paying me to ask questions, are you?"

"No, and I appreciate that. It might be difficult to explain."

"I bet it might." She was at the window, her back to him. "Well, that's all I wanted to tell you. If there's nothing else on your mind, I'm tired and would like to get to bed."

"I guess that's all for now," said Halter. "I'll be over Sunday. Thank you."

"Glad to be of service," she said without turning around.

He hesitated. Standing apart, he watched his body walk across the room and place his hand on her shoulder.

"Please," she said. "I'm tired."

"I want so much to . . ."

"To what?" she said.

"I don't know."

"I'm sure I don't know either."

All the way home Halter knew what he *didn't* want. He didn't want to leave it quite like that.

· 16 ·

Halter was in a cave. Bats rustled on velvet wings. He sat in darkness on a camp seat and waited quietly for his oxygen supply to be exhausted. Nobody would think of looking for him, because the entrance was a perfectly ordinary closet door with a small hole just above and to the right of the keyhole. Terry and he hadn't spoken since he'd been entombed, and he hadn't seen her. His connection with the outside world was the bed that waited with its blanket neatly turned down.

With nothing to do but wait, he had time to think. He found he had nothing to think about, which was ridiculous. It was as if solitary confinement swallowed up his imagination. He could imagine nothing more than being alone, motionless and speechless. It was reasonable to assume (was he thinking?) that when no activity was left to a man he could—in fact, must—still imagine one. Halter felt he must, but he couldn't. He sat, thoughtless, doing his job.

Linkages. Magical extensions that enable him to make his

way hand over hand to memory. Silent-screen projections of Hilda, Gummersell, Terry, Mackey, pride, duty, affection became archeological imprints on his skull. He must have been asked to sit in a closet, because he was doing it. He must be content with the knowledge that many people spent their lives waiting to be asked and never were.

Voices, like phonograph records previously mute in their sleeves, sounded in the other room. He had no idea of how long they'd been on.

"He's a fool, even apart from risking his career," Mackey was saying. "You're more woman than she'll ever be. Believe me, I know. I've known her a long time."

"She's beautiful," said Terry. "The most beautiful woman I've ever seen."

"I know what I'm talking about. She's ugly. She's never thought about anybody but herself her whole life. Her mind's a steel trap. It's no accident she takes to mathematics. People are numbers. Sooner or later they get wise to her. Even Halter will someday, when it's too late. He doesn't know what he's got to lose."

"Me? That's a laugh."

"You don't see me laughing. You're a wonderful girl. You're worth a hundred Hilda Brungards. I mean it. Please don't think I'm just trying to put you on."

"You don't even know me."

"I think I do."

"Well, you're being awfully sweet. It's just that I don't know if I can ever believe a man again."

"That damn Halter. He should be taken out and shot. Those two are made for each other. Between them they've got to work damn hard to find an excuse for living."

"You don't really know him. He's been very good to me. I think she's driven him crazy."

"You still in love with him?"

"All I know is I'm miserable and I don't know what to do about it. Like the letters. It seems like such a terrible thing to do even now."

"Forget the letters. Burn them if it'll make you feel better."
Silence.

"Here," said Terry. "Take them before I lose my nerve. Go on. Do whatever you want with them."

"All right. We'll worry about them later. Right now let's worry about you. Terry, I'd like to help you."

"How can you help me? How can anybody?"

"You're a lovely girl. Maybe I could help you remember that."

Prolonged silence.

"I wish I could believe you really mean it," said Terry. "I can't take it if you're just playing around. If you only knew how much I need somebody right now. Just to like me for myself."

"I do. I really do. Terry, I need someone too. We need each other. I'm pretty miserable myself. My wife divorced me not so long ago. I know exactly how you feel. Like nobody cares if you live or die."

Silences and murmurs. Halter's ears hurt, not from the sounds but the silences.

After a while Terry moved into view of his peephole, sat on the bed and began to take her clothes off. Then Mackey appeared, still clothed, and reached for the bedlamp.

"Don't turn it off," said Terry in a small voice. "I hate the dark. I want you to make love to *me*, not just anybody."

"All right, dear," said Mackey, and moved from view. Halter turned his head and waited a decent interval before screwing his eye back in place. Terry lay naked on the bed, eyes closed. Mackey, stripped, was beside her, kissing her mouth, a hand cupped at her breast.

Halter watched, the camera slack against his chest. This was as far as the blueprint went. Terry lay limp. Halter had Mackey's massive head in his sights but sat bemused and couldn't pull the trigger because no one had told him exactly when. He felt numb.

It was unnerving to be an assassin without a watch. The

victim was ready, the weapon was ready, but how could anything significant happen if nobody had thought of the right time? Halter scanned Terry's closed face for a sign. If she would only call out to him.

Halter, the father of a son, huddled in the closet, and his name became George. Warned never to crawl into secret places, he had slipped between alphabet blocks into expanding darkness. His first impulse was to cry out and be saved, but he was a motherless child. Halter rose, burst through the closet door, and flash cube rotating, took pictures.

He waited quietly while his brain developed the negatives. They arranged themselves in a sequence of Mackey's facial expressions. Mackey's face was blooded and banked. His face was slack and his mouth opened. His eyes widened and the pupils contracted. His eyebrows knitted and fretted, and blood went to his eyes. It was remarkable cinema despite the jerkiness and exaggeration of the performance.

Mackey stood up and reflected upon Halter, then Terry, who lay still and exposed as a corpse. He turned to his pile of clothes on the floor, then sat on a chair and slowly pulled his shorts on, his trousers, shirt, socks, shoes. He shoved his tie in a pocket. His lips moved like the arms of a swimmer about to give up. "It's a strange world, isn't it? Could I speak to you, Mr. Halter? In the other room."

"Of course." Halter walked over to Terry and slid a sheet over her body. He followed Mackey out and shut the door behind them. They sat down.

"Why?" said Mackey. "Why?"

"I'm a lawyer. I'm representing a client. I have a job to do."

"Who the hell you think you're talking to?" Mackey took a deep breath. "You're a son of a bitch. For the first time in my life I'm sorry I'm a lawyer with lawyers like you. Do you realize what you made that girl do? That's the thanks she gets for thinking she's in love with you."

"What's between Terry and me is my affair."

"Like hell it is. From now on, anybody unfortunate enough

to have anything to do with you is my affair. You're a public menace. Doing your *job*. What job? What do you expect to gain by taking some dirty pictures? Show them at a stag? You call yourself a lawyer. Is this the kind of job a lawyer's supposed to do?"

"You call yourself a lawyer and you came after the letters."

"Oh yes. The letters." Mackey went to his jacket hanging over a chair, took out the letters and threw them on the floor. "I don't give a tinker's damn about them and never did. Even if they were genuine I never planned to use them. What for? You think I couldn't take care of you without involving my client in a scandal?"

"What *did* you come for?"

Mackey's lips tightened. "You think I'm like you? I like Terry and I'm sorry for her."

"No," said Halter. "You're not like me. I have nothing to be proud of."

"What's that crack supposed to mean? What could you possibly be proud of?"

"That's what I said. But we're not here to talk about me. Let's discuss you and the pictures."

Mackey shook his head. "There's nothing to talk about. Not you, not me, not anything."

"Try. It might be worth your while."

Mackey stood up. "You've degraded a nice girl by making her the object of a peep show. You've had your kicks. What else is in it for you?"

"You might suggest to Mr. Brungard it would be wise to settle for three million."

"Is that it? You let *her* put you up to this? You're a bigger fool than I thought. I might have felt sorry for you if you were just crazy. You and your so-called client can go to hell."

"She mentioned what you did to her," said Halter. "She says you raped her."

Mackey breathed heavily through his nose. "You believed her? You *believe* that woman?"

"Yes, Mr. Mackey, I do."

Mackey put on his jacket. "There's no point talking to you. Do whatever you want with the pictures."

"I could make up some prints and send them around. What would Judge Banner say? Boys will be boys? Or Judge Dyce. I suppose he'd quote a few Scriptures. Then it would all pass over. Time, they say, is the great healer."

"You just go ahead. All you'll get out of it is disbarment. But I don't suppose that matters to you. What's the deal with Hilda? Twenty-five percent?"

"I like being a lawyer," said Halter. "It seems we both have something to lose."

"Good. Let's find out who has the most." He opened the front door and left without looking back.

"I won't do anything without telling you first," Halter called after him.

What was proved? That Mackey was more than a sense of dignity? It seemed so. Apparently even a false sense of worth might serve to make something of a man.

There was a knock. Halter opened the door. Mackey stood in the hall. "I'll wait to hear from you," he said flatly. "I prefer to believe that we can still be reasonable men."

He turned away and Halter shut the door. He felt drained and rather unsteady. "I prefer to BELIEVE," he found himself muttering. "For every DROP of too much RAIN that falls, a flower GROWS."

He knocked on the bedroom door. There was no answer, and he turned the knob and went in. Terry still lay under the sheet with her eyes closed. Her cheeks were wet.

Halter took out the five-thousand-dollar check and placed it on the bureau. "You were wonderful," he said. "I'm sorry it went so far. I wasn't able to move."

"Why not? Didn't you want to spoil the fun?"

"I just couldn't move. If I let you down, I'm sorry."

"Sure. Well, is it all over? Is that all you want from me?"

"That's all. You did a wonderful job."

"I'm glad for you. I have one more small favor to ask of you."

"Anything."

"I don't want you to come near me ever again. Is that too much to ask?"

"It's very little," he said. "I'd like to understand why you agreed to do it."

Her eyes still closed, she said, "Like the man said, I thought I was in love with you. How's that for a reason? As good as any, isn't it?"

His hands worked with the words. "I suppose so," he said.

"Don't worry," said Terry. "Now I really don't care if you live or die, which ought to make us even."

"I care whether you live or die."

"Tell it to Mrs. Brungard." She buried herself in the sheet. He waited for a moment and then turned to go.

"Tell me something, Mr. Halter," she said. "For the record. In your whole life, did the idea of love ever cross your mind?"

He found himself in a shell, rattling around. "Yes," he said. "It has. Well, Terry, I guess it's good-bye. I appreciate everything you've done."

She didn't answer.

Outside in the night air he moved toward his car, but found himself walking around the block. The camera bounced against his chest. Someone must have planted the idea of locomotion while he was in the closet. He was programmed for the route; an electrode in his brain would make him go around and around until he dropped. Again he approached the front of her building and stopped at the door, waiting for a signal to move him back inside. Instead he was swung away to his car. His hand inserted the ignition key. His foot pressed the starter pedal. His hand released the emergency brake. His hand engaged the gear. His hands gripped the wheel.

He drove home, parked the car, and tried to puzzle it out. Who was it, sometime or other, who had taught his body how to walk and to drive?

part · II ·

Supposing, however, that this were all true and that I were reproached with good reason, what do you know, what could you know as to how much artifice of self-preservation, how much rationality and higher protection there is in such self-deception—and how much falseness I still require in order to allow myself again and again the luxury of my sincerity. . . . In short, I still live; and life, in spite of ourselves, is not devised by morality; it demands illusion, it lives by illusion.

—NIETZSCHE

· 17 ·

Halter lingered over his light blue sport coat with the silver buttons. It was Alice's favorite piece of his clothing, and he wanted to please her. But she was, after all, only a junior officer and he didn't want to offend the high brass. The ultimate question was, what would C. F. Gregory wear under the same or similar circumstances? More crucial, what would he want a foot soldier to wear? The answer seemed obvious; Halter chose his gray suit, the one he wore during trials.

At the front door of the Gregory mansion, the structure loomed over him, menacing and impregnable. If he made a wrong move, boiling oil would pour on him, lances would pierce his flimsy gray armor, arrows would pincushion his heart. Alice was waiting somewhere inside, having been spirited away in the afternoon by liveried minions. The message from her father had something to do with a visiting aunt who was leaving. Alice had given Halter instructions, and he'd had no trouble finding his way this far. It occurred to him that there must be a servant's entrance. He let the knocker fall.

A butler in a tuxedo opened the door. He was a true butler, tall, thin and fitted with an indispensable high-bridged nose. One could perform with the proper condescension only from elevation; it seemed appropriate to Halter that he had to look up to the man.

"Yes?" said the butler.

"I'm Mr. Halter," said Halter without hope. He should have tried the rear door. Dogs usually liked him.

"Yes. Mr. Gregory is expecting you." He offered Halter safe passage into the foyer.

"If you would wait a moment, sir, I'll inform Mr. Gregory that you are here," said the butler; at parade march, he went to a door, knocked and went inside.

"This way, sir," said the butler when he returned. Halter shuffled through the door, and it shut as the fibers of the banked carpet closed over him. Gradually his ears cleared to the sound of harpsichord music tinkling from the fingers of an invisible player closeted in a secret passage. The room was bounded by polished sections of mahogany and equipped with exotic combinations of furniture and draperies. It seemed empty. Halter stood rooted, afraid to move.

A shaft of light beamed down to a heaving chair, and particles of dust, glinting like precious stones, formed the outline of a form. C. F. Gregory sat reading a book.

Halter stood at attention and waited for a sign, and Mr. Gregory sat and gave no sign. It was clear that Halter had to make the first move. He had to demonstrate he'd come in peace and submissiveness, that he had no stiletto or snub-nosed derringer cunningly secreted in a sleeve. Halter passed his hands quickly over his body, frisked his pockets, held out his arms and turned his hands. For good measure, in an unmistakable gesture of good will, he shook hands with himself.

Mr. Gregory looked up and nodded. He slipped a velvet marker into his book, stood up and walked forward with his hand extended. "Mr. Halter, I'm delighted. Come in and sit down."

They shook hands. Halter chose the least dangerous-looking

chair. It gave with docility, but kept giving until he suspected he was in quicksand.

"Some sherry?" said Mr. Gregory. Pouring the liquid into two glasses, he handed one to Halter.

"Thank you," said Halter, and sipped recklessly without waiting for his host. Half hidden in the cushion of the chair, he found himself able to make observations. Mr. Gregory was small and spare. His bones took up little space in the pouch of his skin, but he didn't look soft or spongy. He was, in fact, handsome in the way some older men are, boyishly, until the grim moment when the bones begin to poke through. He didn't look chilling like certain small men, such as jockeys, or toughly fascinating, with the kind of smile that left welts, which he expected of a multimillionaire. He was disarming.

"I appreciate what you're doing for Alice. I want you to know that," said Mr. Gregory.

Halter looked toward the door.

"Don't worry about her," said Mr. Gregory. "She's upstairs. She'll be down in a little while. I wanted to have a chance to talk to you privately. I hope you don't mind."

"Not at all," said Halter and lit a cigarette. He felt suddenly at home, or more properly, at castle. He was proud of the firmness of his fingers.

Mr. Gregory eyed him. "I don't know what I expected, but I didn't expect you. You're handsome enough, but not smooth enough. We might as well be frank with each other."

"All right," said Halter. "To be frank, I didn't expect you either."

"What did you have in mind?"

"Something like your butler."

Mr. Gregory smiled. "That's the trouble with being rich. We ought to look like our butlers." He paused, and said abruptly, "Why did you do it?"

Halter didn't pretend he didn't know what he'd done. He had become impatient with pretences, even small ones.

"Because I was asked."

"By Forrest?"

"Yes."

"And you do anything Forrest asks?"

"I try."

"I suppose Mr. Forrest's opinion is vital to you at your stage of the game. What's the bait, a partnership?"

"I'm already a partner," said Halter. "I'm a junior partner. Which is to say, Mr. Forrest can get rid of me any time."

"Is that your answer? You want to be a Forrest? Get where he's gotten?"

"I shouldn't think so. I've never really thought about it."

"I'm sure Forrest made it clear that if you made me happy, he'd make you happy."

"Yes, sir, he did."

"And yet you don't know if that's why you did it."

"I did it because he asked me to."

"Back to that. What if he hadn't asked you?"

"I wouldn't have taken Alice out."

Mr. Gregory nodded. "You had no interest in Alice personally. She was just another secretary."

Halter thought of Terry. "Yes, sir. She was just another secretary."

"Now that you know she's my daughter, she's no longer merely a secretary, and that's why you've been seeing her such a great deal."

"It began that way, yes, sir."

"Very straight-forward," said Mr. Gregory. "Only a fool would talk himself into lies. I've decided you're not a fool."

"Thank you."

"At this moment what do you think of my daughter?"

"I admire her very much."

"Even if she were only a secretary? Don't be a fool for my sake."

"I won't be."

Mr. Gregory looked at his carpet. "Why did Alice run away from me? Am I the sort of father who would force her to marry a polo player?"

"If you're asking for my opinion, I think she had to be by herself for a while."

"Don't make me change my mind about you. You're beginning to sound foolish. The poor little rich girl who has to find herself? Don't you credit her with more imagination than that?"

"It takes imagination to risk a simple solution."

"You're worse than foolish. You're clever," said Mr. Gregory. "That's risky. Stay simple, bluff and hearty—that's safe. Let's take *your* imagination. You marry the poor little rich girl, you live happily ever after. A simple enough solution."

"I don't know if I have that much imagination," said Halter. "I do pretty much as I'm told."

"Pretty much. What about the rest?"

"I'm not sure about the rest," said Halter. He was getting concerned about his tongue. It was beginning to talk back and he couldn't pinpoint its source material. He felt stirrings at his brain stem.

"Alice likes you," said Mr. Gregory. "She seems to know you very well by now. Nevertheless she likes you. Who can tell? She might go so far as to marry you if you asked her. Have you asked her?"

"No, I haven't."

"Why not? You think Forrest would mind? If I tell Forrest that's what I want, he'd want it. Very much. You can forget about Forrest. Concentrate on Alice, concentrate on me. She ran away from her father and she might run away from her father's choice. What if I told you I'd cut her off without a penny if she settled for you? Marrying her isn't such a simple proposition after all for a clever man. Let me suggest a bird in the hand. Let's say you forget about her, and in exchange I give you a million dollars and your own law firm. I could even provide you with some dignity. Tell her I'd disinherit her if she marries you, that you couldn't let her sacrifice all for love—which she's perfectly capable of doing. She's starved for love. How does that strike you? I'd back you up all the way."

"I promised Alice we'd go on a picnic next weekend. We're looking forward to it," said Halter.

Mr. Gregory smiled. "I'm a patient man. I'd be willing to wait until after the picnic."

Halter's brain made a definite movement. "I think not," he said. "Not on those terms. If you'd simply asked me, nothing more, I might have found it possible to agree."

"You're having trouble talking. Have I embarrassed you?"

"I've embarrassed myself, I think."

"You're a devious fellow," said Mr. Gregory. "Let me give you a tip. If it's selfishness you're resisting, you can't evade it that way. Selfishness is the product of obsession, even of one with a reverse spin. I'll give you another tip. A *big* one. I have a great deal of influence in this world, but little over Alice. With her I haven't even a financial argument. She has three million dollars in her own name. You didn't know that, I'm sure. You see, you're wasting your time even talking to me."

Halter sat silently and the man watched him.

"Can you manage to say you're in love with Alice?" said Mr. Gregory.

"No, sir, I can't."

Mr. Gregory smiled and leaned back. "I don't suppose you've admitted that to Alice?"

"She hasn't asked me."

C. F. Gregory pressed a button. "It should be interesting when and if she does," he said. "You wouldn't lie about it, I suppose? An honest man like you?"

"I don't think I would," said Halter as the butler came in.

"Elkins, you might tell Alice we're ready for dinner now."

"Yes, sir," said the butler, and bowed out.

Mr. Gregory smiled. "The comfort of my old age."

Halter made a remarkable discovery. Mr. Gregory was wearing a pale blue jacket with silver buttons exactly like the one he had hanging in his own closet. He leaned closer. The buttons weren't silver but pale gold, and the quality of the cloth was superior.

When Alice arrived, Halter didn't recognize her because she

looked absolutely the same. The girl moving in the stream during a downtown lunch hour was supposed to be one thing; the same girl, surrounded by mahogany panels, oriental rugs and butlers should be another.

She looked at each of them closely. "Well?" she said.

"I told Mr. Halter you didn't care what I thought," said Mr. Gregory. "I also told him you had three million dollars of your own."

Alice acted as if C. F. Gregory was just anybody; she made a gesture of impatience. "You would," she said. "Is money all you could find to talk about?"

"Not at all," said Mr. Gregory as they went into dinner. "We also discussed honesty."

Alice glanced quickly at Halter and then away as they sat down.

"Mr. Halter is a very honest man," said Mr. Gregory. "I don't believe I'm betraying a confidence when I say that he admitted he didn't love you. You didn't ask me to keep it a secret, did you, Mr. Halter?"

Halter looked at his plate.

"A remarkable young man you have here, Alice. Very likable. I trust you won't hold this against him. There's really so much I could do for him, you know. I could set him up for life. I could make him rich. I could introduce him to the best people. He could join the best clubs. He could go around the world in his own yacht, or mine. He could lunch with the President, or even Frank Sinatra and/or Mia. He could give a party so exclusive that Jackie and Truman would mourn when they weren't invited. Perhaps, Alice, you should explain there are no limits to what I could do for someone."

"It's true," said Alice. "There are no limits." She met her father's eyes. "I didn't want to come here, you know. Neil did. Now I'm glad."

"I'm glad you did too," said Mr. Gregory softly. "I haven't seen you for quite a while." He turned to Halter. "Halter, my boy, how about it? A million dollars and your own law firm. I like to give things to likable people."

Halter surveyed the crystal, the silver, the china. "Thank you for the offer, but I'm afraid I can't accept."

"Interesting. It's getting so you can't even give away the time of day. Elkins," he said to the butler, "how would you like ten million dollars? Your birthday's coming up and you deserve a little extra."

"No, thank you, sir," said Elkins. "You're too generous to me as it is." He filled the wineglasses.

"You see?" said Mr. Gregory. "What good is money if you can't give it away?"

"Father," said Alice. "Stop playing games with us or I'm leaving. Right now."

Mr. Gregory looked at her and shrugged. "Forgive me, Alice. Chalk it up to loneliness. Mr. Halter, listen to me. Never get rich. You'll wind up playing games. Nothing any longer means business. You snap your fingers, and the produce of the earth is drawn, quartered and hung up for you. You have your own fig trees, but you hate figs. You play games. Elkins and I make up one set. Bach and Shakespeare are another." He fingered a button. "This jacket, of course, is a game. There's only one game I'm not permitted to play: the game of love. Nobody, not even his child, loves a rich man." He smiled at Halter. "I hope you don't mind my copying your jacket. It proves I admire your style."

"My jacket has silver buttons," said Halter. "Yours has gold."

"So it does," said Mr. Gregory. "But Alice will tell you. Gold is my color."

"You might tell him the truth about the jacket," said Alice.

"Of course, my dear. You see, Halter, private detectives ransacked your home, looking for clues. I found your silver buttons revelatory. The stuff that dreams are made of."

"Stop it," said Alice. "Neil, Mrs. Gummersell called him and invited him over. And he snooped in your closets."

"I'm flattered," said Halter, "to have C. F. Gregory snooping in my house."

"At Mrs. Gummersell's invitation, I assure you. Your housekeeper thinks very highly of Alice. She feels she would make you a perfect wife. She wanted to make it perfectly clear that your character is above reproach and that we would get the best of the bargain. She has the charming notion my consent is necessary. She demonstrated to my complete satisfaction that you're neat, industrious and of high moral principles. She thinks of you as a son rather than an employer, which indicates you have tact with servants."

"Mrs. Gummersell is very loyal."

"She was somewhat concerned over Alice's religious background. I assured her we ran a good Christian household."

"Mrs. Gummersell has strong religious convictions," said Halter.

"Yes. So I learned. Well. I see that Alice is getting impatient with me."

"Neil, let's go. Haven't you heard enough?"

"No, my dear," said Mr. Gregory. "The question is, haven't you heard enough?"

"Nothing I haven't known before. Neil?" She threw down her napkin and walked out of the house.

Halter stood up.

"You know," said Mr. Gregory. "I wouldn't care to see her hurt."

"I believe you, sir."

He found Alice in the front seat of the car. He got in without a word and drove away.

"I hope you're proud of yourself," she said. "Did you have to get my father to do your dirty work?"

"I'm not proud of myself."

"Money? Is that what I mean to you? I can be as generous as my father pretends to be. Just stop lying to me."

"I've never lied to you."

"You don't think so? I think you've lied every time you kissed me." She twisted on the seat. "I'm not as strong as you think. There's me and there's my money. That's all there is. I'm not proud. I know what I am and what I want. What do you want?"

"Not to hurt you, but that's all I seem to be capable of."

She was silent. "This is no good," she said at last.

"I like to be with you," he said. "There's no one I'd rather be with, and that's no lie."

She exploded her breath. "Isn't it? Look. There's a you and there's a me. Or is there?"

"I need you, Alice."

"You *need* me. Does that mean you *want* me? Is that all you're backing away from? What are you waiting for? Let's put an end to your *need*. I didn't realize I was such a difficult campaign. *I* have needs too. See how simple life can be?"

"You misunderstand me."

"That's a laugh. Not any more. I don't care. Maybe now you'll stop talking about everything but what's on your mind. Okay? Maybe you'll stop treating me like chewing gum."

Halter examined the lamplighted street. A boy and girl, arms locked, swung by; a car's headlights flared in passing. "Lies," he said. "Infinite successions and variations of lies. If love exists, why does it have to be made? What is it? Do I remind you of your father?"

"Who's talking about love? Will you never stop throwing up smoke screens? I've told you—it isn't necessary. I don't need my father and I certainly don't need Freud to tell me what to do. Don't you want even the physical part of me?"

"I don't think *you* do, and that's what counts."

"It's *exactly* what I want. Unless you have something better to offer."

Halter searched his mind, then his body for an answer. "Where would you like to go?" he said.

"Anywhere. What's your usual? Your house—I'm sure it's adequate. Haven't you found *that* to be true?"

"Yes."

"And there's nothing finer than the truth, is there? Don't you feel marvelous, knowing that we're finally feeling true with each other?"

They were met at the door by Mrs. Gummersell, who smiled at Alice and let them in. "George is fast asleep," she said. "Is there anything I can get you? Perhaps a cup of tea?"

"No, thank you, Mrs. Gummersell," said Alice. "We've just had dinner at my father's house."

"A lovely man," said Mrs. Gummersell. "He came to visit one afternoon and we had a wonderful chat."

"Yes," said Alice. "He told me. He's quite taken with you."

"A lovely man," said Mrs. Gummersell. "Well, if you'll excuse me, I have some unfinished ironing in the basement."

They watched her disappear.

"She approves of you," said Halter. "And she doesn't approve of me. She puts inspirational messages on my pillow."

"Aren't you lucky?" Alice was grim. "Inspiring housekeepers are hard to find."

He looked at her. "Would you like to go home?"

"I would not. You'll just have to make do."

"All right," he said. "Shall we go upstairs?"

She'd succeeded, if that was her purpose, in making him angry; he thought he'd forgotten how. There was only one thing to do with it—pass it off on her.

They went to his bedroom. She couldn't intend to go to bed with him. He was being set up once again. She was too good a woman in the same frivolous sense that Mrs. Gummersell was. For people like them there was no such thing as sex; there was only love. She would wait with round eyes for him to collapse into remorse and beg forgiveness. Then she would raise him up and put him on his feet.

A table lamp was burning, courtesy of Mrs. Gummersell. Alice went directly to the bed. "I'd like the light off, please," she said. "I'm not afraid of the dark."

He turned off the lamp, found her body and poked at her clothing. Her arms found his neck. She was strong. His irritation prepared to gather in her strength, but her fingers were poultices.

He became calm and weak and cold. "I'm sorry," he said. "I'd like to call it off."

She lay still. "Do I repel you that much?"

"You don't repel me at all. It's nothing like that. You're entitled to more than this."

She moved away from him. "More than this doesn't leave us with very much, does it?"

"It does for me. I guess it doesn't for you."

"Oh, I don't know," she said. "It's not unpleasant for a woman to have a man around who wants nothing from her. It makes me feel so secure. Thank you for a lovely evening."

She walked out. He lay motionless for half an hour before he realized she didn't have a car.

· 18 ·

By the third day of trial Haggerty had built sympathy for Crowder to the breaking point. Several jurors appeared to be on the verge of tears. There had been Crowder's third- and sixth-grade teachers, his family minister, his parents, the doctor, Garrett, and two specialists. There were neighbors and friends and the high-school basketball coach. Beyond the shadow of a doubt, Crowder had been a splendid physical specimen.

The courtroom was packed. A Haggerty spectacular was always played to standing room only. A juror had yet to yawn. Haggerty looked confident; Halter wondered how *he* looked. He felt as detached from the controversy as the court reporter, taking in everything and feeling nothing. His mind rejected any data irrelevant to the case. He wondered if someday all lawyers wouldn't be like him—calculators that couldn't make a legal mistake, with trials, like wars, conducted by push button.

Haggerty called his next witness. He had finally exhausted the lachrymal glands and was at the cold heart of the case.

Haggerty: What is your name, sir?

Witness: Benjamin G. Granville.

Haggerty: What's your line of work?

Granville: I've been a driver-education instructor for ten years.

Haggerty: Good. In your business, have you become acquainted, through experience and literature, with certain statistics in regard to stopping distances and reaction time and things of that nature?

Granville: Yes.

Halter looked at the jury. It was seventh-inning stretch time, Halter's inning; it was up to him to see that the judge stayed awake.

Haggerty (with a shrug as if to say: it's not my fault if the railroad boys want to worry about this stuff): All right. Are you able to figure how many feet a second a car is moving at thirty miles an hour?

Granville: Yes. About forty-four feet per second.

Haggerty: Then sixty miles per hour would be eighty-eight feet per second. Is that true?

Granville: Yes.

Haggerty: Traveling at sixty miles per hour, or eighty-eight feet per second, what would be the overall stopping distance of a motor vehicle, assuming good tires and brakes and a dry, flat road?

Granville: About two hundred and seventy-two feet.

Haggerty: How long is a Ford Falcon station wagon, last year's model?

Granville: Fifteen and a half feet.

Haggerty: A fifteen-and-a-half-foot vehicle traveling forty-four feet a second, how long would it take to pass a given point?

Granville: About . . . well, sixteen forty-fourths of a second.

Haggerty: Between a third and a half of a second, is that correct?

Granville: Correct.

Haggerty: I have no more questions. Your witness, Mr. Halter.

He smiled at Granville and returned to the lawyer's table. Before he sat down he raised his eyebrows at the jury and grinned. They smiled back as Halter got up.

Halter: Mr. Granville, did you graduate from college?

Granville: Yes, sir.

Halter: What degree?

Granville: Bachelor of Science.

Halter: Any engineering in that?

Granville: No.

Halter: Not an engineering degree?

Granville: I told you, no. Education.

Halter: Bachelor of Science in Education?

Granville: Yes.

Halter: You mean you were trained to be a schoolteacher?

Granville: Yes.

Halter: Not to be an engineer?

Granville: That's right.

Halter: And is that the extent of your formal education?

Granville: Yes.

Halter: I see. What is the formula you apply to determine how many feet per second a car goes at one mile per hour?

Granville: Well, it's a rather rough formula. You take the number of miles per hour and add half that number to it, and you get feet per second.

Halter: Why do you add half to it? What is the mathematical basis for it?

Granville: It's just a set formula. It works out. I don't know why.

Halter: Does it work out precisely?

Granville: No, it isn't exact.

Halter: Well then, what is the formula? I believe you said that at thirty miles per hour a car would go forty-four feet per second.

Granville: Right.

Halter: You tell me it's about a half. Your figures don't jibe. It would be forty-five per second, right? What is the formula?

Granville: I don't know the exact formula for it.

Halter: You don't have the slightest idea?

Granville: I guess I don't.

Halter: Let's see if we can't work one out.

Granville: All right with me.

Haggerty (jumping up): Just a minute. Your Honor, I'm going to object. Is Mr. Halter asking questions or is he going to give everybody a lecture? I thought Mr. Granville was the schoolteacher around here.

The crowd chuckled and nudged each other. This was what they had come for, laughs or tears, and both had gotten thin. The response was more than Haggerty deserved.

Judge Dyce: What exactly is your objection, Mr. Haggerty?

Haggerty: He's not asking questions, your Honor.

Judge Dyce: All right. Mr. Halter, put your lecture in the form of questions.

Sanctified by the court, this got an even bigger laugh in which Haggerty joined.

Halter: How many feet are there in a mile?

Granville: Five thousand two hundred and eighty.

Halter: How many seconds are there in an hour?

Granville: Oh, sixty in an hour, wait a minute, I mean—

Halter: Sixty minutes in an hour and sixty seconds in a minute, thirty-six hundred seconds in an hour, is that what you mean?

Granville: Right.

Halter: If we divided thirty-six hundred into five thousand two hundred and eighty, the number of seconds in an hour into the number of feet in a mile, we'd get the number of feet in a second, wouldn't we?

Granville: Golly, I believe you're right.

Halter: Isn't the formula one point four seven instead of one half as you stated? Would you like some time to work it out?

Granville: Oh, I'm sure you're right because, as I said, my formula's a rough one, but it suits our occasion, it suits our needs.

Halter: But it isn't exact.

Granville: No, I guess not.

Halter: All right. Now you were asked by Mr. Haggerty how long it would take a sixteen-foot car to pass a given point at thirty miles per hour. Remember that?

Granville: Yes, sir.

Halter: Instead of taking that anonymous point, let's say the car is going across in front of an eleven-foot-wide locomotive and it has to pass in such a way that the back end of the car clears the front of the locomotive. How many feet would that be?

Granville: Let's see. Eleven feet, and sixteen feet for the car. Twenty-seven feet. Is that right?

Halter: I'm asking *you*.

Granville: That's right. Twenty-seven feet. Isn't it?

Halter: Your answer is twenty-seven feet.

Granville: Yes.

Halter: Then how long would it take for the car to clear?

Granville: Let's see, that would be the twenty-seven over, you want thirty times one point four seven, that would be forty-four point one o. It would take twenty-seven over forty-four point one o of a second. Am I right?

Halter: Is that your answer?

Granville: Well, yes.

Halter: Twenty-seven forty-fourths of a second. That's more than half a second by a good deal, isn't it?

Haggerty (jumping up): Just a minute. Slow down there. It's five forty-fourths of a second more. If that's a good deal I'll eat my hat. On second thought, I'd rather eat Mr. Halter's.

Halter glanced at the jury. This time they sat on their hands. Unlike Hilda Brungard, they were impressed by Halter's mathematical ability. One juror managed an anxious grin for his leader. Their momentary deference was more than Halter expected and nothing he could depend on. Still, it was nice to stand up and be counted.

Halter: It's over six/tenths of a second, isn't it?

Granville: Yes, sir, I guess so, if you say so.

Halter: Is it or isn't it?

Granville: Yes, sir.

Halter: Thank you. One last question. When it's a matter of a life-and-death collision, a matter of inches, much less feet, a sixth of a second can make a lot of difference, can it not? The moment of impact is a split second that a sixth of a second could avoid, isn't that true?

Haggerty: I object, your Honor. First a teacher, and now Mr. Halter's trying to be a philosopher.

Judge Dyce: The objection is sustained.

Halter: I have no further questions, your honor.

Haggerty faced the courtroom. "Arnold Tryon," he called.

Haggerty was employing an enemy troop in violation of the maxim: Never prove the case by the other lawyer's witness. But he really had no choice, and he had long ago outgrown legal maxims. The witness was sworn in.

Haggerty: Your name, sir?

Tryon: Arnold Tryon.

Haggerty: You're employed by the Sunflower Railroad?

Tryon: I am.

Haggerty: In what capacity?

Tyron: Locomotive engineer.

Haggerty: For how long?

Tryon: Eight years.

Haggerty: How old are you?

Tryon: Fifty-six.

Haggerty: You were operating a railroad engine when it was involved with an auto on June eighteenth of last year?

Tryon: That is correct.

Haggerty: I've asked you questions before, haven't I? Under oath at your deposition?

Tryon: Yes.

Haggerty (using a pointer on a diagram agreed upon between counsel): You were coming down this track in a southwesterly direction?

Tryon: Yes.

Haggerty: The intersecting road runs in a northeasterly direction, does it not?

Tryon: Yes.

Haggerty: What kind of engine were you driving?

Tryon: A Baldwin switcher-type locomotive.

Haggerty: What were the weather conditions that day you collided with Mr. Crowder's car?

Tryon: Fair. The sun was shining.

Haggerty: Level track?

Tryon: Yes.

Haggerty: Straight?

Tryon: Yes.

Haggerty: As you approached the intersection from about a quarter of a mile, at what speed were you traveling?

Tryon: About thirty miles per hour.

Haggerty: All right. There's no speedometer on that locomotive, is there?

Tryon: No.

Haggerty: So we're relying on your best judgment?

Tryon: That's right.

Haggerty: Okay. As you approached the intersection, did you see a moving automobile on the highway approaching the track from the south?

Tryon: I did.

Haggerty: Where was the car when you first saw it in relation to the track?

Tryon: As it came out from behind the house.

Haggerty (indicating on the diagram): This house down here?

Tryon: Yes.

Haggerty: Do you know the distance the car was from the intersection when you first saw it?

Tryon: Around eight hundred feet.

Haggerty: All right. When you first saw it, did you estimate its speed?

Tyron: Oh yes. I estimated it as sixty miles per hour.

Haggerty: Very well. When you first saw the car back by the house, some eight hundred feet from the crossing, where was your engine?

Tryon: Back some point around a tree that stands on the left there, about four hundred feet from the intersection.

Haggerty (indicating): Is this the tree you have reference to? A sycamore tree?

Tryon: Yes.

Haggerty: Were you traveling at thirty miles per hour at the time?

Tryon: Yes.

Haggerty: What do you do to keep a locomotive moving?

Tryon: You open the throttle.

Haggerty: Is that a lever-type arrangement?

Tryon: Yes.

Haggerty: Worked with the hand?

Tryon: Yes. The right hand, going in reverse.

Haggerty: When you saw the car for the first time, did you have your hand poised on any part of the braking system?

Tryon: When I first saw it, no, but right after I saw it.

Haggerty: Which hand?

Tryon: My left.

Haggerty: Is the brake valve a hand lever like the throttle?

Tryon: Yes.

Haggerty: Did you continue to watch the automobile from the time your first saw it up until the time it reached the track?

Tryon: I did.

Haggerty: As it traveled the last two hundred feet to the track, did you see it change its rate of speed at any time?

Tryon: Yes, when it sloughed to the right.

Haggerty: You're describing the movement demonstrated by the skid mark?

Tryon: That's right.

Haggerty: How fast was the car traveling at the time of impact?

Tryon: From twenty to thirty miles per hour.

Haggerty: On your deposition you said thirty miles per hour.

Tryon: Well, I don't exactly recall, but it would be in that range.

Haggerty: Would you say thirty now?

Tryon: Okay.

Haggerty: Fine. Were you alerted to the situation and aware the car was approaching the crossing?

Tryon: Yes.

Haggerty: And you continued to watch it?

Tryon: Yes.

Haggerty: Do you have any idea as to the stopping distance of a car that's traveling about sixty miles per hour?

Tryon: Oh, perhaps two hundred and seventy-five feet.

Haggerty: Did you at any time while Mr. Crowder was traveling that last, terrible eight hundred feet make an emergency application of your brake?

Tryon: Just about the time of impact.

Haggerty: As you were traveling this distance from the tree to the point of impact, at no time did you make an emergency application of your brake? That's what you're saying, isn't it?

Tryon: That's right.

Haggerty (nodding): Very well. Now listen carefully. When you make an emergency application of the brake, is there any lapse at all between making the application and feeling a reduction in speed of the train, under the conditions prevailing at the time of the accident?

Tryon: Well, there's a reaction time of several seconds before there's any application of the brake shoe to the wheel. And that would be several seconds for the air to be reduced in the train line so as to set those brake shoes against the wheel. They're constructed so that the application won't apply all at once, so it will apply gradually.

Haggerty (wagging his finger): This isn't the first time this question has been asked you, is it? Didn't I ask you the same thing on deposition?

Tryon: I believe you did.

Haggerty: Do you recall what you said then?

Tryon: No.

Haggerty: Let me help you out. On page twenty-seven you said, 'Emergency application gives an immediate reduction.' Remember now? Sure you do.

Tryon: I may have said it, but I don't recall it, and it don't.

Haggerty: You don't recall it even though it's down here in black and white?

Tryon: No, I don't, and that's a fact. Anyway it don't.

Haggerty (shaking his head at the witness, then several times at the jury, several jurors nodding in response): I have no more questions at this time. Your witness, Mr. Halter.

Halter: When the brake lever on a railroad engine is moved, Mr. Tryon, so as to apply the brake, is there a time lag between the time when you move the lever to decrease the brake-pipe pressure and the time when the brake shoes on the individual cars and engine grasp the wheels sufficiently to cause a reduction in speed?

Tryon: Oh yes. There's a reaction time.

Halter: You're not referring to the human reaction time here but the brake reaction time. Is that correct?

Tryon: The brakes, that's right.

Halter: How long a period of time is this?

Tryon: I'd say five or six seconds.

Halter: Will it depend on the speed of the train?

Tryon: Regardless of the speed of the train.

Halter: And do you recall being asked these questions on your deposition?

Tryon: No.

Halter: Are you sure you weren't asked?

Tryon: Well . . .

Halter: Let me refresh your recollection.

Haggerty (jumping up): Your Honor, I object to Mr. Halter attempting to impeach his own witness.

Judge Dyce: This is not his own witness.

Haggerty: Your Honor, I'd like to make a record on this.

Judge Dyce: Well, come on up here.

(Counsel approach the bench.)

Haggerty: Your Honor, this is an employee of the railroad, and certainly not equally available to plaintiff.

Judge Dyce: He was put on by you.

Haggerty: Under the adverse-witness statute.

Judge Dyce: Nobody has shown he is an adverse witness.

Haggerty: He's been shown to be an employee of the railroad.

Judge Dyce: That's all right. Nobody has shown him to be adverse. I overrule the objection. Get on with it.

Halter (back with the witness): Mr. Tryon, I'll read from your deposition on page—

Tryon: You don't have to. I didn't understand what you meant. Sure, I remember those questions from the deposition.

Halter: All right. When you apply an emergency application, does that stop the train as soon as you make your application?

Tryon: Well, it takes a few seconds in there before the brakes take hold.

Halter: Do you remember saying that in answer to my question on deposition?

Tryon: Yes.

Halter: Is it correct that it takes a few seconds?

Tryon: Yes.

Halter: And after you start getting some reduction in speed, after these few seconds, is it true that the reduction starts gradually and builds up?

Tryon: Yes.

Haggerty: I want to object to the leading nature of these questions. This is an employee of the railroad.

Judge Dyce: Come up here, gentlemen. Mr. Haggerty, do you have any law that says that just because the witness is an employee of the railroad he can't be led on cross-examination?

Haggerty: No, sir, but I think under these circumstances the court should be very careful as to the way in which the interrogation is done, particularly with the use of a deposition.

Judge Dyce: Thank you for telling me my job. Do you have any law?

Haggerty: No, your Honor. I have no law to give you.

Judge Dyce: The objection is overruled.

Halter (to the witness): During what you refer to as the reaction time of the brakes, is there any reduction in the speed of the train?

Tryon: No.

Halter: If your train is going thirty miles per hour, can you estimate how fast it will be going for the six tenths of a second after the reaction time?

Tryon: I'd say at least twenty-five miles an hour. I'm sure it's more.

Halter: So that it would travel in that time another twenty-two feet?

Tryon: About that.

Halter: All right. I believe you testified you were at the sycamore tree, four hundred feet from the crossing, when the automobile was eight hundred feet away, at the house. Is that correct?

Tryon: Yes.

Halter: And your speed was thirty miles per hour, and the auto's sixty?

Tryon: Yes.

Halter: In other words, the automobile was twice as far away and going twice as fast?

Tryon: Yes.

Halter: So that while the auto is covering six hundred feet you would be traveling three hundred.

Tryon: That's right.

Halter: Accordingly, when the car was two hundred feet from the crossing, where were you?

Tryon: I'd be a hundred feet away.

Halter: And how fast was the car going at that point?

Tryon: Sixty miles an hour, as far as I could see. It hadn't slowed down.

Halter: So you knew, didn't you, at that point, with you

one hundred feet from the crossing and the automobile two hundred, that the auto couldn't stop in time?

Tryon: Correct.

Halter: All right. From the time you first saw the auto at eight hundred feet away and you were coming past the tree, were you doing anything with your diesel horn?

Tryon: Sure. I was blowing the horn. I blew it all the way to the point of impact.

Halter: When the auto was two hundred feet away and you knew it couldn't stop in time, why didn't you apply your brakes?

Tryon: It wouldn't have been any use.

Halter: Why not?

Tryon: I was only a hundred feet away. Like I said, the brakes don't take hold for a few seconds. I'd go over two hundred feet before I'd even begin to slow down.

Halter: No further questions at this time. Thank you, Mr. Tryon.

Haggerty: I have a few more. Mr. Tryon, you said you knew that an auto going sixty miles per hour would take about two hundred and seventy-five feet to stop.

Tryon: That's right.

Haggerty: And you told Mr. Halter that you knew when Mr. Crowder was two hundred feet away he couldn't stop.

Tryon: No, I didn't know that.

Haggerty: I thought you said you did know.

Tryon: I meant he couldn't stop if he kept going.

Haggerty: Where in blazes would he go?

Tryon: He could have taken off to the side of the road. Then he would have been all right.

Haggerty: Is that what you were relying on instead of your brakes—that he'd take off to the side of the road?

Tryon: No. You don't sit around in an emergency like that and figure.

Haggerty: You didn't figure, all right. Isn't it true that when that car was two hundred feet from the crossing, going sixty miles per hour, he couldn't stop?

Tryon: I just knew *I* couldn't. You don't know what he's going to do. There was a possibility of him clearing the crossing if he'd kept going sixty.

Haggerty (raising his arms): Did I hear you right? Do you have people racing you at crossings all the time? You like to play Russian roulette?

Tryon: *I* don't. *They* do. They do it quite often.

Haggerty: Are you telling this court and jury you like to gamble with people's lives?

Tryon: No, sir. I didn't know about him. I was hoping. I just knew I couldn't stop in time.

Haggerty: You also knew he couldn't make it if he tried to stop, didn't you?

Tryon: I just knew I couldn't stop in time.

Haggerty: Would it have hurt you to try? Would it have strained your arm?

Tryon: It wasn't any use. None at all.

Haggerty: And Russian roulette is more exciting. That's all.

Halter: A few last questions. Mr. Tryon. On this occasion were you on a local service run?

Tryon: Yes.

Halter: How far had you traveled from the time you started your run until you reached the place of the accident?

Tryon: About eighty-five miles.

Halter: Do you have any idea as to the number of railroad crossings that exist on this distance?

Tryon: From fifty to sixty.

Halter: I believe that's all.

Judge Dyce: This is as good a time as any to adjourn for lunch. The court will reconvene at one o'clock. Will the attorneys approach the bench?

Judge Dyce: Mr. Haggerty, how much more will you go?

Haggerty: I have just one more witness, your Honor.

Judge Dyce: What about you, Mr. Halter? How much more time will you need?

Halter: I won't need more than the afternoon, your Honor.

Judge Dyce: Fine. I'd like to finish up today. I have to

be in the state capitol tomorrow, if possible. Understand, only if it's possible. I'm not trying to rush you.

Halter: Yes, sir.

Halter went to lunch by himself. He dawdled with a ham sandwich and a glass of milk, but when he was finished he still had half an hour before court reconvened. He went to the park adjoining the courthouse and sat on a bench. It was a warm, sunny day, and the park was crowded with people and birds. The sparrows clustered around bread crumbs until their pecking order was disrupted by a raiding grackle. There was even a cardinal timidly waiting for a vacancy that might never come. Halter wished he'd remembered that the Crowder trial was not the world and had brought part of his sandwich along for the cardinal. No one, people or birds, cared whether Crowder got some money from the railroad or not. He turned to ask Judge Dyce, sitting on his bench, whether he realized that the courtroom was really an open-air theater, and discovered the judge to be a man in a striped sport shirt, beard and sandals, feeding the birds. The man smiled and held out crumbs to Halter, who shook his head and looked away. He couldn't afford to accept charity or be charitable; he had a case to win. It wasn't proper to accept a kindness.

Haggerty was still confident. "You've got the judge, and I've got the jury," he'd said on his way out. "Fair enough."

Halter watched the bearded man sprinkle crumbs. He might be a juror, if not this time, then the next. Jurors were the Communists of the American personal-injury system. From each according to his ability, to each according to his need. The railroad was able to pay; Crowder needed to be paid. What could be more equitable? Yet there was the grackle, powerful in the chest, bumping sparrows aside to gobble every crumb in sight, and the cardinal, powerful enough, standing by.

Halter gave up on the sun and grass and surrendered to the courtroom. He was almost late; the crowd was on its feet, and the judge was settling in his chair.

Judge Dyce: Call your next witness, Mr. Haggerty.

Haggerty: He's waiting in the hall, your Honor. I beg the court's indulgence while he's wheeled in.

Halter: Just a moment. If it's the plaintiff, I'm going to object.

Judge Dyce: Counsel approach the bench . . . All right, Mr. Halter. What's the objection?

Halter: Your Honor, Billy Joe Crowder, the plaintiff, is incapable of testifying, due to his condition. He wouldn't add anything material as a witness because, the court will recall, Mr. Haggerty admitted in his opening statement that the plaintiff is nothing but a vegetable.

Haggerty: I intend, your Honor, to call Billy Joe to the stand to ask him whether he knows anything about the accident, in order to assure the jury that we're not trying to conceal any information from them, and to show them that he has no recollection of the accident. That is going to be the extent of my interrogation. I believe he would be competent and his testimony material for the purpose for which I intend to use him.

Halter: The only effect and purpose of such an exhibition would be to excite the jury's sympathy and to create an atmosphere of passion, bias and prejudice.

Judge Dyce: What exactly is the matter with him, Mr. Haggerty?

Haggerty: He's totally paralyzed as a result of the accident, your Honor.

Halter: His mind is totally gone, your Honor.

Judge Dyce: Well, I'm inclined to overrule your objection, Mr. Halter. He has a right to be heard. I do it with this reservation, that he will be in the courtroom only during the period of his testimony. Is that understood?

Haggerty: Yes, your Honor.

Halter: Well, for the record I'm objecting to the plaintiff appearing in front of the jury at all.

Judge Dyce: All right. I overrule the objection. You may move for a mistrial right now if you want to.

Halter: To keep my record, I have made my objection in

advance of the witness' appearance, so that everybody is fore-warned. I'd like to reserve the question of moving for a mistrial until after the testimony.

Judge Dyce: Very well. Mr. Haggerty, summon the witness.

Haggerty walked rapidly through the courtroom and out the rear. He returned slowly with Crowder on his hospital bed, pushing it with painstaking care down the central aisle between the masses of spectators. The room was still. Halter coughed. Haggerty concluded his pilgrimage in front of the witness stand.

Haggerty: I'm afraid, your Honor, the witness will have to testify from here. He's totally incapable of movement.

Judge Dyce: All right. Swear in the witness from there.

Court Reporter: Do you solemnly swear to tell the truth and nothing but the truth?

Crowder: Nobody loves ME cuz nobody KNOWS me.

Haggerty: Your name, please, Billy Joe?

Crowder: Well, it's a GROOVY WORLD, girl.

Haggerty: You're the plaintiff in this action?

Crowder: The clothes you're WEARING, girl.

Haggerty: One last question. Do you recall being hit by a railroad locomotive while you were driving your automobile?

Crowder: YEAH.

Haggerty (stiffening; a wind sighed through the window): You do?

Crowder: YEAH, there's thirteen hundred and FIFTY-two guitar cases in Nashville.

Haggerty (bowing his head): No more questions. Your witness.

Halter: I have no questions, your Honor.

Judge Dyce: The witness is excused. Please remove him, Mr. Haggerty.

Haggerty: Yes, your Honor (slowly wheeling Billy Joe out and returning). That concludes plaintiff's case, your Honor.

Halter: Your Honor, at this time I would like to move for a directed verdict for defendant.

Judge Dyce: Approach the bench . . . All right, Mr. Halter, repeat your motion.

Halter: I move for a directed verdict. The plaintiff has failed to make a submissible case. The defendant must be shown not to have exercised ordinary care, and the plaintiff has failed to do so in any degree.

Haggerty: Your Honor, Mr. Tryon, defendant's own employee, admitted he made no effort to apply his brakes. He further admitted on his deposition that he could have slowed down as soon as he hit his brakes. That would have been all Billy Joe needed to be a whole human being today.

Judge Dyce: All right. Mr. Halter, I'm overruling your motion at this time. I'd like to hear your evidence. You may renew the motion at the close of your case, if you like.

Halter: Very well, your Honor . . . Will Mr. Gunther please come forward?

Mr. Gunther walked past Halter to the witness stand and sat down. At the same time Terry Rauscher ran through the crowd toward Halter.

"I'm terribly sorry," she whispered. She handed him a folded note and then darted away. Halter unfolded the note. It read: *I must see you at once. It's extremely important.*

Halter considered the words and turned slowly to the judge.

Halter: Your Honor, with the court's indulgence, I request a ten-minute recess on a matter of considerable urgency.

Judge Dyce (frowning): All right. The court will recess for ten minutes. Do you have any objection, Mr. Haggerty?

Haggerty: None whatsoever, your Honor. I'm always ready to accommodate a fellow barrister.

Halter looked for Terry in the crowd, but she wasn't there. He encountered rude stares. They didn't like him very much, a man who kicked cripples when they were down.

He went outside into the hallway, and Terry pressed his arm. "I'm sorry, Neil. You'll understand when I tell you what's happened."

They were standing a few feet from Crowder, who was laid out next to a window. His father and mother were with him, gazing out at the park. "Let's try the courtroom across the hall," said Halter. "I think it's empty."

They sat in the last row. "What is it?" said Halter.

Terry leaned forward. A round knee caught his thigh, and he realized that she'd never lose the power to move him. "There's been an accident," she said.

"What kind of accident?"

"Don't be upset. Please. George is going to be all right. It's Mrs. Gummersell."

Halter watched tears form in Terry's eyes and was startled. How could she care about Mrs. Gummersell?

"She saved George's life. She ran into the street and got him away from the wheels of a car. He's in the hospital, but Alice says he's going to be all right. She's there with him. But Neil, *she's* dead. Mrs. Gummersell is *dead*. She was killed right away. Thank God, she didn't suffer. She must have been a wonderful woman."

Halter watched the dazzle of words pouring from Terry's mouth. The stories that people had to tell. The mountains of language they had to climb because they were there.

"Where's George?" he said finally. "He's never been alone before."

"I told you. It's all right. Alice is with him at the county hospital. They're sure he'll be all right. As soon as Alice heard, she went right over. She's waiting for you. She won't leave him. He's quieted down, she says, but he keeps asking for you."

"Where is Mrs. Gummersell?"

Terry stared at him. "Oh, Neil. She's dead." She hesitated. "If you don't think you can drive, I can take you."

"No, it's all right," said Halter. "If it wouldn't be too much trouble, you might tell Alice that I'll be there as soon as I can. As soon as the trial's over."

"*Listen* to me, Neil. They'll understand. George needs you. He saw the whole thing. He needs you very much right now."

"I'll finish up as soon as I can. Will Alice stay?"

"You don't need to ask a question like that. If she couldn't, I would. That's not the point. George wants *you*."

"Is George all right?"

"I'm sure he is, but go to him. Right away. *Please*."

"You really must excuse me," said Halter. "I have to get back now."

He left her, went back to the courtroom and sat down at the counsel's table.

Haggerty grinned. "Got the case cracked?"

"Yes," said Halter. He mustn't be rude to Haggerty; he owed him more than small talk. "It was Salisbury Street all along."

"What or who is Salisbury Street?"

"Where someone hit me. Where I live."

"You like to talk in riddles," said Haggerty good-humoredly. "Like if a train four hundred feet away is going thirty miles an hour and a car eight hundred feet away is going sixty, what color are the engineer's eyes? It looks like I'm getting to the jury, boy, and when I do, you know, you're dead."

"I'm sorry," said Halter. "I really am."

"I've got to hand it to you," said Haggerty. "You never give up." He paused. "You know something I don't know?"

"No, nothing," said Halter. "The same old sixty-six," as the judge resumed the bench. Mr. Gunther sat down in the witness stand and was sworn in.

Halter was very impressed with himself. His mind was certainly a remarkable instrument. If called upon, it was capable of bowling a perfect game, of bouncing a golf ball a foot from the hole every time. If employed as witness, it could answer like a shot and hit the bull's-eye. It was *the* precision instrument upon which all precision instruments depended. Without it, who could have even dreamed of a moon shot? Guiltily, Halter commandeered it for the trivial job it had at hand.

Halter: What is your name?

Gunther: Felix Gunther.

Halter: And what is your occupation?

Gunther: Professional engineer.

Halter: In connection with your profession, do you have occasion to deal with the times it takes objects to move at certain speeds?

Gunther: I do.

Halter: Did you have occasion on February eighteenth of this year to conduct certain tests at the intersection of Howard Street and the Sunflower Railroad track?

Gunther: I did.

Halter: Would you describe the tests?

Gunther: We clocked the travel of the railroad diesel engine, flatcar and caboose involved in this accident. We conducted measured time tests through measured distances for the train running at various running speeds and braking.

Halter: Was there a speedometer on the train?

Gunther: Yes.

Halter: Did you run a test to determine whether the speedometer was accurate?

Gunther: Yes. In the first test, we ran the train southwest toward the intersection. Mr. Gridley was stationed at the intersection. I was down track two hundred and twenty feet. Mr. Gridley stood with his arm raised, and when the train came even with him he dropped his arm, while I clocked with a stopwatch the time it took the train to travel from Mr. Gridley the two hundred and twenty feet to where I was.

Halter: And what time did your stopwatch show for that train to travel two hundred twenty feet?

Gunther: Exactly five seconds.

Halter: How many feet per second does a train going thirty miles per hour move?

Gunther: Forty-four feet per second.

Halter: And you clocked this in five seconds.

Gunther: Yes.

Halter: For two hundred twenty feet.

Gunther: Yes.

Halter: So how fast was the train going?

Gunther: Thirty miles per hour or forty-four feet per second.

Halter: Was a further test conducted to determine the

ability of the train to stop when emergency brakes were applied at thirty miles per hour?

Gunther: Yes.

Halter: Describe this test, please.

Gunther: We stationed men at measured distances along the track. Mr. Gridley was at the intersection, myself two hundred and twenty feet down track, others further down and between us. The engineer was told to run this train down the track, reach thirty miles per hour at the intersection and to apply the emergency brake at that point on signal from Mr. Gridley.

Halter: Was this done?

Gunther: Yes.

Halter: Did you clock the time it took the train to travel the two hundred and twenty feet after it was emergency-braked at the intersection?

Gunther: Yes.

Halter: What did your stopwatch show as to the time?

Gunther: Exactly five seconds.

Halter: The same as when the brakes were not on?

Gunther: Correct.

Halter: What is your conclusion from that?

Gunther: There was no reduction of speed after application of the brakes for two hundred and twenty feet.

Halter: How long was it before this train finally did come to a stop at thirty miles per hour?

Gunther: Four hundred and ninety-seven feet.

Halter: Thank you. I have no further questions. Your witness, Mr. Haggerty.

Haggerty: Okay. As an engineer, you're aware that there's a reaction time in the handling of instruments by human beings, aren't you?

Gunther: Yes.

Haggerty: Did you consider this when you were testing the validity of the stopwatch?

Gunther: Yes.

Haggerty: How? Just how? Didn't you say you waited until

Mr. Gridley's arm dropped before you started the watch? And the engineer waited for Mr. Gridley's drop before he braked? You'd have to see the arm drop and respond, wouldn't you?

Gunther: We were prewarned. We were expecting it.

Haggerty: Even though prewarned, doesn't it take some time for you and the engineer to respond to a stimulus?

Gunther: Well, if I understand your question, there is some reaction time for anything we do.

Haggerty: And wouldn't that distort your test considerably, since we're dealing with seconds?

Gunther: No. We were prewarned. It would be infinitesmal.

Haggerty: But it would be a factor in the test unaccounted for, the reaction time, right? Speak up.

Gunther: I suppose so.

Haggerty: And the same holds true for Mr. Gridley, doesn't it? He'd have reaction time too before he dropped his arm, wouldn't he?

Gunther: He was also prewarned.

Haggerty: But he'd also have to react?

Gunther: I suppose so.

Haggerty: Thank you very much. All of a sudden we have all kinds of time on our hands, instead of those very precise and scientific five seconds. That's all.

Halter: One moment, Mr. Gunther. Just a few more questions. If Mr. Gridley had a reaction time, this would mean a delay before he dropped his arm. Is that correct?

Gunther: Yes.

Halter: And your reaction time, if any, would also be a delay?

Gunther: Yes.

Halter: So that if he had a delay at the start and you had one at the end, they would tend to cancel each other out, isn't that right?

Gunther: Yes. Yes, that's so.

Halter: That leaves us with the reaction time, if any, of the engineer. By the most generous calculation, what part of a second do you estimate as his possible reaction time?

Gunther: Oh, let's say a thousandth of a second.

Haggerty: Your Honor, I object to that as speculative and highly improper.

Judge Dyce: All right, will the lawyers approach the bench . . . Mr. Halter, do you have any further witnesses?

Halter: Only the other men conducting the tests, your Honor.

Judge Dyce: Do you intend to put them on?

Halter (thinks a moment): No, your Honor. They would merely be corroborative. That closes my case, your Honor, and at this time I'd like to repeat my motion for a directed verdict.

Judge Dyce: Mr. Haggerty, the only evidence you've introduced to show lack of ordinary care by the railroad defendant is the statement by the engineer in his deposition that there was an immediate reduction in train speed upon emergency braking. He amended this in the deposition upon questioning by Mr. Halter to say there were several seconds' reaction time of the brakes. He has maintained this position here during your interrogation. He appears to be an honest man, giving as honest answers as he can. I take his honest answer to be that there are a few seconds' delay, and I take it to be the fact, as proved by the tests of Mr. Gridley, that there is a five-second delay. The uncontradicted testimony is that the train was one hundred feet from the intersection when the engineer first knew that the car, at two hundred feet, allowing for the driver-reaction gap, wouldn't stop in time. By no stretch of his imagination could his braking have done the slightest bit of good. His only recourse was to keep blowing his horn and pray. I am inclined to grant Mr. Halter's request for a directed verdict.

Haggerty: Your Honor, please. Let me point out that we don't know what shape the brakes were in during the test. A lot can happen to brakes in the time that's elapsed. We don't know how long it took the engineer to apply the brakes. And the engineer did say—it's in the record—that there was an immediate reduction of speed on emergency application of the brakes. It's there, your Honor, for the jury to consider, and you have no right to take it away from them. The credibility of the witness is up to the jury to pass on.

Judge Dyce: Have you any further comments, Mr. Haggerty?

Haggerty: Just what I've said, your Honor. This is a terribly tragic case, and your Honor should be very careful before he invades the province of the jury.

Judge Dyce: Mr. Halter, your motion for a directed verdict for defendant is sustained. Please prepare the memorandum while I address the jury.

Haggerty: Your Honor, I beg of you.

Judge Dyce: That's enough of that, Mr. Haggerty.

Halter, disengaged, watched Haggerty's face smooth into blankness; his shoulders sagged and began to shake violently. Judge Dyce's lips tightened. Haggerty was laughing. A flat layer of sound emerged and spread into a sob. Haggerty was crying.

"For God's sake, man, control yourself," said Judge Dyce. "Remember where and what you are. Save your tears for another jury. Mr. Halter, get him out of here. Bring him back when he remembers he's a lawyer. Mr. Haggerty, you're a respected member of the bar. Behave like one. If you don't like my decision, appeal. In any event, pull yourself together."

"Haggerty," said Halter, and took his arm. The other lawyer allowed himself to be led through the speechless room.

"He's right, you know," whispered Halter. "You can appeal. I'm sorry. It's just another case."

Haggerty raised his head. "Just another number on the docket?"

"That's right. Some you win, some you lose."

"Tell his folks that. They're waiting for me in the hall."

"I'm sorry. What else can I say?" said Halter. "I'm just doing my job."

Haggerty wiped his eyes. "What the hell," he said. "Like that bastard said, we can appeal. It won't stand up. You'd better believe it."

"I guess I'd better," said Halter. "Good luck."

As they passed through the swinging doors, Haggerty turned

to Halter and worked up a smile. "You did a hell of a job," he said.

"So did you."

He watched Haggerty approach Crowder on his bed, and the parents standing, their rural faces scrubbed and patient.

"Trusty sword is HANGING at his side," yelled Crowder at Haggerty. "With a RUSTY blade."

· 19 ·

Conscious of the need for speed, Halter drove to the hospital slowly. He was more out of favor with his body than ever before. It was contemptuous and went about its duties with any icy indifference. A car passed him; as it pulled parallel, the driver shook his fist and moved his jaws as if he were chewing licorice. He was trying to tell him something, and Halter smiled regretfully. The other car moved ahead and in a moment would be out of range. By a supreme effort, Halter put his head against the door frame; perhaps he would pick up a communicable vibration. The metal throbbed against his ear, and his body jerked the car as its foot slipped off the gas, but he picked up what sounded like two words: *is dead*.

Halter struggled to become alert. It was a vital clue: . . . *is dead*. What, who? God is dead, Crowder is dead, Justice is dead, Morality is dead, Pity is dead, Truth is dead, Haggerty is dead, Mackey is dead, Terry is dead, Alice is dead. It was too easy. He'd have to work harder than that to crack the code.

Your son George is dead. Halter's body tightened on the wheel. George was in the hospital, alive and doing fine; Terry had said so.

Mrs. Gummersell was dead.

Halter's body's joints froze. Undirected, the car stopped. Mrs. Gummersell was white-haired, spiderweb-cheeked, cued by soap operas, the woman of the bison nostrils. With her white hair, pink skin and buffalo nose, she was a Walt Disney creature. She was the creature who had run into the path of a steel-nerved murderer, snatched George from its Duco-enameled teeth and satiated it with her own marrow.

Cars behind Halter honked in a furious overture to Mrs. Gummersell while Halter sat and listened. Mrs. Gummersell was being canonized by the miracle of the horns. All around him was the sound of klaxons. The Sunflower Railroad bearing down on Howard Street gave every toot it had for Mrs. G. Crowder, lying on his hospital bed, jerked erect and spoke a song for Mrs. G. Judge Dyce blew his nose for Mrs. G. The noise was tremendous. As drivers inched past Halter he could see that their faces were contorted with emotion. He imagined that at this very moment Mr. Trevellyan was shaking hands with Mr. Pilchuck and telling him that he could park his camper wherever he wanted to. Mrs. G. would have liked that. And Mr. Grasser, who was so upset about the chains being up on Clapper and not on Salisbury, would . . . would . . . would get his chains on Salisbury. He would be very grateful to Mrs. G. for proving how dangerous it was on Salisbury without chains. Halter was so happy about Mr. Grasser getting his chains on Salisbury that he couldn't contain himself any longer. He burst out crying and couldn't stop. He knew once again what a lawyer was: a crybaby. Look at Haggerty if proof was needed. "Mrs. Gummersell," he whispered, "we'll have chains on Salisbury. I'll put that in writing on your pillow tonight."

A policeman appeared at Halter's window. "What's the matter here? You're blocking traffic. Your car stalled?"

"No. I've fixed it. I'm sorry I caused any trouble."

"Just get it moving," said the cop.

At the hospital, Halter was told that George was in 402. Alice met him with a finger to her lips. "He's fallen asleep. Just bruises. No worries."

Halter approached the bed and looked at his son. The face, forehead and a cheek bandaged, still bloomed. Halter leaned down to feel his son's breath on his cheek, and his own breathing stopped. George was terribly still. But the cheek was warm to his lips. George was all right; he was only asleep.

He straightened, regarded his son and turned to Alice. "Could I speak to you in the hall?" he whispered.

She followed him out. "He kept asking for you," she said. "You should have come sooner."

"I know," he said. "Look, I have a favor to ask. Have they said when George could go home?"

"Tomorrow. What's the favor?"

"Could you stay with him for the next few days?"

She eyed him calmly.

"Mr. Forrest would give you time off for this," she said.

"George will need more than me. He'll need a woman."

"You're a great one for needs, aren't you?" she said. "Why me? Can't you get anybody else?"

"He likes you and trusts you."

"And he needs me. Of course I'll stay," she said rudely. "And without even asking Mr. Forrest's permission."

"Mr. Forrest will be tickled to death. He's anxious to show you every courtesy." He hesitated. "Would it be possible for you to sleep over?"

She stared at him. "I'm beginning to see. You need another housekeeper. Mrs. Gummersell saved George's life, but you lost a housekeeper."

"I know she did."

Alice sighed. "Have you at least notified her relatives?"

"She has no relatives. George and I are as close as she comes. I'll take care of things. Will you stay?"

"You've asked me to, haven't you? All you have to do is ask me. Congratulations. You've found yourself another house-keeper."

"Thank you very much."

Alice watched him a moment. She shrugged. "Is the pay good?"

"Mrs. Gummersell got eighty dollars a week."

"Good enough. I'll charge the same. Of course I don't have much experience."

Halter looked away. "One last favor," he said. "Could you stay with him here a little while longer? There are some things I must do. I'll be back as soon as possible."

Alice shook her head. "What do I tell George when he wakes up and you aren't here?"

"Please," said Halter. "I'll leave a note for him."

"You do that. Do anything you want. Leave him a note."

Halter took out his memo pad and wrote:

Dear George,

I was here and you were asleep. I have some work to do but I'll be back very soon. I kissed you while you were asleep. Alice is going to come to our house and stay with us awhile. She's very nice.

Love,

Daddy

He handed the note to Alice, who read it and then looked at him. "Love?" she said.

"Thanks again for staying."

"Nuts," she said, and went back into the room.

Halter left the hospital and drove to Mackey's office, weaving in and out of traffic, braving changing signal lights.

"I'm sorry," said the secretary. "He's in conference. Did you have an appointment?"

"No. I think he might see me anyway. Could you tell him Mr. Halter is here?"

"He isn't taking any calls," the girl said. "Would you care to wait?"

"Try. Please. It's urgent."

"Well, all right." She picked up her phone and pressed a buzzer.

"Mr. Mackey, I'm terribly sorry to disturb you, but there's a Mr. Halter here who says it's urgent that he see you . . . What? Thank you. I'll tell him."

She nodded. "He'll be right out. Won't you have a chair?"

Halter shook his head as Mackey emerged, glanced quickly at Halter and pointed to a door. "We can talk in there," he said.

Inside, Mackey sat down behind a desk, and Halter took a visitor's chair. The man had grown bags under his eyes.

"Before you say anything," said Mackey. "You'll be interested to know I've discussed the matter with my client. He's willing to pay Mrs. Brungard the three million dollars. I want you to know further that I advised him against it."

Halter took out the roll of negatives and placed them on the table. "I'm sorry I may have caused you some anxiety," he said. "The negatives are there, and there are no prints. About the settlement: Mrs. Brungard doesn't want any money. She never did. Just the divorce."

Mackey looked at the roll and made no effort to pick it up. "I'm getting awfully tired of your games. You don't know enough to quit when you're ahead."

"It's no game. The negatives are yours, and the matter is closed."

Mackey reached out, picked up the roll and weighed it in his hand. "Another of your so-called jokes?"

"No, but you can call it that if you like."

Mackey leaned back. "You might tell Hilda," he said grimly, "that she has a rare sense of humor." He met Halter's eyes. "I hope you got the kick out of this you expected. We once discussed pride. Myself, I don't think either of us has anything to be proud of."

"I don't think so either."

Mackey fingered the negatives. "That's the end of it, then? Anything else on your mind?"

"I have nothing else," said Halter. "Good-bye, Mr. Mackey. As I said, I'm sorry to have troubled you."

Halter drove to Hilda's house and found her outside on the front lawn, snapping pictures of a little girl. She'd never looked more beautiful. She was dressed in a purple, sleeveless dress and leather sandals; her hair was loose and fell to her shoulders.

Halter realized that the little girl must be Sylvie. She too was beautiful and auburn-haired. She was wearing a white starched dress with a blue ribbon in her hair, and posed as if a massive advertising budget depended on her.

"What have we here?" said Hilda. "Sylvie, this is the family lawyer, Mr. Halter, come to advise us that we're stepping on the grass."

"How do you do, Mr. Halter," said Sylvie.

"I'm pleased to meet you, Sylvie. Mrs. Brungard, may I talk to you a moment?"

"Talk," said Hilda, snapping another picture.

"Could we go inside?"

Hilda turned and inspected Halter. "You mean, talk privately? I haven't any secrets from Sylvie. Do I, Sylvie?"

"No, Mother."

"I've just returned the negatives to Mackey," said Halter. "I told him the matter was closed."

"*Did* you? Wasn't that my decision to make? You gave him the negatives before I had a chance to see the prints? You're much too independent. You never seem to learn."

"I saw no sense in prolonging matters," said Halter.

"You're not paid to see. You're paid to do what I tell you." She turned to Sylvie. "Darling, go pick flowers. Lawyer Halter and I have something to discuss in private."

"Yes, Mother."

Hilda went into the house without waiting for Halter. He followed, and she confronted him in her elegant living room.

"I'm very angry with you. I didn't ask to be in your fantasy. It was all your idea, remember?"

Halter nodded.

"All right," she said. "First of all, I've changed my mind. I do want three million dollars from Vince."

"I gave Mr. Mackey my word you wanted nothing."

"*Your* word. What's it worth? What's the current market value of the word of a fool?"

"I gave him my word. I can't go back on it."

Hilda laughed. "You keep aching for me to fire you so you can slink off somewhere with your word. The answer is still no. I want you to pick up the phone right now and tell Mackey you want three million dollars. I also want you to tell him you're stupid and ridiculous."

"I'm sorry. No."

Smiling, Hilda lifted her arm and slapped him hard on the cheek. "Yes, you will."

Halter shook his head.

She watched him. "All right," she said. "I'll do your dirty work. God knows what I'm paying you for. I'll tell Vince and he'll tell Mackey." She unwound the camera strap from her neck. "Here. I want you to take my picture."

He focused the camera. She made a face. He took the picture.

"Another," she said.

This time she stuck out her tongue as he took the picture. Sylvie, peonies in her hand, was standing beside him, looking at her mother. Hilda smiled. "Mr. Halter is taking my picture, dear," she said.

"Here are your flowers, Mother."

"Thank you, darling. Would you put them in a vase and take them up to my room like a good little girl?"

"Yes, Mother."

Hilda watched her go. "She has exquisite manners, don't you think?"

"She's very pretty."

Hilda moved so close to him that their noses almost touched. "Listen, Halter," she said. "Think of my little girl. We can't let her see me fooling with a man and simply forget all about it. Think of the trauma. We've got to do something about it."

"What would you like to do?" said Halter.

"How should I know? Good Lord. You're the squarest, weirdest man on earth."

"I'm sorry. I can't help the way I am."

Hilda laughed and put her head against his chest. "You," she said. "Tell me your secret. Where will I find another one like you?"

"I don't know."

She looked at him and shook her head in awe. "You're beautiful," she said. "Positively beautiful."

"Thank you," he said. "I have to go."

"Well, good-bye to you, Lawyer Halter. When the pictures are developed I'll send them to you. Something to remember me by?"

"Thank you. I'd remember you anyway." He opened the front door and walked along the porch toward the front steps.

"Hey," she shouted.

He paused.

"You know what I want to be when I grow up? Cinderella, before she met the prince. Can you fix it for me?"

Halter shook his head and stumbled on the steps. His arms flailed the air, and he almost fell before regaining his balance. She was laughing very hard as he walked to his car.

· 20 ·

Arms fluttering, Miss Benton ran to greet Halter as he entered the office door. For the first time since he'd started working at the firm he was late. He looked at his watch; it was ten-fifteen.

Miss Benton wore a wispy, cobwebbed dress. From her manner he expected her to alight on his arm, but she did something more surprising. She captured his hand and squeezed it. "We're all so proud of you," she said. "The railroad people have been calling all morning, and Mr. Forrest wants to see you as soon as you come in. Guess what he said to me?"

Halter retrieved his hand.

"He said, 'A brilliant piece of work. That Halter is going places.' Those are his exact words. What do you think of that?"

"It's nice of him to say so," said Halter, and went into his office.

Miss Benton followed him in. "You can go right over," she said. "Mr. Forrest is waiting for you."

"In a minute. Tell Mr. Forrest I'll be there in a minute,

would you? And please shut the door after you, Miss Benton. I'd like to be alone for just a few minutes."

"Well, all right. Don't be long."

Halter sat down and flipped through the files on his desk. *Fletcher* vs. *Fletcher,* the sticky divorce case. The joint-accounts memorandum. The barred promissory note. Acme Tool and Die, revised shareholders agreement. Several new personal-injury cases. He piled them together and filed them away alphabetically in his cabinet. He surveyed his desk. His mail was opened and spread out; he put the stack in the center drawer. The desk top was clear except for his pen; he put that in the top right-hand drawer and stared at his closed door. Miss Benton had honored his request. Nobody moved in on him. His old enemy, the door, stood quietly at attention, impassive as Elkins, the butler, perfectly satisfied with the terms of its employment.

Halter walked into the outer room. For a moment he couldn't imagine where he was; the place was deserted and looked like a battlefield after the last shot was fired. Sheets of paper were poised in typewriters; a box of Kleenex was sitting on Miss Benton's desk; files were opened everywhere.

Terry emerged from Crenshaw's office just as Miss Benton's feathery hand arrived at his elbow. She'd been waiting for him outside his room, guarding the entrance. Terry sat at her place without looking at him.

"Hurry," said Miss Benton. "He can't wait to see you. He's terribly proud of somebody named Neil Halter."

Halter moved across to Forrest's door, escorted by Miss Benton, and he raised his knuckles.

"*You* don't need to knock," she said. "Go right in."

Halter turned and took inventory of Miss Benton's stock. She quivered under the appraisal and lowered her eyes. She had regular features—a nice nose, widely spaced eyes, a decent mouth and chin. Once pretty perhaps, but time and Mr. Forrest had traced lines in her skin and laid a film of dust across her blue eyes. She'd never married; neither had Forrest. At night under her hair net, Miss Benton read fairy tales while Forrest counted his money.

Halter knocked on the door, and Miss Benton faded away.

"Come in," said Forrest.

He stood at a window, his back to the room. Halter sat down and made do with Forrest's rear. When he examined the man's jaunty buttocks for the pride in Halter Miss Benton had spoken of, he discovered the curve of C. F. Gregory's cheek. It told him something about the way of money. It talked best when it talked least. Silence was golden; it commanded attention by what it *threatened* to buy. Gregory was smarter than Forrest, for he knew there were silences money couldn't buy.

"Halter," said Forrest to the window. "My intention was to congratulate you on the Sunflower job. It's too bad you had to spoil it."

Halter waited, tongue bedded in his mouth.

"Why didn't you tell me Gromm died? His widow had to call me." He turned and faced Halter. "You pulled a fast one, didn't you? Made yourself executor and me only successor. Got yourself a big, fat twenty-thousand fee at my expense. You sat down one night and read the fine print in our partnership agreement, saw that executor's fees were excluded and got real busy. Well, sir, you may have outfoxed yourself. I had big plans for you. I mean *big*. I had to go to bat for you too, I'll have you know. Crenshaw was raising hell about the way you handled the Acme Tool and Die matter."

"I didn't know Gromm was dead," said Halter. "I'm sorry to hear it. About the will: it was his idea, not mine. That's the way he wanted it."

"And you couldn't see your way clear to refuse," said Forrest. "You obey your client's wishes. Let me remind you he was *my* client, not yours. *Mine.* You found it convenient to forget that, didn't you? Let me tell you, Halter, this puts you in the soup, and I don't know of one reason I should bail you out."

"I understand your position. Maybe the Sunflower people can find me something to do."

Forrest pressed his lips together. "What do you mean? Have you made a deal with them behind my back?"

"Not yet."

Forrest sat down, picked up a desk pen and chewed its

casing. He set a smile in motion. "Okay. O-*kay.* I was testing you. You've gotten tough. That's all I wanted to find out. No sense playing any more games with you. You're *in,* Neil. All the way. A full partnership." He nodded. "That's the way I like my partners. Tough and smart. We'll shake on it and go announce it to the others. They're as tickled about it as I am." He winked. "You see, it was all arranged before you came in here." He extended his hand across the desk.

"I appreciate the offer," said Halter, "but I'm sorry. I'll have to turn it down. You see, sir, I'm leaving the firm to get married. I wanted you to be the first to know."

Forgetting his outstretched hand, Forrest stood up. He looked like an usher showing Halter to a seat. "You getting married? To who?"

"Alice Gregory."

"Good God," said Forrest, retracting his hand and wiping his face with it. "You really hit the jackpot, didn't you?"

"I think so," said Halter. "I haven't told her yet because, as I said, I wanted you to be the first to know."

"You're *that* sure she'll have you? What makes you think so?"

"Well, you know. People know these things."

Forrest trotted around his desk and came to a halt in front of Halter. "Okay, okay. Look. You're holding some mighty fine cards. But what's that got to do with the firm? We're good for each other. We *need* each other. We're a team. We'll hire men, bright young fellows from Harvard and Yale. As many as you need. You won't have to lift a finger if you don't want to. Hell, with the Gregory business we'd need five, six men right away. I tell you what. You're getting married? Fine. Take a nice long honeymoon. Say, two, even three months. A cruise, maybe. The full partnership starts as of now. How about it?"

"What if Alice turns me down?"

"You think she might? I thought you said it was in the bag."

"Well, you know, people don't always know these things."

Forrest thought a moment. "Either way. I told you. The full partnership was in the bag even before you brought up Gregory."

"What about not lifting a finger and the three-month honeymoon?"

"Say now, let's be fair. We've got Crenshaw and Rucker to think about. Let's not forget *them*. If it was just me, it'd be different. I don't have to tell you that. I tell you what. No matter how it goes, you get six weeks on full pay. How's that?"

"I'm afraid not."

"Damn it, man, be reasonable. How far can I go with what might be a pig in a poke? You'd have to pull your weight without Gregory. You can see that."

"I can see that. You don't understand. I'm not trying to make a deal. Your offer is more than generous, but I've decided to quit the firm and take it easy for a while."

Forrest threw up his hands. "When I said you've gotten tough, I didn't say the half of it. You win. Marriage or not, the same setup. God help me if we don't get Gregory."

"You still misunderstand me," said Halter patiently. "I'm quitting the firm. Period. No ifs and buts."

Forrest froze. Ice formed on his eyeballs. Halter, comfortable in his skin, felt like a thermal-suited Arctic explorer.

"Just like that," said Forrest. "We gave you a start. Gave you a partnership. Groomed you until you were ready. Arranged the Gregory affair. None of that mean a thing to you?"

"I appreciate all your kindnesses."

"You think you're smart now, do you?" said Forrest. "I can play rough too. You're forgetting something. We've got a partnership agreement. You pull out, and I don't care if your father-in-law is Jean Paul Getty, I'll see to it that no firm in the city hires you."

"I was thinking of starting my own firm."

"I'll have you up before the disbarment committee."

"I don't think so."

Forrest retired to his desk chair. He was silent for a while, and then looked up. "You going after the Sunflower Railroad business?" he said.

"No. I have no intention of stealing your clients. If they ask me, I'll refuse."

Forrest looked alive. "You mean that?" he said.

"Yes, I do."

Forrest hesitated. "I guess you're entitled to the Gromm estate," he said.

"Oh no. I'll sign a waiver on that if you like. You'll be the executor—on one condition."

"What's the condition?"

"I walk out of here clean. I don't even get a telephone call about any of the cases I was working on."

"That's kind of rough. We'd go crazy, trying to pick up the pieces."

"I figure you owe me quite a bit of money on the books," said Halter. "You won't owe me a cent."

"Fair enough. That's fair. Fair is fair. All right."

Halter stood up.

"Wait just a minute, Neil," said Forrest, and pressed his buzzer. "Miss Benton. Bring in a waiver form of right to administer. Immediately." He smiled at Halter. "Might as well take care of it now."

Miss Benton entered with the form and put it on the desk. She tried a smile on Halter as she went out. Forrest wrote on the form and handed it to Halter, who signed without looking at it.

"By the way, Mr. Forrest. I talked to Mr. Gregory about switching his law business. He said that for the present he'd stick with Mackey but that he'd think about you for later on."

"Don't kid around," said Forrest. "Not with a new son-in-law."

"I'm not interested," said Halter. "I don't believe in having relatives for clients."

Forrest's eyes rounded into coins. "Well, I've got to hand it to you. I guess I underestimated you all along. I don't know what you're after, but one thing's sure. You're your own man."

"Good-bye, Mr. Forrest."

"Keep in touch. You'll always have friends here."

The door to Rucker's office was open, and Halter walked in.

Rucker was sitting over his fingernails. He smiled broadly at Halter, his crevices doing mazurkas and polkas, as he jumped up and hugged him, then held him at arm's length.

"My God, Neil, did you ever do a job. The Sunflower crowd can't stop talking about it. You know Collins over there? Well, you will. He's the top dog and hasn't cracked a smile in ten years. You should have seen him. Grinning from ear to ear. Is it true? Was Haggerty bawling like a baby?"

"He took it pretty hard."

"Ain't that tough? He's done it himself to enough people. You'd think he'd have learned how to grow up. They tell me Dyce chewed the hell out of him."

"He didn't like it." Halter looked at the hands on his shoulders, and Rucker dropped them.

"I think it's great. I guess Forrest's given you the big news. How does it feel to be on top of the world? Pretty good, huh? No more Halter this, Halter that. Did Forrest spring it? We're scouting around for one, maybe two, guys to do the shit-work."

"I'm leaving the firm. I came to say good-bye."

The music stopped. Rucker's face settled into place. "What do you mean? What's gone wrong? Did that goddamn Forrest try to jockey you? We all agreed, a full partnership, nothing less. And a couple of guys to help you out. Listen, I'll go in right now and straighten him out."

"It's not Forrest," said Halter. "He made a very generous offer. I'm just leaving, that's all. I'm going to take it easy for a while."

"On what? Don't be a screwball. I'm with *you*. You think I don't get fed up with the rat race and want to chuck it all? You get to the point where you say the hell with it. If all life is work, what good is it? Don't I know? Listen, you've been in there plugging. You've worked your ass off. Don't I know Crenshaw? It's different now, I'm telling you. You'll be able to start sticking it into somebody else." He managed a grin but his ridges stayed put. "You're conning me. Man, I fell—hook, line and sinker."

"No," said Halter. "This is for real. I'm leaving."

"What would you do? What would you live on? Don't be a fool."

"I'm getting married. To Alice Gregory."

Rucker let out a low whistle. "Wow," he said. "So that's it. A brand-new ball game."

"That's about it. We thought we might spend some time just moving around. C. F.'s very kindly promised us the use of his yacht. We'll probably go to the Riviera first, I imagine, and then drop in on a few people. C. F.'s fixed us up with letters of introductions to Princess Grace, Mr. Onassis, Mr. Getty, a few people like that. Jackie may go along with us, just for the ride."

"Come on, buddy. Don't fool with the old fooler."

"Why not? Don't you think C. F. can swing it?"

"Sure, sure," said Rucker. "Give it a chance to sink in, will you? I'm just a country boy. You're marrying Alice. Christ."

"By the way," said Halter. "I asked C. F. about getting you into the Province Club. You still want to, don't you?"

"I wouldn't exactly turn it down, if you're on the level."

"He says he'll see what he can do."

Rucker took Halter's hand and gripped it hard. "Okay, but that's not what I really care about. Just don't forget your old buddy, will you? That's what really matters."

"You know I won't," said Halter. "Maybe sometime later on we can get together on the yacht. You think you could get away for a while?"

"Just try me," said Rucker. "Anytime. For you I'd drop any goddamn thing I'm doing. You better believe it."

"I do. When we get back I'll give you a ring."

"I'll be here," said Rucker. "I guess you'll have some stories to tell."

"I imagine so."

"Give my love to Alice. Tell her we sure are going to miss her around here. To tell you the truth, I had a hunch something was in the works. Terry told me Alice was staying at your place for a while to take care of the kid. I figured, people like the Gregorys, what do they care about the rules? They do what they feel like. I'm tickled to death for you. I think it's great."

"Thanks, Ben. I'll give you a call."

Rucker grinned and shook his head. "Wait till I tell Mary. She'll be tickled pink. Maybe when you get settled, the four of us can go out on the town and have ourselves a ball. You think Alice would go for that?"

"Sure she would."

Halter went to Crenshaw's office, started to knock, stopped, turned the knob and walked in. Crenshaw was alone, speaking into his dictaphone. He gave Halter one hard glance without breaking his stride. He moved through his stack of files as if they were pancakes, gobbling up each in turn. Halter sat down and waited. For five minutes he listened to the sound of Crenshaw's voice. Having concentrated previously on the words, he had never really heard it before. It was precise, with no ragged edges or suggestion of a thicker sound underneath. It was a sheet of metal—thin, yet capable of carrying with ease the bulk of legal vocabulary.

The sound stopped, and again he was attacked by silence. Crenshaw was the master of silence. Halter counted the lunches consumed in the perfection of Crenshaw's art.

"Don't think you've made it with *me*," said Crenshaw. "You may have conned Forrest and Rucker, but in my book you're still the same fuck-up. The next time you walk in here without knocking, I'll beat the shit out of you—and don't think I can't do it."

"I'm bigger than you are."

"You think that makes any difference? Go ahead. Go outside and come through the door without knocking."

"No, I guess it wouldn't make any difference."

"Just so you know where you stand. Forrest doesn't know it but he's put you on a trap door, and I'm holding the spring. Sooner or later you'll be flat on your ass. Don't forget it."

"What have I ever done to you?" said Halter. "I'm curious. I'd really like to know."

"You're a fuck-up. I lay it on the line for you and you still don't know how to do a job right. I can't stand to work near a fuck-up."

"I do the best I can."

"It isn't good enough. You don't win wars with the old college try. Your trouble, Halter, is that you're not a professional and you never will be."

"I guess you're right."

"You bet your ass. You've got to learn to take orders before you can give them."

"Your orders?"

"That's right."

Crenshaw put a lock on Halter's eyes. "Hand me my pen," he said. Halter examined the pen in its holder. All Crenshaw had to do was reach.

"Mr. Forrest offered me a full partnership. He's happy about the way I handled the Sunflower Railroad case."

"Hand me the pen."

"He says I can take it easy from now on because I'm bringing in the C. F. Gregory business."

"You fuck-up, hand me my pen."

"I'm leaving the firm," said Halter. "I'm going out on my own. I'm thinking of hiring five or six lawyers to help me out."

Crenshaw reached for his pen and began signing his outgoing mail. He smiled. "That's the best news I've had in a long time. I give you a year, maybe less. Save your money. You're going to need it."

"I won't need money. I'm going to marry Alice Gregory."

Crenshaw grinned. "I had you tagged for a rich bitch's lap dog. Let me give you some advice. Get yourself a penthouse apartment on the top of some building. Then maybe nobody'll shit on you. Stay inside when a plane flies over."

"I'll need a good man to run herd on the younger fellows," said Halter. "How about coming in with me? I'll start you at a hundred thousand a year."

"Go to hell," said Crenshaw, signing his letters without looking up. "That's where your firm will be inside a year."

"Won't you wish me luck?" said Halter, standing up.

"Sure. Good-bye and good luck." He awarded Halter a final glance. "I might have made a lawyer out of you if I had a thousand years to work at it. Go to it. Work at it yourself. See how much good it will do you."

"I hope you have more success with your next trainee," said Halter. "I hope he's everything you expect."

"Close the door on your way out."

Halter returned to his own office, pulled out the bundle of accumulated mail and flipped through it, placing two letters in his briefcase, leaving the others on top of the desk. He pressed his buzzer. Miss Benton answered—another first.

"Miss Benton, could you please put Miss Rauscher on? I'd like to talk to her."

In a moment, Terry's voice said, "Yes, Mr. Halter?"

"Terry," he said. "I wanted to say good-bye. I'm leaving the firm. I don't know if you've heard."

"Good-bye, Mr. Halter."

"If there's ever anything I can do for you, I wish you'd let me know. Someday I hope you'll give me the chance."

"That's very considerate of you, Mr. Halter."

"I couldn't say good-bye without telling you that."

"You've told me. Good-bye."

Halter stared at each of his four walls, picked up his briefcase and walked out for the last time.

· 21 ·

A child's mind, Halter reflected, was a marvelous mechanism, organically quite different from the adult's. It was an India-rubber ball, tough and resilient, that dealt with experiences only as it bounced against them, and erased their impact as soon as contact was lost. A child might recall them, but unless they were dreams, he discounted their significance.

George never spoke of Mrs. Gummersell. He didn't appear to find her among his toys or clothes, in his bed, or at meals. They had no picture of her, but even if they had, it was likely that George would get impatient with trying to remember her.

Sipping cognac and smoking a cigarette, Halter watched Alice at play with George. It was a game she must have bought for him because Halter had never seen it before. It involved wooden shapes under tension; the idea was to pick up each piece without releasing the spring and shaking up the remaining ones.

"You win again," said Alice. "I just can't beat you. Come on. Time for bed."

"One more time," said George.

"I don't think so. Let's ask your father. Is it time for bed, or may George play one more game?"

"It's time for bed, George. Give Alice a kiss."

The boy threw a kiss at Alice's cheek and ran to Halter. "Carry me."

"All right." Halter picked George up. "I'll be right down."

"Take your time," said Alice. "I'll do the dishes."

"Wait for me. We'll do them together."

She had been at the house for three weeks and asked no questions, not even about the office. As far as he knew, she hadn't even called Terry to find out why Halter was still home, why no one made contact about cases or even to say hello. They'd settled down to the domestic routine of a man at home with his family, even to making love with no questions asked. With one variation: she slept in Mrs. Gummersell's room.

Alice got George up, washed and dressed him, and prepared breakfast for the three of them. Except for one morning with George at the playground, Halter went to his bedroom and read. Alice found playmates for George on the block and sat with the mothers. Then there was lunch, and in the afternoon Halter took George to the zoo or the playground. After dinner they did the dishes and then sat down to read and listen to music. They talked from time to time—about George, about the house, about the world, but never about themselves or the office. Then they made love.

George, from time to time, engaged Halter in stalling tactics at bedtime. He demanded his paper cup of water and got it. His story was told. His fear of being left alone was recognized, and Halter rocked him in the chair for a few minutes before he put the boy to bed and patted his behind.

"Kiss."

Halter kissed him.

"Handshake."

Halter shook his hand. "Good night, George. Sleep tight."

"I don't want to sleep tight."

"Then just sleep." Halter turned off the overhead light and put on the shaded table lamp.

"Daddy," said the small con man's voice from the bed. "I love you."

"I love you too, George. Good night." The rituals were completed and Halter went downstairs, picked up a towel and joined Alice at the kitchen sink. "If you have a minute, I'd like to talk to you," he said.

"I figured you would, sooner or later."

"I've quit the firm for good. I told them you and I were getting married."

She scraped a dish. "I know," she said. "Let's see. Mr. Forrest, Mr. Rucker and Terry all called to wish me luck. Oh yes. And my father."

"What did you tell them?"

"I said thank you very much. What else is there to say at a time like that?"

"I didn't want my quitting to have anything to do with you. I only wanted them to think so. It's the only reason they couldn't argue about."

She stopped doing the dishes. "Let's see. In soap operas they have coffee now. You want some?"

"No, thank you."

"Then let's go into the living room, where I can sit down hard."

"All right."

They went into the living room, and Alice sat down hard. "Let me tell you something," she said. "I don't care what they think or are supposed to think. I made up my mind some time ago that if you could bring yourself to ask me I'd marry you. If you didn't, I'd be perfectly satisfied with the way it is. Of course I hardly expected to hear about it through the grapevine."

Halter's eyes wandered around the room and settled on one of George's blocks in the center of the rug. What would Mrs. Gummersell say? "Alice," he said. "Will you marry me?"

"I'm flattered, I really am, that you bother to ask. I know how hard it is for you. You make me feel so happy, so proud. As if I had a voice in the matter."

His mind wouldn't sit still. He found himself back in Mackey's office delivering negatives. He bent down and picked up the block. "That's what we live on," he said. "The 'as if.' The fictions we call reasons to be. Without them we're something else. Call it real, but it isn't human. Playing dumb is playing dead."

"Is it human to ask you what you're talking about?"

"Yes. 'As ifs.' Things I've found I can't live without. Like a false sense of worth. All I can do is try to choose my own brand."

"Of what? Poison? What are you trying to tell me?"

"I *want* to marry you, Alice."

She looked at him. Finally she stood up and kissed him brusquely on the mouth. "You do like to punish yourself," she said. "Let's finish the dishes."

"Give me a minute," he said. "I have some things upstairs to clean up first. I'll just be a minute." He paused. "Thank you, Alice."

"What for? I like to do dishes."

Halter walked upstairs and sat at the desk in Mrs. Gummersell's room with his two pieces of mail from the office. He reread them carefully.

One was from Legal Mountains, Inc.

Our unique service, utilizing Univac 418 and Honeywell 200 computers, takes over the plodding search through the vast and ever-expanding archives of case law. No longer will you have to spend tedious hours searching volume after volume to find the applicable citations to the case at hand. The time you save is monumental. This is valuable extra time you can spend with clients, creating new approaches, making important contacts. Acclaimed by both the law profession, its critics and the press, legal research by computer is the tool you've been looking for to climb that legal mountain.

Halter took out stationery from the right-hand drawer. Mrs. Gummersell used pink paper with blue rosebuds at the top. He wrote:

Dear Mr. Legal Mountains:

I am very interested in your services and would like to know more. I have been climbing legal mountains for years and I've found that it's not so hard going up as in coming down. I am sure that Univac 418 and Honeywell 200 have valuable comments on this. I anxiously await their reply.

He turned to the other letter, a Bar Association questionnaire.

FRUSTRATIONS

(1) Too much to do?
(2) Financial troubles?
(3) Loss of prestige?
(4) Unappreciative clients?
(5) Unreasonable adversaries?
(6) Marital problems of clients?

SATISFACTIONS

(1) Grateful clients?
(2) Respect in the community?
(3) Service to mankind?
(4) Personal independence?
(5) Enjoyment of people?
(6) Congenial colleagues?
(7) Good results?
(8) Pride in profession?

At the bottom Halter wrote:

Rockabye, baby, in the tree TOP
When the wind BLOWS, the cradle will ROCK

When he looked in the drawer for envelopes he found a card in the making from Mrs. Gummersell:

A living dog is better than a dead lion. For the living know that . . .

He replaced the card, tore up the letters, shut the drawer and went downstairs to join Alice.

ABOUT THE AUTHOR

Born in St. Louis, Missouri, where he still lives, ALBERT LEBOWITZ graduated from Washington University and from Harvard Law School. During World War II he flew combat duty as a navigator with the Fifteenth Air Force stationed in Italy.

Mr. Lebowitz and his wife, who is an associate professor of literature at Washington University, have two children. He is a moonlighting writer, dividing his time each week between practicing law and working on his third novel.